Finding
Our Way
Home

**Center Point
Large Print**

Also by Charlene Ann Baumbich and available from Center Point Large Print:

Snowglobe Connections Series:
  Stray Affections
  Divine Appointments

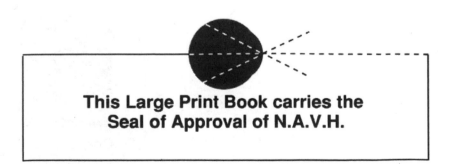

Finding Our Way Home

CHARLENE ANN BAUMBICH

CENTER POINT LARGE PRINT
THORNDIKE, MAINE

This Center Point Large Print edition is published in the year 2012 by arrangement with WaterBrook Press, an imprint of The Crown Publishing Group, a division of Random House, Inc.

Scripture quotation is taken from the Holy Bible, New International Version®, NIV®. Copyright © 1973, 1978, 1984 by Biblica Inc.™ Used by permission of Zondervan. All rights reserved worldwide. www.zondervan.com.

The characters and events in this book are fictional, and any resemblance to actual persons or events is coincidental.

The text of this Large Print edition is unabridged. In other aspects, this book may vary from the original edition. Printed in the United States of America on permanent paper. Set in 16-point Times New Roman type.

ISBN: 978-1-61173-331-0

Library of Congress Cataloging-in-Publication Data

Baumbich, Charlene Ann, 1945–
Finding our way home / Charlene Ann Baumbich.
p. cm.
ISBN 978-1-61173-331-0 (library binding : alk. paper)
1. Female friendship—Fiction. 2. Large type books. I. Title.
PS3602.A963F56 2012b
813′.6—dc23
2011042267

One of our most sacred duties
is to be open and faithful
to the subtle voices of the universe
which come alive in our longing.
From Eternal Echoes *by John O'Donohue*

Dedicated to the following
Lad and Ladies of Dance:

Kenneth von Heidecke,
who lived the loss and affirmed the story

Tresa Mott,
whose willingness, encouragement, and vetting
helped me get it right

Misty Lown,
whose good fruit, faith, and dedication
bring my tiny-dancer grandgirlies to the stage

Sondra Forsythe,
whose sparkling passion for dance
struck my mind's eye

Kim Moss,
who teaches novices how to dance with the stars
and dancers how to take flight.
You are much beloved in a little town
very near Wanonishaw.
and to

Bret and Jackie,
whose love came alive

Leaving Nazareth, he went and lived in
Capernaum, which was by the lake in the
area of Zebulun and Naphtali—to fulfill what
was said through the prophet Isaiah:
"Land of Zebulun and land of Naphtali,
   the way to the sea, along the Jordan,
   Galilee of the Gentiles—
the people living in darkness
   have seen a great light;
on those living in the land of the shadow
   of death
   a light has dawned."

MATTHEW 4:13–16

One

Sasha readjusted the multicolored shawl until it was high and tight around her neck. As she secured it in place with her palm, the tip of her long, slim index finger landed on one of the dozens of glass pearlescent beads hand-worked into the elegant crocheted garment, complete with satin trim. She repeatedly tapped the bead with her fingernail. The sound, very close to her ear, reminded her of the familiar tick of a metronome.

No, it sounds more like the ticking of clock, counting down to death by regret.

She shook her head to dismiss the dark thought and stared at the snowglobe on her side table, on which she set her ever-present cup of hot tea. It didn't matter if the outdoor temperature was twenty-five or ninety-five: "Hot tea, please. That will do." On this midsummer Saturday in Wanonishaw, Minnesota, even though it was a humid eighty-seven degrees outdoors, Sasha did not turn on the air conditioning, and still she felt a slight chill.

Pinning her eyes on the ballerina in the snow-globe, she slowly rolled the bead between her thumb and index finger, as if fine-tuning a memory on a radio dial. She rocked back and forth in the rocking chair, the only chair in the house that, for the most part, didn't hurt her back. She nearly lived in it since she'd moved back in. It had been her mom's favorite chair, the one she used to rock in while nursing Sasha.

Her mom loved to tell the story about how Sasha often fell asleep while she fed her, how she had to tap the arch of her tiny bare foot to wake her. Sasha could hear her mother's gravelly voice, see the spark in her Paul Newman–blue eyes. "You were such a tiny little bird, yet from the get-go, you were so uncommonly strong."

On the rare occasions Sasha visited home, her mother always proudly showed her the most recent clippings and photos she'd added to the latest scrapbook. She had started the scrapbooks when Sasha was a child, the program from her first dance recital leading the way. Across the top of one of the pages of that first scrapbook, in her loopy handwriting, her mother had written, " 'I could twirl forever!' The first words out of Sasha's mouth this morning."

Quickly the scrapbooks began to document the life of an emerging professional ballerina. "Seems impossible," Sasha's mother would say, "that such a tiny little bird could grow into such a majestic swan." She'd point to the recent pictures and the lean muscles in Sasha's calves, marvel at her balance, revel in her glorious costumes and top-flight billing.

As the sound of her mother's voice faded away, the rhythm of Sasha's rocking and the roll of the bead between her fingers began to fuse with the arpeggio of orchestra music rising within her. She closed her eyes, rested the back of her head against the support pillow, and envisioned the ballerina in the snowglobe—elegant neck extended, feet in perfect fifth position—suddenly lengthen her ankles and elevate to pointe. The dancer, a perpetual and wonderful smile on her face, floated her arms to shoulder height. She tilted her delicate head and demure eyes toward the floor, slightly stage left. At the swell of the vibrating string section, in one velvet-smooth motion, the dancer lifted her chin, elongated her neck, raised her chest upward, and leaned toward the audience as she extended her right leg high up behind her and reached her left arm forward. Only her agility, strength, and the tip of her pointe shoe on her arched left foot anchored her to the floor as she performed a stunning *penché arabesque*.

The dancer was acutely aware that the stage lights brought to life the sparkles sewn into her pink, three-quarter-length tutu, flared like an elegant fan between her legs. She rejoiced in knowing she looked as stunning as Maria Tall-chief, the prima ballerina in the picture she had, as a child, tacked to her bedroom wall, right above the ballerina snowglobe she kept on her bookcase headboard.

With perfect timing, Sasha's partner's large, warm hands surrounded her waist as he lifted her like a plume readied to fill the air with poetic movement and words. Her spirit and body sailed with the rising crescendos and quieting lulls of the melody as together she and Donald soared across the stage, his strength repeatedly lifting and lowering her, the box of her pink satin pointe shoe barely tapping the floor, her tutu flaring during each quick descent of their grand *pas de deux*, and . . .

CRASH!

With a lightning fast series of tumultuous thuds, Sasha and her partner fell to the floor. Disoriented, Sasha darted her eyes from here to there to lock in her bearings. Excruciating pain riveted her tailbone, hip, and leg. *Please, God, don't let either of us be injured! We have three more stops this tour!*

It wasn't until her vision focused on a pair of young hands picking up china shards and the dish towel soaking up a spreading circle of tea that reality sank in, yet again. She was no longer Sasha Davis, glitterati, principal dancer at Mid-Central Festival Ballet in Boston, one of the largest and most prestigious ballet companies in the United States. She was no longer traveling the world, performing to standing ovations. She was simply

Sasha Davis. A near invalid living in her deceased mother's home, the home she grew up in, with shelves full of scrapbooks in an upstairs bedroom she could neither get to nor stand to look at.

She was back in Wanonishaw, Minnesota, a town—a *life*—she'd left when, at age seventeen, she'd been accepted into Juilliard.

She put her hands on the arms of the rocker and leaned forward. The shawl slid down behind her back. "I'm sorry," she said to the top of Evelyn's head. Evelyn, nineteen, was on her knees, cleaning up the mess. "I can't believe I spilled again. How many teacups have I gone through in the two months since you've been with me?"

Evelyn looked up and chuckled. Beads of perspiration dotted her forehead, dripped off her nose. "Your share of them," she said. She carefully set pieces of china in the metal garbage can she'd brought from the kitchen. "But no worries, Ms. Davis. Your mom had so many teacups and saucers in this house, you could break one a day, live to be a hundred and fifty, and still not run out! I haven't seen so many cups and saucers since the last time I went to the cities and dreamed about setting up my bridal registry at Macy's. I bet there isn't a china department in any store in the whole *world* that has as many unique teacups as your mom!" Evelyn swiped at the remaining puddle of tea with the towel, which she wrung out in the garbage can. She dabbed at a few drops splattered on the fringe of the nearby area rug.

Sasha noticed the way Evelyn managed, at regular intervals throughout the day, to maneuver her hand in order to catch another glimpse of her own engagement ring. At least that's what Evelyn had called it when she jutted her finger in front of Sasha's face during her interview for this dreadful job. "My *engagement* ring from my *fiancé,*" she said dreamily, as if the diamond could rival one of Elizabeth Taylor's. If there was even a chip of genuine diamond in the middle of that thin band, Sasha would be surprised.

"I'll bring you another cup of tea," Evelyn said, startling Sasha as she sprang to her feet and headed toward the kitchen. "The water's still hot in the kettle," she said over her shoulder. "Sit tight for a minute."

Sit tight? After exhausting herself simply pulling the shawl from behind her, wrestling it over her shoulders, and tucking it up under her neck, Sasha slumped back in the chair. *Who would have imagined that at only age thirty-seven, that's nearly all I'd be able to do? I might as well be ninety.*

Through the window, a large bird caught Sasha's eye as he floated onto the porch rail. His blue iridescent head and bright eyes glistened in the sun. The colors, including his jet-black body, reminded her of one of the dramatic costumes

14

she'd worn during a solo performance in Venice. Organza, chiffon, tulle, beads, the music . . . She fingered a bit of the satin that trimmed her shawl, recalled the exact tiara she wore for the sequence.

The bird took a few hops, then began to bathe in the warped aluminum frying pan she'd instructed Evelyn to get rid of after the dramatic incident just days after Evelyn moved in. The next morning, when Evelyn drew the drapes, Sasha saw the old pan, its handle half-melted, on the porch railing. It was filled with water and a handful of glass marbles. She opened her mouth to chastise Evelyn for once again not following her instructions, but before she could emit a sound, a bright small bird, its head the color of coral, landed on the handle, hopped to the rim of the pan, and took several delicate drinks of water. As soon as he was gone, a small, brilliant, gold, black, and white bird took his place and broke out in song. *Such beauty. So many colors.*

Such tiny little birds.

When she looked up, Evelyn was smiling, nodding her head in that annoyingly knowing way of hers.

Ever since the pan first appeared on the rail, a constant parade of birds drank and bathed, splashed and vied for space. The expensive birdbath Sasha sent her mother one Mother's Day—a departure from the usual teacup and saucer—sat empty in the middle of the yard.

Utterly entertaining, these tiny dancing birds. And now, a large yellow-eyed one, swooping in like the handsome Prince Siegfried in *Swan Lake*. A few bars of Tchaikovsky's glorious score played in Sasha's head, then quickly faded. By the time the grackle, which Evelyn had identified for her, was done with its raucous bath, the pan was nearly splashed empty.

Just like my life.

"Time to refill the pan again," Evelyn said, as she settled a new teacup and saucer into their usual spot. "Funny how much the birds love that old thing. Wonder why? Maybe the sun warms the metal, which warms the water."

"Maybe," Sasha said, careful to sound like she didn't care, which she didn't.

"Or maybe it's the marbles. I read birds are attracted to shiny glass, which is why I put the marbles in there."

"Maybe." Sasha frowned, shook her head, pursed her lips. "Perhaps I should have someone create a cement birdbath decorated with all the shards of glass I've produced lately."

"Just to remind you, Ms. Davis," Evelyn said, positioning herself right in front of Sasha, encroaching on her personal space by nearly standing on her toes, "you won't be in that rocking chair forever, you know. Allowing yourself to get all pity-partied up just saps the energy your body needs to mend itself."

16

Sasha studied the large, big-boned young woman standing before her, who, hands on her hips, boldly studied her right back.

Sasha's chin jutted slightly upward as she felt her anger rise. "Who do you think you are?"

Evelyn backed up a step.

"Not only my aide, but a mind reader too? My cheerleading squad? My *shrink?* May I remind you that I pay you to assist me. To do what I *instruct,*" Sasha said, her eyes momentarily diverting to the frying pan she'd *instructed* Evelyn to get rid of. "I do not pay you—and I pay you well—to lecture me or to override my decisions."

Evelyn straightened, letting her hands fall to her sides. "Yes, Ms. Davis, you do pay me well, and I thank you. I'm sorry if I overstepped my boundaries. I'll try to do better next time. It's just that I hate to see you get so down on yourself." She bit her lip. "If there's nothing else you need"—Evelyn paused, waited until Sasha shook her head—"I have some errands to run. Maybe you can enjoy a nap while I'm gone."

This wasn't the first time Evelyn had reminded Sasha that she was cranky when she was tired. At least this time she was more subtle about it.

"I'll be back around four-thirty to prepare dinner. And again, I'm sorry. My mom's often told me I have a short circuit when it comes to boundaries." Evelyn reached back, grabbed her long blond ponytail, and twirled it around her

17

index finger. "But my fiancé says he adores my spunky attitude. I guess I have to figure out a happy medium, or where to be what or who or how. Or something like that." She shrugged and grinned. "Sure you don't need anything before I go?"

Sasha shook her head and flicked her fingers in dismissal. Shortly after she heard the back door close, she saw Evelyn whizzing down the street on her bicycle. Her pink Life is good–brand back-pack clung tightly to her body. Her ponytail sailed behind her like a kite tail. *Isn't everyone supposed to wear a helmet?*

But what was the point of playing safe in life? Look where it had gotten Sasha. All those years. All that practice. All that pain.

As much as that girl annoys me, why is it she's right about nearly everything? Pity party, indeed. Knock it off!

Sasha sucked in her stomach and tried to flatten her back to the chair. Although the action caused her to grimace, she straightened her right leg and lifted it parallel to the floor. She pointed her toe, rotated her foot to the left, then to the right. She pointed her toe again, studied the line of her slim leg beneath her long rayon skirt, thought about all the times she'd stood at the barre while studying the stretch of her legs in the mirror, the angle of her arms, the tilt of her head and carriage. She shook her head, closed her eyes, and repeated the exercise with her left leg. She sucked in her breath and tried to will herself to lift both legs at once, an action that hurt so badly it made her whimper.

After five months, her body still wasn't ready for that much rigor. The doctor told her to let the pain be her guide, not to rush the process lest she risk setting back her healing. Absolutely no pushing herself until physical therapy began. But how could she sit there and do nothing? The life of a dancer was fraught with aches and pains, twitches and bruises. One learned to bandage up, ice down, and gut it out. Doing nothing wasn't acceptable!

Then a sickening thought struck her. Pain wasn't a guide. Pain had become her best friend. At this point in her messed-up life, without the pain, she would have nothing. Nothing at all.

She squeezed the chair arms, pushed her spine into the back cushion, and tried to lift both legs. Again and again and again she tried, until at last she broke into sobs, not an ounce of strength left in her body.

Two

Evelyn Burt twisted her ponytail while she stood in line at her grandfather's butcher shop. It was Saturday and the place was packed. Her grandpa was in fine form, joking and weighing, slicing and winking. Betty, his new wife, to whom he'd been married less than a year, rang up purchases. She didn't often help out in the shop, but when she did, Grandpa Burt smiled even more than usual.

"What do you need, Sweet Cakes?" he asked when he called out number forty-seven and Evelyn handed him her ticket.

"Two of your best T-bone steaks, a half pound of Lorraine Swiss cheese, two chicken breasts, and a hug."

"Get yourself around here, honey!"

She scooted behind the counter, saying "excuse me" several times and stepping on one gentleman's toes before diving into her grandpa's open arms.

He kissed her on the cheek, said he was sorry he couldn't visit, and that she and that fiancé of hers should stop by for dinner. "How about . . . Betty? We busy next Tuesday?"

Betty shook her head, nodded, and smiled at Evelyn.

"It's a date. Well, actually, I can't speak for Jorden, but I'll be there, even if he can't make it. They've been changing his work schedule around."

"Think old what's-her-name would like to come too?"

"Gramps!" Evelyn blushed, which she was not prone to doing. Of course he was kidding by referring to Ms. Davis like that, but nonetheless . . . "Lower your voice please, Gramps. You want me to get fired?" she whispered through her teeth. "If anyone heard you and word gets back to her, I'm finished. I'm always in enough trouble with her without that. In any case, I seriously doubt she'll come. In fact I am one hundred percent sure of it. But I'll extend the invitation anyway. It's nice of you to think of her. I'll let you know tomorrow about both Jorden and Ms. Davis." She moved back around to the customer side of the counter.

She watched as her grandpa selected two of the choicest steaks. They both knew that for Ms. Davis price was never an issue and that Evelyn would be eating one of them. He sliced the cheese super thin, just the way Ms. Davis liked it, and wrapped two chicken breasts. Betty rang up the charges to Ms. Davis's account and said she'd see Evelyn on Tuesday. Evelyn tossed the meat in

21

the green bag she kept folded up in her backpack. Today it contained two frozen bottles of water she nabbed out of the freezer before she left the house to keep the meat cold. She stuffed it all back in her backpack, then threw her grandpa a kiss.

Next stop: Jorden's! She couldn't stay but a minute, since the deadly combo of fresh meat, stifling heat, and the sun beating down needed to be taken seriously. But a quick kiss would be better than no kiss. Plus, now she needed to invite Jorden to her grandpa's next Tuesday.

As she traveled the mile to Jorden's family's house, using her arm to signal her turns, she thought about the way Ms. Davis had reprimanded her. Evelyn was grateful for the job and decided she would have to try harder to not always say what she was thinking.

All her life, she'd just blurted things out, which had gotten her into her share of trouble, especially in high school. Her mom said it was just the way she was wired, but her dad spent a lot of time raking his fingers through his hair when they argued. She was as stubborn as he was.

But when, two weeks after her high school graduation, she blurted out that she was engaged *and* that she was no longer interested in going to college, at least not now, her dad blew a gasket. She'd already been accepted at three of her four top college picks. She was only nineteen and her fiancé a mere twenty.

"We're not getting married for at least two years," she told her folks, which helped settle them a little.

But still her parents, both teachers, admonished her. "Get an education, Evelyn!" her dad eventually bellowed.

Evelyn stood firm, which they should have been used to by now. "I need to get out of here and see a little of the world before I settle down."

Get out of here? Where was she going if not to school, they wanted to know.

Well, nowhere, really. But she needed to make her own stand in life. And she was in *love!*

Shortly thereafter, an inspired vision popped into her head, and she began to design her own business card.

EVELYN BURT'S
HELPING HANDS, HELPING YOU.
NO ODD JOB TOO ODD.

She included her phone number and the word "REFERENCES."

"Mom, Dad," she said when she showed them the first draft of the card, "you know I'm a hard worker, right?"

They could not disagree.

"Grandpa," she said one day when she stopped in the shop, "okay if I use you as a reference too?"

Of course.

Taking advantage of her artistic talents, which

her art teachers had always lavishly praised, she drew a picture of her own hands reaching toward the readers of the card. She took a photo of the drawing, then used a graphics program to incorporate it into her design. She bought Avery business-card stock and printed the cards herself. She tacked the cards on bulletin boards around town, set some on the counter in the butcher shop, and knocked on doors throughout her neighborhood.

Immediately her phone began to ring. More requests poured in than she at first thought she would be able to handle. But never short on determination or lacking in enthusiasm for a new experience, she handled them anyway.

She mowed yards, ran errands, and delivered groceries. She helped clean an attic, drove a senior citizen to her sister's house in the cities, baby-sat, painted a cupboard, dug a trench, sorted weekly pills into pill containers for Gerald McCarthy, cleaned gutters, washed windows, and trimmed Doris K. Phibbs's disgusting toenails with a giant toenail trimmer. When she didn't know how to do something, she looked it up on the Internet.

Aside from the splurge on her Life is good– backpack she found at T.J. Maxx ("How perfect is *this,* Jorden!?"), she saved her proceeds for her upcoming great adventure, whatever and wherever that would be.

But mostly, she saved for her wedding.

Then one day she saw the ad in the newspaper for a temporary live-in aide, no name mentioned. "Errands and light cooking. Some personal care. Room and board included. Duration uncertain. Only females need apply."

Maybe she couldn't yet afford to get out of town for her adventure, but she could at least get out of her parents' house. A step in the right direction. She loved her folks dearly, but a girl had to *live*.

In her usual impulsive style, without giving it another thought, she called the number.

"Sasha Davis," the voice said.

"Whoa! Is this really *the* Sasha Davis?" She heard the clearing of a throat. "Well hello, Ms. Davis. Evelyn Burt here, calling about your ad in the paper."

"Burt," Ms. Davis said, her voice flat. "Any relation to Burt Burt the butcher?"

"Yes, ma'am. His granddaughter. Bob, my dad, is Burt Burt's son."

The line was quiet for a long while, which piqued Evelyn's curiosity. She wondered if being a Burt was good news or bad news to Ms. Davis.

"How old are you, Evelyn?"

"Nineteen."

"I certainly did not expect someone so young to respond."

"Well, life is just like that, isn't it? Full of surprises." Evelyn delighted in life's surprises and therefore assumed everyone did the same.

"No college for you?" Ms. Davis sounded disapproving.

"Not right now. I'd like to experience a little independence before I get married. My fiancé agrees that it will be good for both of us to have our own lives before we wed. Still, we just can't bear to be apart, not now."

"Fiancé? At *nineteen?*" Ms. Davis sounded incredulous.

"Ms. Davis, love is as love does, and believe me, our love *does.* I am a woman who knows my own mind. Always have. I have a goal: to birth two children by the time I'm twenty-five, and to always and forever be in love with my one and only husband. Somewhere in there, a college degree will be mine too. I'm physically strong, wholly reliable, have an entrepreneurial spirit, come with countless references, and I'm very interested in this position. I can't imagine a more wonderful opportunity than to spend time both serving and getting to know *the* Sasha Davis. You do know you are the most famous person to launch out of Wanonishaw, right? And that people used to report their rare Sasha Davis sightings when you came to town to visit your mom? Well, okay, maybe we didn't always actually see *you,* but we'd hear you were here, and one time we saw that limo! And by the way, I am sorry about both the loss of your mother and your injury."

The line was silent for a long while.

"Ms. Davis, are you still there?"

"Yes. Yes, I am. You are a lot to take in, Evelyn."

"I imagine I am."

"Yes, well . . . When might you be available for an interview?"

"I can come right now!"

"Oh, no. That's impossible. I need time to . . . Today won't work. How about tomorrow morning at nine?"

"I'll see you then."

"Don't you need my address?"

"Ms. Davis, everyone in Wanonishaw knows you're living in your mom's old house while you recuperate. In fact, everyone in Wanonishaw knows pretty much everything about you and everyone else."

At exactly nine the next morning, Evelyn rang Sasha Davis's doorbell. She waited a moment, then rang it again. Perhaps Ms. Davis couldn't *get* to the door. She cracked it open and poked her head in.

"Ms. Davis? Evelyn Burt is here!" she announced with the flair of a grand *ta-da!*

"I've been saying come in. I guess you couldn't hear me," Evelyn heard from down the hall.

Although Evelyn remembered Genevieve Davis, Sasha's mother, from church, she'd never been inside the house. The entryway was dark. Dark wood. Old wood. Rich looking. She didn't recall them having money. She cast her eyes from one piece of furniture to the next, peeking around corners, stopping a moment to stare at the old console radio with brown push buttons. She'd seen one like it before in an antiques store. She loved wandering around in those musty smelling places, viewed them as the caretakers of millions of stories that fired her creative juices. On that sighting, she'd rested her fingers on the buttons, wondering how many others had done the same throughout time. She was going to push one of those buttons, curious how the click sounded, but the owner of the store had glared at her, so she put her hands in her pockets.

The temptation now to push one of these radio buttons was strong, but she restrained herself by clasping her hands together, in case Ms. Davis could see her. Evelyn hadn't laid eyes on her yet. It was so dark, she could be anywhere.

"In here," came the voice. "Keep walking straight back, please. I'm in a small room near the kitchen. You'll see me."

Evelyn couldn't get over how dark everything was. Every drape pulled tight. Depressing, if you asked her. All this dreariness would be difficult to live in. The walls could use a good coat of yellow or cream, maybe even a mint green. She'd watched enough HGTV—research for the business, she told her folks—to know just how to perk the place up. Maybe she could talk Ms. Davis into letting her have a go at redecorating.

It never occurred to her she wouldn't get the job and move right in.

It never occurred to Evelyn Burt she wouldn't get any- and everything she wanted out of life, which she told Ms. Davis. And right now, she wanted this job, which she told her too.

Ms. Davis looked like she might be ready to say no, so Evelyn kept right on talking. She told her she could not only type—well, *keyboard,* she explained—but could do so with blazing accuracy and speed. Then she showed Ms. Davis her business card.

"You designed this yourself?"

"Yes, ma'am. Original artwork, too."

"You could handle correspondence, then?"

"I can handle anything, including cooking a mean steak on the grill."

Ms. Davis raised her eyebrows. "Can you maintain confidentiality, Evelyn?"

"Absolutely. I'm a talker, but I'm not a gossiper. You can ask anyone who knows me. That is the gospel truth."

Ms. Davis stared at her, unblinking. She rearranged her beautiful shawl, which seemed completely out of place to Evelyn. She shifted in her rocker and fingered a stack of mail on her side table.

Evelyn could, Ms. Davis told her, begin moving personal belongings into the room at the top of the stairs, to the left. She should consider the upstairs bathroom her private bathroom. She could have flex hours off as prearranged and agreed upon. As she told Ms. Davis, "I am in love, Ms. Davis, and I take that commitment seriously." But in general, she needed to be available during the day and always present at night. And she needed to maintain confidentiality. Unless otherwise instructed, nothing that took place in the house moved outside the walls. Period.

Evelyn gave her head one firm nod, and just like that, she'd struck out on her own.

Already, she thought, thrusting out her arm to turn into Jorden's driveway, she was becoming more self-aware and mature, and in good ways. For instance, no matter how perfect or brilliant the concept, she now understood it was not a good idea to go against your boss. Exhibit Number One: the impromptu frying-pan birdbath.

Sure, it was old-fashioned looking, an inspired idea, and the birds' favorite—plus, it had the whole recycling thing going for it. But she'd gone against her boss's wishes by a) keeping it after the explosive incident, even though she'd been asked to dispose of it, and b) putting it right in front of Ms. Davis's face, which she thought would be soothing.

Sometimes I am too inspired for my own good.

When she returned to Ms. Davis's house on

Fourth Street—*her* new abode, she reminded everyone—she'd have to remember to take that pan off the porch rail and toss it in the garbage.

By the time she knocked on Jorden's front door, she had also decided that as soon as she arrived home, she'd ask Ms. Davis if there was anything else she'd done since moving in that Ms. Davis would like undone.

And she would apologize.

But first, she needed to kiss Jorden's wonderful crooked grin of a mouth, and there it was right there, waiting for her, right between those magnificent dimples.

Three

Donald Major went to the gym three times a week. The aesthetic body of a dancer was most appreciated long and lean. Yet when partnered, males had to lift hundred-pound bodies—often sweaty bodies with interfering costumes—and make it look effortless. In order to keep Donald strong without having him bulk up, Jeff Kronkite, company physical therapist for the Mid-Central Festival Ballet, had him working on machines and with free weights.

"Repetitions, repetitions, repetitions. Yes, I

know repeating the word is redundant, but doing the reps is not."

When Jeff spoke, Donald listened. Donald also did Pilates several times a week, as did many in his company.

Like all dancers, out of necessity and for survival, Donald had always been dedicated to keeping his body strong, which wasn't to say he'd never dealt with aches, pains, and injuries, all ongoing side effects of the career. At thirty-eight, although his body reaped the physical rewards of many years of hard work and performance, it also took a little longer to fully recuperate from strains.

No matter, he still followed the rules: Never miss class, usually seventy-five minutes long; work hard at rehearsal, often six hours without a break; eat right; get rest. But since the terrible fall five months ago, he'd become über-obsessive about his health and stamina. Although he knew in his head that the tragedy was not his fault, the *what-if*s of it still haunted him.

And there was so much more.

Maybe if he'd known about Sasha's heart condition, if she had trusted him enough to confide, he could have talked her into seeing the doctor earlier or counterbalanced the sudden limpness in her body. Been more prepared for the possibility of such an event.

Talked her into hanging up her pointe shoes earlier.

Maybe they'd still be together.

He toweled off his forehead, his neck, and under his arms. "Good session today," Jeff said when they passed on his way to the locker room. Yes, it had been. Donald felt strong, capable, ready for the day's class and rehearsal, the evening's performance. A small miracle, really.

Sometimes, if he thought about it hard enough, he wondered how any dancer withstood the rigors, including him, especially with all that was on his mind. Long days, sometimes two performances a day for weeks on end, especially around the Christmas season, plus all the exercise, classes and rehearsals. Go. Go. Go.

But all too soon, it would be over for him too. At best, he had only a couple of years left to perform. Professional dance was a short career. But unlike Sasha, he at least would make the choice to quit—assuming his body held up and he didn't go down again.

He walked toward the showers as thoughts of Sasha hammered at him. Even with all the busyness and the constant company of the corps, he was desperately lonesome for her, sometimes feel-ing like he might go insane without her. During idle moments, a dichotomy of emotions ravaged his brain. As much as he regretted her casualty and the loss of her presence, he also raged with anger that she'd not confided in him at the first signs of her heart ailment.

During the month of hospitalization after their fall, and after two surgeries on her broken sacrum, tailbone, and multifractured leg, Sasha had become increasingly despondent and remote.

Then one day during an awkward visit, she told him, "Donald, I can't do this anymore. Don't come again, and don't call me either. *Seriously,* Donald." She withdrew her hand from his and slipped it beneath the covers, then closed her eyes. "If you truly love me, you'll honor my wishes. You need to keep your career on track, and I need to be alone." He started to protest, but her eyes opened, filled with sudden and fierce determination. "If you try to fight me on this," she said, her voice stony, "I'll give the hospital a no visitations order. You know I'll do it too."

After a dozen years of marriage, there was one thing he knew to be true about Sasha: when his otherwise happy-go-lucky wife made up her mind about something, fighting her only caused her to dig a deeper trench, even if she ended up burying herself in it.

She'd explained everything to him—the arrhythmia, dancing against the odds—and begged him to understand that the accident wasn't his fault. But then to completely cut him off like that? To demand he no longer contact her? How else could he interpret her desire to be left alone? Either he was guilty of causing the accident after all, or he was a painful, constant reminder of the way her life—their life—used to be.

Thus, he'd kissed her on the forehead and left her room in silence. He'd honored her wishes, given her time and space to adjust. Time to rethink, heal, and change her mind about seeing him.

Come to her senses.

They'd eventually get back together. They were so happy before the accident—why wouldn't they reunite? Sasha was a fighter. She'd recover. She always did. This time it was just more complicated. She might not take the stage again, but she'd return to her old cheerful self. She just had to.

After three weeks of leaving her alone, of waiting for her to break the silence and give him a call, enough was enough. He was worried sick. She was his wife!

Once he'd fully recuperated from the nasty hip pointer he incurred during the accident and was back to performing, he tried to phone her from the road and was shocked to learn that she'd left not only the hospital, but the state. He'd spent hours sleuthing before he tracked down her where-abouts. Why in heaven's name had she moved back to Minnesota? Her mom had died a couple of months before her injury, and her dad died when she was a baby. She'd kept no close friends in her little town. After twelve years of marriage, he ought to know.

He sat on the bench in front of his locker and put his head in his hands. *Then again, considering how long she hid a heart condition from me, perhaps I didn't know her at all.*

He rubbed his eyes and began to peel off his sweaty clothes. Did she move just to get away from him? Was that her plan when she dismissed him from her hospital room? Did she want him to stay away forever?

Surely not.

But to this day, she would not answer his calls, which didn't stop him from trying. Sometimes when he left a message, he said only, "It's me again. *Please,* Sasha." Other times, especially if he called late at night, he rambled as long as her voice mail would allow, talking about anything and everything that came to his mind—anything but dance. He'd talk low and quiet, the way he sometimes did after they made love, their strong legs entwined, defenses down.

He got a towel and headed for the showers, recalling times they'd bathed together. But now there were several states between them, and Sasha was still determined to keep him locked out of her life. Perhaps he knew her too well. To fight her head on—to go gallivanting in like a knight in shining armor—would only widen the gap.

He needed to give her time to find her way back to him.

As much as he longed to toss everything aside and be with her, first and foremost was this: he understood that the worst thing he could do for Sasha was to stop dancing himself, a decision he knew would further crush her. Were the circumstances reversed, he had no doubt she would continue on. After a lifetime of tireless dedication and hard work training body and mind, it would be intolerable for him to watch her sacrifice her last years on the stage, simply because *he* went down. There would be two tragedies in the family then. He felt the anger and guilt rising within just thinking about that possibility.

They were dancers. He had to dance now, for both of them.

His steps quickened as he entered the shower and let the tepid water pour onto his head while tears rolled down his cheeks. As he lathered up he wondered how long this could go on. He wanted to cry out from the emotional torture. What worried him most was that by now, maybe he'd given her enough time and space to fall out of love with him.

Why won't you at least talk to me? He smacked his hand against the wet wall. *Why is there always someone in the middle?*

Soon after she disappeared, a stranger's voice, not always the same one, sometimes answered her phone. Each said she was a home health-care worker and that Ms. Davis was not taking calls.

Good Lord! Did she still need home health care? From the surgeries? Or was it her heart?

More recently, however, he always heard the same determined voice of a woman claiming to be Sasha's *assistant*—the word spoken with haughty authority. The first several times she answered, she asked who was calling and put him on hold. Despite his momentary hope he might get through, in the end it didn't happen.

On his last call, the *assistant* again answered. Rather than put him on hold, she simply stated that Ms. Davis had instructed her to remind him that she did not wish to take his calls. That yes, she had received his letters. No, he was *not* to come for a visit. *Absolutely* not.

"Sir," the assistant said, speaking in a voice that sounded rehearsed, "Ms. Davis has instructed me to inform you that she wishes you well, that she is grateful for your ongoing concern and especially your patience."

Patience? A hopeful sign?

How long could—how long *should*—a man wait to see his own wife and continue to call her that?

He finished showering, got dressed, looked at his watch, and grabbed his dance bag, grateful for what came next: class, rehearsal, performance. He had the lead, Conrad, in *Le Corsaire.* He would have to do it all over again tomorrow and the next day and the next day and . . .

There was room for nothing else in his life. Not now.

Not yet, he told himself as he headed to the studio. For now, no matter how bizarre his personal life, the show must go on.

When Sasha opened her eyes and oriented herself, she smelled something cooking on the outdoor grill.

Given the chance, which didn't happen often, Donald loved to cook out on the little hibachi they kept on their high-rise patio in Boston. They were sometimes away from home for months at a time. But when they performed locally, they lived within a mile of the studio and even closer to the opera house where many of the performances were held. Meat or shrimp, fresh veggies drizzled with olive oil, wrapped in foil and cooked on the grill, salad . . . She inhaled deeply and closed her eyes, blinking back a tear.

Her neighbors must be cooking out. Then she heard Evelyn thrashing around in a kitchen drawer. There was nothing restrained about that girl. Nothing.

She took a sip of her tea. Cold. How long had she slept? After she set the teacup in its saucer, she noticed the frying pan was gone from the porch rail. At once, she missed its presence. What was wrong with her, spiting herself to make a point? *I should have outgrown that by now.* But since when did Evelyn listen to her anyway? In the kitchen, the banging of metal against metal continued.

"Evelyn! What on earth are you looking for?" she hollered. "Such a racket!"

She heard a drawer slam shut. She'd witnessed Evelyn hip-checking the old sticky drawers before, implored her to stop the unladylike behavior. "Not only is it a bad habit, but you're going to break either the drawer or your hip!" Why did she waste her breath?

Evelyn appeared in the kitchen doorway. "I'm sorry, Ms. Davis. Did I wake you?"

"What makes you think I was sleeping?"

"Maybe the snoring and the drool?" Evelyn smiled.

Sasha turned crimson and swiped at the corners of her mouth with the back of her knuckle.

"Or maybe there was no drool or snoring," Evelyn said, her eyes twinkling with mischief. "In fact, to be honest, there wasn't. I knew you were sleeping because you didn't open your eyes or answer me when I returned home and called your name. You were so asleep, you didn't even know TuTu was curled up on your lap—unless he hopped up there before you dozed off. When I came in and he jumped to the floor, you still didn't wake up," she said, nearly breathless from the surprise of it all. "A cat on your lap! For *real!* I could hardly believe it myself. First time in the two months I've been here that I saw either one of those cats even get close to you, and there it was on your *lap,* curled up in the sweetest little ball."

"Evelyn Burt! You are utterly insolent," Sasha said, examining her skirt. Much to her dismay, there did appear to be black cat hair on it, which she began to swipe and pick from the fabric. It unnerved her to think one of those hateful cats had crept up on her like that. *On* her. If TuTu and Arabesque hadn't been her mom's cats, rescued by a neighbor after her death, then plopped into her hands two days after she moved in, they would be gone. It was creepy, the way they slipped around the house. She feared one day they'd team up, hide on top of a bookcase or kitchen cabinet, and pounce on her.

"I was just joking with you about the drool, Ms. Davis. But seriously, TuTu was on your lap, and your hand was resting on his back, and . . ."

"Evelyn!" Sasha said, vigorously wiping her hands against each other as if they were covered with deadly bugs.

"If you don't mind my saying so, Ms. Davis, sometimes you take yourself a little too seriously. You looked so relaxed with TuTu on your lap. And to answer your question, yes, I did find what I was looking for in the kitchen." She raised her hand triumphantly and stepped closer, opening her fist to reveal four corn-on-the-cob tongs. "When I stopped by Jorden's, he gave us six ears

41

of fresh corn. He picked up a couple dozen for his folks' party tonight, but they only need eighteen. I put ours on the grill with the steaks."

"All six of them?" Sasha was nearly dizzy from trying to keep up with Evelyn's constant change in topics.

"I figured since you barely eat anything, two for you and four for me. But of course if you want more than two, you can have them. I also figured I should do a better job of following your orders, so I put the frying pan in the garbage. I'm sorry for my . . . insolence, Ms. Davis." For a moment, she sounded truly remorseful.

"Yes, well . . . Now you can follow my orders and put the pan back."

"Good!" Evelyn closed her hand around the tongs. In a flash, she was gone.

The grill was just out of Sasha's sight on the back porch. She heard the grill lid bang shut. Evelyn whisked across the porch the other way, toward the back of the garage. She quickly returned with the pan, set it back on the rail, pulled a few marbles out of her pocket, and plunked them in.

Back toward the grill she went, glancing at her wristwatch, which was as big as any man's. In fact, Sasha was pretty sure it was a man's. Evelyn flashed seven fingers toward Sasha as she passed by the window. Sasha took it to mean that was how long she had before the steaks would be done. Time to start toward the bathroom to wash up for dinner.

She pulled the walker in front of her. The hardest part was getting out of the chair and transferring her weight to the walker. Along with the warm memories the chair evoked, and the way it made her feel close to her mother, another reason she chose this chair for her daily encampment was its relatively high arms, which she used as leverage.

The first home health-care nurse approved of the chair, as long as Sasha put tacky strips on the bottom of the rockers so the chair didn't scoot out from beneath her when she transitioned to the walker. Either that, he said, or she'd have to rearrange the room so the chair was on the area rug. But then she wouldn't be close to the window. Sasha was grateful when a nearby neighbor and dear friend of her mother's picked up the strips. The neighbor's husband came over and applied them.

Every time Sasha pushed up out of the chair, she was thankful for the home health-care nurse's recommendation. The last thing she needed was to land on her back again. Two surgeries were quite enough, thank you.

By the time she finished taking baby steps to the bathroom, getting on and off the toilet— grimacing at the ongoing humiliation of the high-rise toilet seat—and then making her way to the kitchen table and seating herself, she was sweating.

Sweat: at least that was something familiar to a dancer.

She dabbed at her forehead with one of her mother's cloth napkins. Once Evelyn had discovered them in the bureau drawer and claimed them to be "very green," there had been no more paper napkins. For a moment, with her eyes closed and the napkin at her face, Sasha was back at the barre, dabbing her brow with the towel she often kept wrapped around her neck during class.

The screen door slammed and in came Evelyn with a tray full of food. She set it on the kitchen counter, where she divvied up the steaks and corn onto the china plates already set in place.

Sasha had no idea how such a young woman could be so adept, albeit clunky, at so many things. As often as Evelyn said, "I've read where . . . ," it was beyond Sasha why she didn't want to go to college. Evelyn was forever seeking knowledge of one kind or another, bringing home armloads of books from the library, each new set on a different topic. Once when Sasha asked her why no college, the response came quick and simple.

"Love and life. That, and I couldn't be here if I was there, right?"

Sometimes no matter how preposterous the things Evelyn said, they were unarguable.

Evelyn set Sasha's plate in front of her, then

brought her a glass of fresh-squeezed lemonade. Once she'd served herself, Evelyn sat down, bowed her head, put the palms of her hands together, and said her usual premeal prayer, a prayer that covered many things during the day too.

"Grace. Amen."

The first time she'd uttered that prayer at the dinner table, Sasha had said, "That's it?"

"What else do we need or need to remember?" Evelyn had looked truly perplexed, as if the question was absurd.

"How about healing and wellness, an end to war, or thanks for the food, or . . . something about forgiveness?"

"Grace covers it all. Easy-schmeasy and amen."

Sasha had blinked a few times, tried to think up an argument—for instance, where was the grace in what had happened to her?—but knew it would be pointless. By now she knew better than to question many of the acts of Ms. Evelyn Burt.

Evelyn dug right in and encouraged Sasha to do the same.

"Good job, Evelyn!" Evelyn exclaimed after the first bite of her meat. "Superb!"

Sasha took a bite, chewed, held it in her mouth a moment, chewed some more, and swallowed. "I have to agree."

"And don't forget Grandpa's perfect cuts of meat!"

"True."

45

"Oh! That reminds me," Evelyn said, nearly yelling. "Grandpa invited us to dinner next Tuesday night."

"By us, you mean you and Jorden, correct?"

"That too. But also you. Hey!" she said, chuckling. "Poet and know it!" She loved cracking herself up. "Wait till I tell Jorden that one! So, wanna come?"

"Why on earth would your grandfather invite me to dinner?"

"Because he's kind like that," Evelyn said while slathering two tablespoons of butter onto her first ear of corn. "I told him odds were one hundred percent you'd say no, but I'd love it if you surprised me." She sprinkled the ear with what appeared to be a tablespoon of salt and began to gnaw her way down a row, as if trying to set a new Guinness World Record for corn eating. "Oh, man, that is divine."

"I was going to say I hate to disappoint you," Sasha said, "but one-hundred percent odds against anything pretty much covers the bases. So, no surprises. As you very well know, I can barely get around in my own house without doing myself in. Getting to my doctor appointments is trial enough. I'm hardly up for a night out." *Especially with someone I barely know.*

"Whatever you say."

Sasha raised her eyebrows. "Are you questioning my abilities?"

46

"Oh no, ma'am! Not right now." Evelyn wiped her mouth with her napkin and buttered her next ear of corn.

"Now?"

"Once they let that physical therapist have at you, things will change, and likely pretty quickly. When my aunt had her knee replaced, I think they had her up and at it within hours after the surgery. I couldn't believe how quickly she started getting around, and with only one crutch, then a cane, then *blamm-o!*" She said the word so loudly, it caused Sasha to jolt. "Off to the grocery store she went, and to her Bunco club and canasta parties and the casino and . . ."

"Hoping you're soon out of a job?"

"Of course not! I love it here!"

Sasha could not imagine why. She was so miserable and cranky, she could barely stand herself much of the time. "You know, Evelyn, a knee replacement is nearly a routine procedure these days. They have it down to a science. My issues are not that pat."

"Issues. Let's discuss." Evelyn placed her ear of corn on the corner of her plate. "You know, Ms. Davis, you've never really explained the whole thing to me. Did you break something, like your back? Or do you have a disease, or did you have a heart attack? Everybody in town knows there was a terrible fall, but everybody thinks there's more to the story, something the press doesn't know." She picked between her two front teeth with her little fingernail.

"Really, Evelyn. Please get yourself a tooth-pick."

"I'm sorry, ma'am. You're right." She hopped up, retrieved the china toothpick holder, set it on the table and selected a toothpick. Before she could get it to her teeth, Sasha raised her hand to her mouth as a gesture to remind Evelyn to cover hers. They'd gone over this before. Evelyn obliged.

Did I break my back? Do I have a disease? Will I recover?

Perhaps the better question is, do I have an ounce of courage? Did I ever?

"This is all I'm going to say to you about my condition, Evelyn, and I'm only going to say it once, so please listen carefully: There is a condition, and there were multiple injuries, and it was complicated, even for the doctors. There is no easy answer. Yes, once I get into physical therapy, better mobility might come quickly. But how much mobility remains to be seen. There. Now you know everything about my condition that I do."

Except that it's the regret that most terrorizes and paralyzes me.

Four

Quilt folded on the bed rack, teeth brushed, pajamas on, a pile of books nearby, Evelyn stacked up all four fluffy down pillows and sank into them, ready for a readathon.

She loved this old bedroom with its tall ceiling. The space was nearly three times as large as her room at home. By comparison, the entire house was palatial, really. She loved the small childhood ranch home of her youth, the one her folks still lived in. But a girl could get spoiled by a room this size—although she and Jorden had already talked about renting a trailer in the trailer park just west of town when they were married. That way when they were home, they would never be too far apart, and she could continually bask in the light of his brightness. Cozy. Romantic. The mere thought rosied her cheeks.

She hopped out of bed and threw open the window, glad for the break in the stifling heat. The evening breeze felt wonderfully refreshing. Even so, she kept the old oscillating fan turned to high.

It was difficult, living in a house filled with stale air. She sometimes stuck her head out the back door just to inhale a few breaths that didn't feel already used up. How Ms. Davis could stand it so warm, and drink hot tea to boot, was beyond her. Evelyn had cleared it with Ms. Davis to buy a ten-pound bag of ice from the Kwik Trip and keep it in the freezer. For Evelyn, it was iced tea and iced water. When temperatures rose, it was iced everything.

She hopped back into bed and drew the pile of books up beside her. Wiggling her toes, she studied her fat ankles, ragged toenails and extra-wide feet shaped like her father's. She drew the bottom of her feet together and noted the dry skin on the back of her heels, something she'd never given thought to until earlier today.

Ms. Davis paid a young woman named Dawn to drive from her salon two towns away to give her a weekly pedicure. Evelyn longed to tell Jorden about the decadence, but what happened in this house stayed in this house. Period. Any talk of such activities would be nothing short of gossip. Since Ms. Davis bothered to hire a nail technician from so far away, it seemed evident she did so for privacy reasons.

Today was the first time Evelyn had passed through the room during the pedicure. Aside from the fact that primping wasn't Evelyn's thing, knowing her services wouldn't be needed for at least an hour, she usually seized the opportunity to get out of the house. But that morning, Ms. Davis had told her she expected a few important phone calls on her landline, asked if Evelyn could please stick around and field them, and gave her specific instructions how to handle them. She was to tell the physician Sasha needed to see him and to go ahead and make the appointment. And she was to tell that insistent media person who called every morning at the same time that no, Ms. Davis was *not* interested in an interview, and she was thinking of filing harassment charges if he didn't stop calling. She would let him know if/when she changed her mind. In the meantime, stop calling!

"I especially do not wish to be interrupted during my pedicure appointment, Evelyn. Ever. Make it clear to that man that I mean business about filing charges."

Evelyn was carrying an armload of clean sheets to Ms. Davis's bedroom when she came upon the remarkable scene. Dawn sat on a short stool at a slight angle to Ms. Davis, a soak tub on the floor between them. She held one of Ms. Davis's slender feet in her hands. The back of Ms. Davis's calf rested on a towel draped over Dawn's thigh.

This was the first time Evelyn had seen Ms. Davis's feet without a shoe or slipper. Her skirt was pushed up to the bottom of her knees, her long thin calves exposed. For someone who danced in front of hundreds of thousands of people wearing a tutu, she was always so draped, as if hiding her body. Even though the exposure was slight, Evelyn felt embarrassed, as if she'd stumbled upon Ms. Davis nude. The scene felt so intimate, so private.

The technician squirted what appeared to be oil onto the top of Ms. Davis's foot, which she began to massage. Evelyn passed by, into Ms. Davis's bedroom just off the kitchen, keeping her eyes on the action as long as she could without rotating her head, lest she be perceived as a gawker. She quickly set the sheets on the bed. Since the technician's back was mostly toward her from that viewpoint, she dared a peek around the kitchen corner. She wouldn't have done so had she not noticed as she passed that Ms. Davis's eyes were closed. Otherwise she'd be looking right at her.

Ms. Davis's head rested on her support pillow in the rocker, eyes thankfully still shut. Her arms rested relaxed at her sides, forearms and hands in her lap, the back of one hand in the palm of the other. Evelyn heard Ms. Davis release an audible sigh. Due to the angle, Evelyn could only catch glimpses of what the technician was actually doing. She worked so gently, kneading, rubbing her thumbs into the bottom of the foot, slowly bending the toes, massaging the back of the heel.

Evelyn held her breath. The look on Ms. Davis's face was nothing short of a beatific transformation. Ms. Davis actually smiled. All the hard and ever-present frown lines softened and melted away. The massage must feel wonderful. But Evelyn felt sure there was more to her contentment than just a pedicure. Ms. Davis appeared transported, as if engaged in an out-of-body experience.

Although Evelyn had previously caught glimpses of this same phenomena—especially when she saw Ms. Davis staring at the ballerina in the snowglobe, and again the other evening when she'd entered the kitchen with the steaks—this was the first time she'd witnessed what appeared to be a . . . surrender to whatever "it" was. Memories? Daydreams?

Sometimes when Ms. Davis appeared "out there," her fingers rhythmically tapped against her leg, or she hummed or nodded her head.

Was she dancing?

In bed, Evelyn rotated her heels so she didn't have to see their wide calloused form, wiggled her toes again, imagined what it would feel like to have someone massaging them. Maybe she should call her Aunt Patty, owner of the Beauty Barn, to see how much a pedicure cost. She wondered if Jorden would notice if her toes, sprouting through her Birkenstock sandals (when she wasn't wearing gym shoes), suddenly sported pink polish, a thought that made her cheeks flush again.

Although she and Jorden engaged in their lavishly fair share of smooching and cuddling, Evelyn had made it clear when they started dating that she was going to be with only one man in her lifetime and that man would be her husband—

and then only after he was her husband. Thoughts of crawling into bed with pink toenails in a cozy little trailer caused her to shudder, then quickly reach for the book on the top of her stack.

Albert Einstein: A Biography. The perfect distraction. She flipped to her bookmark and began to read, faster than she'd ever read before, and she was fast.

Who knew Mr. Einstein played Beethoven on the violin, and so well? I love *Beethoven!*

Although Jorden's taste ran toward country western, he was kind enough not to insist on blaring it when they were together. She'd always loved classical music, which she listened to when she worked on art projects. Jorden would fake yawn whenever she turned it on.

Music! That's what we need in this house!

She'd tried a few times to listen to her MP3 player, but Ms. Davis didn't approve of her wearing earbuds while she was on duty. When Ms. Davis had delivered *that* lesson in the fine art of manners, Evelyn was disappointed, but she understood, mostly, and accepted the judgment.

Tomorrow she would ask Ms. Davis if she could, at the very least, see if the old radio worked. The dark, dreary house was too quiet all the time. Evelyn had a small TV in her room, but it was usually too hot upstairs to relax in the evenings to watch it. In truth, although Jorden loved any and all reality shows, she wasn't much of a TV person anyway. Obviously, neither was Ms. Davis. Evelyn had only seen her turn on the television a few times, occasionally watching something about history or a short bit of news. But she'd usually quickly turn it off, complaining about the mindless chatter and shoddy reporting.

Ms. Davis spent a good deal of her time reading too. She subscribed to several newspapers, all but the local rag delivered by mail. They came from cities around the country, including two from New York and one from Boston. Twice Evelyn had noticed pages folded to articles about breakthroughs in heart disease. *Yes, there must be something more.*

Ms. Davis used to subscribe to a couple of dance magazines too, but shortly after Evelyn came to work for her, Ms. Davis had her cancel the subscriptions. This month they'd arrived anyway, which caused Ms. Davis to get on Evelyn's case. But when Evelyn showed her the printed pages from the Internet cancellation—she'd had to take her laptop to her folks' house to use their Wi-Fi and printer—the situation infuriated Ms. Davis.

"What is wrong with businesses today? Is no one reliable?"

"I am, Ms. Davis. You can always count on me."

One day Ms. Davis had casually inquired about the stacks of books Evelyn brought home from her frequent library visits, then asked if she might read one while Evelyn looked at another. Soon, they'd begun trading off volumes on Evelyn's current topical interest, both finishing most of the books before their due dates. Evelyn asked Ms. Davis if she had her own library card (no), then if she'd like her own library card (no), then told her she'd be happy to pick up whatever she wanted. But Ms. Davis declined all such requests, saying that, for the most part, she found Evelyn's taste enlightening, albeit eclectic and occasionally peculiar—especially the time she brought home a stack of books on how to build a chicken coop.

"One day," Evelyn had explained, "when Jorden and I can afford it, I see our family buying an eight- to ten-acre piece of property, growing most of our own food. Organic, of course. We'll have chickens, maybe a pig or two. Get the kids in 4-H."

"Interesting," Ms. Davis said in response. "Is Jorden reading about organic farming too?"

"No," she said, then chuckled. "He's not much of a reader. When he does read, he's more into steampunk."

"Steampunk?"

"It's kind of like a subculture—subgenre, if you will—of sci-fi. But different."

"I take it you don't read steampunk, then?"

"No. I do not." A look of pain crossed Evelyn's face. "I tried, to be supportive of Jorden and all. It's not that there's anything wrong with it, of course," she said, fanning her enthusiasm. "It's just not my thing. This," she said, holding up one

56

of her chicken coop books, "all nonfiction, really, is closer to my heart."

And so, Ms. Davis read about building chicken coops too. The woman, Evelyn decided, was impossible to figure. She had another of the Einstein books downstairs with her right now.

Evelyn closed her book, finding it difficult to concentrate. She tapped her fingers on the title, the action reminding her of Ms. Davis's finger-tapping bliss-out moments, leading her back to her quest to get some music in the house.

She'd spied a large collection of vinyl albums shelved in a built-in bookcase in the dreary living room where she sometimes sat to read. It was too difficult to decipher most of the spines on the thin sleeves, which looked well worn, but they appeared to be classical music. There must be a record player somewhere, perhaps built into the top of that old radio console, which had a hinged lid. She would have lifted it by now, but feared that, like the floorboards, it might squeak. Perhaps some Beethoven was among those albums.

As she turned off the light, the happy strains of "Ode to Joy" from Beethoven's Ninth Symphony played in her head. Tomorrow, one way or the other, she would dedicate herself to getting some music in this house. It would be good for both of them.

Maybe while the music played, she'd even talk Ms. Davis into letting her repaint that dungeony living room. She'd waited long enough to ask.

Five

Sasha was awakened by the sounds of Evelyn banging around in the kitchen. She looked at the clock. Six-thirty. If she'd slept well last night, it wouldn't have been that big a deal; she usually got up around seven anyway. But she'd tossed and turned in her rental bed, complete with twin-size air mattress designed to relieve pressure and pain, not sinking into a restful sleep until the wee morning hours, sometime after she jostled her way to the kitchen to take a pain pill.

For the past several months, she had tried to do without pain pills, giving great consideration to the question, how bad is the pain, relative to pain I often danced with? She'd heard the stories. It was too easy to become addicted to those pills, especially when not much else was going on in her life. And idleness, she'd found, rendered too much time to dwell on pain.

When she'd been performing, there was no time to sit around and feel sorry for herself, no matter what ailed her. She had Donald to cheer her on, rub her shoulders, knead her feet, apply soothing lotion to the small of her back, all of which she in turn did for him.

Now, between heart meds, vitamins, and an antidepressant, which she more often than not stubbornly refused to take, she had enough pills to swallow every morning. Still, sometimes, like this day's wee morning hours when she could not sleep, pain relief was necessary.

Although her pedicure had been wonderful—heavenly, really, the sense of touch delivering its own medicinal magic—during the many coats of polish and drying time, the particular angle of her right leg caused a twitch near the site of the second surgery. She did her best to ignore it. But after the technician left and her polish dried, the twitch turned into a spasm, then a throb, which when combined with her racing mind, meant no sleep.

For next week's pedicure appointment, she thought as she pulled her pillow closer under the curve of her neck, she'd have to remember to readjust her hips in the chair more often, a procedure that sometimes stirred up its own pain issues. She wouldn't wish a severely fractured sacrum *and* a fractured coccyx on anyone. Anti-inflammatories prohibited bone growth, surgeries brought risks of infections, healing fractures prohibited cardio rehab. There was always a Catch-22. She'd just need to be more mindful of her position throughout her next pedicures, navigate the waters as best she could.

It was not an option to cancel her standing

pedicure appointment; the small yet new-to-her pleasure was worth any consequences. Since her earliest childhood dance classes, she'd been told what wonderful feet she had for dancing, a prerequisite if she was to pursue a career in dance: square toes, excellent plantar flexion, and a "soft" Achilles tendon. But she'd also been warned about the hidden risks of allowing someone else to care for those precious feet.

"And never, but never," one of her teachers said, "wear nail or toe polish, which catches the light on the stage." The teacher went on to both regale and horrify the entire class with tales of hideous infec-tions and fungi left in the after-math of pedicures gone bad. "If you want to be a serious dancer," she said, her face stern, her tone of voice verging on hysteria, "be smart, and care for your *own* feet!"

Although Sasha had encountered dancers in the company who treated themselves to pedicures, the very idea scared her to death—until now.

Funny, she thought, rubbing her toes together under the covers, *this small defiance in the presence of such overall cowardice.* But now, what did she have to lose, even if her pedicure did go bad? She'd never dance again anyway, not as a professional. No matter what hopeful gibberish any of the doctors told her, she knew better. Even if by some miracle she did eventually heal, by then she would have aged out.

When the pot-banging in the kitchen finally died down, Sasha tried to go back to sleep. Just when she'd slipped into a twilight state, the loud meowing of cats—their usual morning routine of bugging Evelyn until she fed them—and the smell of sausage wafted her way. *No, that's bacon.* Better to just get up now and go to bed early tonight.

By the time she did her morning duties, got dressed, and made her way to the table, the cats were back in hiding. But as if Sasha had stepped back in time, a full English breakfast filled the table, complete with juice, a cup of thick porridge, bacon and sausage, eggs, beans, tomatoes, and mushrooms.

The girl is amazing.

Last week, dreamy-eyed and expectantly sitting on the edge of her chair, Evelyn had asked Sasha about her favorite travel adventures. The two of them had just finished responding to a stack of fan letters that had been accumulating for months. They were from all over the world, which piqued Evelyn's curiosity and seemed to give her permission to inquire. Sasha had dictated and Evelyn typed, fast enough to keep up with her. Sasha had hoped the frantic pace of their task would throw Evelyn off her growing inquiries, but no such luck. The only good thing was that Evelyn never asked why Sasha didn't do her own correspondence.

When Sasha moved to Minnesota, she'd been so long in the hospital without her laptop, she decided to leave it behind. She found removal from the ability—the temptation, really—to instantly send an e-mail to Donald or to Google his name emotionally easier. She didn't have it in her to read online reviews about his performances and those of the dancers who filled her shoes.

Sasha usually rebuffed Evelyn's personal inquiries. But that day, for whatever reason (was Evelyn's persistency finally wearing her down?), rather than flag Evelyn off or divert her to dance highlights during her travels—like staying healthy, first-class accommodations, standing ovations, magnificent reviews, performing with the Kirov in Russia, or heady honors such as twice being chosen to play the fiery Kitri in *Don Quixote*, set to Ludwig Minkus's superb score—Sasha had instead surprised herself and extolled the delightful discovery of a full English breakfast.

Three years ago, she and Donald, whom she did not mention—*never* mentioned—had appeared at the Royal Opera House in London. When the short run was over, they spent a wonderful week traveling through the Yorkshire countryside, staying at cozy, even rustic, bed and breakfasts. They enjoyed the time off and especially each other. Every morning they were greeted by the most wonderful hosts and a full English breakfast. Evelyn said she'd never heard of such a thing but that it sounded *yum.*

Apparently Evelyn had since read a book on the topic or spent time Googling, as she was fond of saying, on that ever-present laptop of hers that she occasionally reminded Sasha she had to take elsewhere to hook up to the Internet. This morning, she'd delivered the meal to perfection. Her Grandpa Burt must have cut special wide, meaty bacon slices. English bacon looked nothing like the bacon typically served in the states.

Even though Sasha was still yawning, the meal ushered in peaceful memories of beautifully haunting moors and dales, skittish sheep in the middle of the road, laughter . . . serenity. The trip and time off had been such an uncommon and sweet time to share with Donald.

A month ago, Sasha had finally gathered enough courage to go through one, and only one, of her mother's dresser drawers. Therein, she discovered stacks of postcards she and Donald sent from around the world, ones that didn't make the scrapbooks, but which her mom nonetheless kept. A line here, a highlight there. *Interesting, yet heartbreaking,* she thought, *reading tidbits from one's own exciting past.*

But the notes on the cards from Yorkshire were so different, detailed and filled with lightness. Such tiny print on those cards, as if she'd attempted, was compelled even, to cram all the day's joy into the small space. Perhaps finding those cards was why she'd mentioned the full English breakfast to Evelyn.

Breaking Sasha's spell of Yorkshire reminiscence, the memories drawn closer to the surface with each perfectly presented portion of the meal, Evelyn began to fidget. When they were done eating, she catapulted from her chair, cleaned up the dishes, put away the leftovers, then scooted upstairs, announcing she was off to make her bed.

By the time Sasha settled in her rocker, Evelyn was standing before her, asking if there was anything she needed. Chores? Phone calls? Special instructions for anything? Laundry? Correspondence? Sasha began to think the eager-to-please Evelyn was setting her up for something. *Perhaps that's why the breakfast?* It only took another second to learn her hunch was correct.

"You know, Ms. Davis, I discovered a bunch of record albums in the living room. I wonder if there is a record player somewhere, like perhaps hidden in the top of that old console radio? It's awfully quiet around here. How about I check on a few things, get us set up for some music in this house? Or perhaps you'd like to come in the living room with me to supervise my explorations?" Evelyn said, her enthusiasm unbridled.

"Evelyn. I haven't yet gone through that room myself. After my mother died last December, I needed to get back to my tour as quickly as possible. I decided to just leave everything the way it was, thinking I'd tackle it later this summer when I had some time off." *After I emotionally settled. When perhaps Donald and I could do so together. And now look at me: alone, nearly crippled and cowering, one drawer emotionally doing me in.* "But the way things turned out, it could be awhile."

"Let me help you with that project, Ms. Davis. I'm strong. I can move furniture. I'm good at decisions. Whatever it takes. I can get some boxes, sort things out . . ."

Sasha pounded the side of her clenched hand on the arm of her chair. "Does it *ever* occur to you, Evelyn, that sometimes you need to think before you speak? My mother hasn't been gone even nine months, and I am a dancer who can no longer dance, leaving me stripped of two of the most precious things in my life. And here you are, practically a stranger to me, prattling on about sorting—dare I say to give away?—private belongings in the house in which I was raised, the house in which I live—the house in which *you* are but a temporary *guest*."

Evelyn bit her bottom lip. "I am so sorry," she said, her voice low and weak. "I was thinking about how quiet it is in here, how nice music would be—how much *you* must miss the music, especially after all those years dancing. When you said you hadn't had a chance to go through things, I thought you were implying . . .

"Never mind." Evelyn cast her eyes to the floor. "The more I say, the more assumptive I realize I've been. Again." She looked up at Sasha. "I am so sorry."

Sasha stared at her hands, which were trembling. She clasped her fingers together. "I could not get to sleep last night. I was awakened too early by your insistent banging in the kitchen. After such a large breakfast, I am not only weary, but now uncomfortably full. Right now, a *completely* quiet house sounds divine to me. I'm sure you have some errands you need to run—or a need to visit your family or your fiancé—so I'm giving you the rest of the day off."

Evelyn swallowed. "Yes, ma'am. I'll make up a couple of sandwiches for your lunch and leave them in the fridge. I'll bring you a carafe of hot water and a selection of tea bags before I head out too. I'll be back in time to make dinner."

"I have enough leftovers from breakfast to last me a week, but I'll take the hot water. No need to return for dinner. I'll be fine."

Evelyn swallowed again. She looked like she was about to say something but thought better of it. "Yes, ma'am. If you need anything, you have my cell number. I'll be gone soon."

Quiet as a mouse, Evelyn went to work in the kitchen. Soon Evelyn delivered the carafe and tea bags, as well as a small plate of cookies she'd baked the day before. She ran upstairs, came down with her backpack, and out the door she went.

Not until Sasha saw Evelyn disappear down the street on her bicycle did she notice it was pouring rain.

Not until Evelyn had been gone for ten minutes did she notice how quiet it was in the house—how very quiet.

Not until she'd cried for five minutes and nodded off in the chair did she stop asking herself why she kept turning everyone away, especially those who tried the hardest to please and help her.

Those she needed the most.

Between the rain and her tears, Evelyn could barely see where she was going. Worse yet, she had no idea where that would be.

It wasn't even 8:00 a.m. Jorden was working the day shift today, which for him started at seven. She couldn't go to her folks' house either, since they likely hadn't left for work yet. The last time she'd dropped by, they tried to milk information about Ms. Davis out of her (everybody in town did), then started in again about college. They wanted to know if Jorden had any plans to "better himself" and if she had come to her senses yet and given the current direction of her life a second thought. She'd left in a huff. She was not ready to engage in *that* battle again. Especially not today, not when she felt at least one of her recent impulsive decisions to strike out on her own balanced on shaky ground: she'd just been sent packing.

The torrential raindrops landed so hard they pressed the hood to her slicker down half over her eyes. She pulled the garment back off her face a little. The winds gusted so strongly, she felt as if the rain and tears might drown her.

She held out her arm and turned toward the library, then decided she wasn't in the mood for more quiet. Because of the rain, she hadn't packed her laptop anyway.

She needed music. Color. *Something* with life to it!

She needed the company of someone who wouldn't get on her case or correct her. Someone who simply accepted her for who she was.

Grandpa!

The butcher shop wasn't open yet, but he was always there early. She checked behind her before pulling a U-turn in the middle of the street. By the time she leaned her bike against a lamp-post, scurried beneath the awning in front of the shop, and pulled off her rain slicker, she'd thankfully quit crying.

She couldn't remember the last time she'd cried. Listed as "Ms. Happy-Go-Lucky" in her high school yearbook, a phrase she thought was likely a tongue-in-cheek slam, she was still proud to call herself an optimist. Her mom always said her positive, go-get-'em personality rivaled that of her grandpa. She couldn't receive a better compliment.

But moreover, crying was for wimps, not worldly women.

She pasted on a smile and banged on the door. "Grandpa! It's me, Sweet Cakes!" She pressed her drenched nose to the glass door and peered in, giving the door another solid rap. "Gramps! Open up!"

He appeared from the back room, wiping his hands down the front of his white butcher's apron, then smiled and waved. After he unlocked the door, she fell into his arms.

"Goodness!" He grabbed her in a big bear hug and gave her a couple of aggressive squeezes. "Aren't you out and about early, and as wet as a car wash." He wiped water from his face and playfully flicked it at her. "How'd the full English breakfast go over?" he asked. "Today was the day, right?"

"She loved it," Evelyn said, breaking eye contact.

Grandpa raised an eyebrow. He knew her too well. "But . . ."

"But . . . Let's just say the meal was yum, but there were a few bumps in the road, having nothing to do with food. Nothing I can't handle, though."

"Got a minute to give me a hand?" he asked,

checking the clock, then nodding toward the back.

"I'd love to." She hung her slicker on the coat tree, taking note of the trail of water she'd left behind. "Let's have at it. Whatever you need, I'm your gal."

"How long you got?" He pulled a loose sliver of ham from the slicer and handed it to her.

Even though she was stuffed, she popped the ham into her mouth. Some of her earliest memories of her Grandpa Burt took place in the comforting surroundings of this very shop, most including the constant delivery of slivers of meats and cheese. "How long have I got? The whole day long. And you are the lucky one who gets me." She grabbed an apron off a hook and tied it on.

"Mr. Fiancé working?"

"Yup."

"All is well in Love Land then?"

"Lovey dovey," she said, giving him a wink, which he returned.

"How about you wash your hands, slip on a pair of those disposable rubber gloves, and start weighing up a few two-pound packets of beef stew meat? It's on special, starting today. I got it all cut up, right over there." He pointed at the pile.

"Consider it done." She retrieved a short stack of white cardboard-boat containers from a shelf, washed up, donned the gloves, and set to work. She knew the drill; she'd done it before.

70

"Seen your folks lately?" he asked as he began to cut pork chops.

"I can tell by the tone in your voice," she said, turning to look at him, her enthusiasm deflated, "that Dad's been talking to you, right?" She shook her head.

"Right. But you know I'm in your corner, Sweet Cakes. Just remember, your folks only want the best for you."

"I know," she said, sounding unconvinced. She grabbed a handful of beef chunks and slammed them into one of the cardboard boats. "How about some music, Gramps?"

"That's just what I was thinking," he said. When he turned the radio on, it was set to a morning talk show, but he quickly tuned to a classical station. "We got us almost forty-five minutes before I open. Let's crank this baby up." He revved the volume as loud as he could take it.

"Thanks, Gramps. You are exactly what I needed this morning. Exactly. Let it rain; let it pour; let the joyful, music-laden meat-market games begin!" She removed one chunk of meat from the package, and the scale showed exactly two pounds. "Scooooore!"

She looked up toward the heavens, winked, and whispered, *"Grace! Amen."*

Six

Sasha poured herself a fresh cup of hot water. She surveyed the tea bags and opted for a Black Cherry Berry from Celestial Seasonings. The tea bag had no string or tag attached to identify it, but Evelyn had stuck Post-it notes around the edge of the plate to inform Sasha of her choices. The simple kindness of the girl, even after Sasha had rudely ousted her, nearly did Sasha in.

What kind of wretch have I become? The thick, dark cloud that encompassed her rendered her incapable of overriding her own abysmalness.

Even though she'd napped on and off for nearly two hours, nightmares and a few rounds of thunder kept her sleep from being restful. She yawned, looked out the window, dunked the tea bag with the spoon, finally took a sip. *Mmm.*

Despite the rain, which had momentarily let up, the bright yellow goldfinch couple (Evelyn was teaching her to identify the species) was at the frying pan again, one bathing while the other kept watch.

That's the way life's meant to be: equally able.

Soon a robin appeared, sending the goldfinches fluttering off. She watched the robin splash and bathe, puff out his wings, toss water in the air, keep an ever-watchful eye out for predators.

"Feeling vulnerable?" she asked, as though she expected him to turn and nod. "I know what that's like," she said, taking another sip. The robin hopped up on the pan's half-melted handle.

The pan. What a fiasco, one she'd tried to block from her memory. But there the pan sat, returned to the porch rail by her own dictum. Evelyn had handled the ridiculous "throw it away, take it away, bring it back" orders without batting an eye. If the girl was anything, she was resilient— although Sasha knew that everyone had a threshold, including Donald. She hoped Evelyn hadn't reached hers today. Right this minute, she might be securing plans to quit and get the heck out. How much correction, admonishment, and displaced anger could one person put up with before deciding enough was enough?

If Evelyn quit, even if she didn't say anything about her treatment, it wouldn't take long for people in town to figure out why. No matter what the age of her replacement, should Sasha even be able to find someone who could put up with her, she doubted she'd ever secure anyone as talented at so many things as Evelyn. Although the girl was headstrong, during the interview her tenacity had given Sasha a good feeling about her capabilities, productivity, and loyalty. She hadn't been wrong. From phone calls to nosy knocks at the front door, as a protector, she was a warrior.

Sasha glanced at the short stack of cookies, picked one up, took a bite. A small bird, one she didn't think she'd seen before, landed on the rim of the pan. She thought about grabbing the bird book Evelyn had given her as a gift, saying she'd already memorized it. Instead, Sasha studied the tiny creature's sweet profile, his thin, fragile, dancer-like legs, and savored the delicious flavor in the pecan-laden cookie shaped like a crescent moon. The cookie was as light and tasty as any professional bakery's goods. What had Evelyn called them? Cosmic Wonders or something like that. She said she'd taken a few liberties with the ingredients in a recipe she found on the Internet, had renamed them, and "made them her own," a phrase she admitted she'd stolen from *American Idol*, a show she said her Jorden was addicted to. Evelyn didn't seem to watch that much television. At least not while she was at the house. She must have watched with Jorden.

Thunder rattled the house again. Sasha picked up another cookie, held it to her nose, inhaled, thought she whiffed a hint of almond before taking a bite.

Evelyn was impulsive, seemingly unaware of her clunkiness (in an odd way, a refreshing departure from all the delicate and precise movements of the uniformly shaped dancers Sasha spent her life with), a little socially inept, and occasionally

74

impertinent. But she never meant to be any of those things, likely couldn't help being all of them. She was just . . . Evelyn. Strong, independent, enthusiastic, gutsy, and artistically gifted. Fast-typing, fast-talking Evelyn. Whom Sasha had dismissed for the day, as if Evelyn were a pesky fly on the skin of her life.

She looked again at the tea labels, each so carefully printed.

To what depths have I sunk to treat another human being with such disregard?

She sighed, brushed the crumbs from her hands, then off her lap, diverted her eyes to the pan again. Rather than relive *that* incident, she picked up the snowglobe.

She'd caught Evelyn staring at it a few times, curiosity brimming. Sasha never offered the story, one she was sure Evelyn would enjoy—at least until the creepy part. Even Sasha hated to think about that. And yet, like a scab one can't resist picking, the memory itched until she scratched it.

She was so regretful and guilt-laden about so many things. If only she'd heeded what, in retrospect, felt like the snowglobe's ominous premonitions for her own life. Maybe everything would be different.

She settled the globe in her lap, looked at the pan again, then down at her weak legs. It didn't take idle muscles long to lose their strength. These legs used to hold her up on pointe and were admired by critics—their length, along with her short torso inherited from her father, gave her the proportions considered perfect for a dancer. Oh, how she'd taken so very much for granted!

How long can a person strive to keep from constantly reliving every horrible incident, every bad choice, and not go insane?

No wonder she often didn't sleep well. Her subconscious was likely busy all night trying to bring to life everything she spent her days striving to forget: the crash, rounds of post-op pain, the end of her career, her treatment of Donald, the death of her mother, the caustic fumes from a melting pan handle, her cruelties to Evelyn, the way the dancer inside the snowglobe tried to warn her . . .

How many times did I send you off to be repaired? she asked, looking straight into the blue eyes of the dancer in the globe.

The snowglobe repairman had often asked her if she'd dropped the globe or left it exposed to direct heat for any length of time. No, she had not, she assured him each time she fielded one of his calls. He could think of no other explanation for it continually and inexplicably coming apart. The strong metal wires that hinged the arms and legs to the torso of the dancer—*near the dancer's heart and tailbone*—just seemed to . . . unlink.

"It's like a Houdini trick," he said. "I've never

seen anything like it, and I've seen a lot of peculiar things. I just don't get it."

She'd had the snowglobe for thirty-two years. It was a gift from her mother on her fifth birthday.

"You have to be very careful with this, honey. It looks very old, so Mommy will keep it on *her* dresser until your eighth birthday. By then, you'll be more naturally careful. You let Mommy know when you want to look at it, okay?"

Although disappointed to learn it would usually be out of her reach, Sasha was mesmerized. She'd never seen such a thing. The dancer's jointed-at-the-shoulders arms were rounded, her fingertips almost touching in front of her pelvis. *"It looks like she's holding her own invisible snowglobe, Mommy!"* She later learned the dancer's arms assumed first position. Her jointed-at-the-hip legs, slightly outturned, were long and delicate. The dancer stood on her toes.

Sasha watched as her mother turned the globe upside down. Slowly, the dancer's arms floated up over her head and her legs split out, stopping hip high. When the globe was upside down, the dancer looked like she was cartwheeling on the stars, little particles within the globe swirling around her head. When her mother righted the globe, together, in silence, they watched until the dancer resumed her original serene pose and the last tiny speck of snow settled at her feet, making it appear as if she were perched on a cloud.

"Where did you get this, Mommy?" Sasha asked, gently putting her finger to the glass, feeling a bolt of excitement race through her.

"Remember when you and Grandma and I went to the fairgrounds last fall?"

Sasha nodded.

"While you and Grandma were looking at the baby dolls, the sun bounced off this round globe at another booth and caught my eye. When I saw the dancer, I just knew it was for you. So when you and Grandma got in line for hot dogs, I snuck over and bought it. The man I purchased it from said, 'I knew you'd come over to get this for your daughter, who will one day become a famous ballerina.' He said, 'Tell her to keep her eye on the ballerina. She will lead you.' And you know what? I believe he was exactly right!" Her mom set the globe on the table and drew Sasha's hands into hers. "But that's not the whole present, not even the best part. To go along with this, Mommy signed you up for dance classes! They start next week."

Sasha squealed with joy. From the time she could stand and hang on to a footstool for balance, whenever she heard music, her legs bounced and she wiggled her bottom. As she grew, she danced, twirled, adored costumes— sometimes changing dress-up clothes, purchased by her grandmother at a resale shop, several times an afternoon—and naturally pointed her toes.

She'd begged her mother for ballet lessons from the moment she understood what that meant. In the whole wide world, there could not be a better gift! She wrapped her arms around her mother's neck and squeezed until she was out of breath.

"But there is one condition to all of this, Sasha, my little bird," her mother said, drawing Sasha's face near.

"What?" Sasha asked, her hazel eyes locked on the painted blue eyes of the dancer.

"You have to give me your blanket." Her mom looked somber.

The blanket was a secret only she and her mom knew about. The pink fabric, rather large for a baby blanket, was worn thin from years of cuddling, its satin trim long gone. Her father had brought it to the hospital the day after Sasha was born. He'd shopped for it himself. Thus, the gift was a precious treasure for both of them, laced with the memories of love freely given and too soon lost. He'd died when Sasha was only four months old.

"You're going to be in kindergarten this year," Sasha's mother said. "Big girls don't need blankets."

Sasha said okay. Anything to keep the snow-globe, to start dance lessons—to become the famous dancer someone she did not even know proclaimed she would be. From the moment she laid eyes on the beautiful lady in the globe,

Sasha never doubted the prediction; her mother's words echoed a sacred truth already buried deep in her soul. Each time she touched the globe, her body came alive, as if empowered to fly. Without batting an eye, she marched to her bedroom and dragged the pink blanket out from under her pillow.

Thirty-two years ago, Sasha thought, as she turned the globe over, then righted it and watched as the dancer leaped in the air and settled back onto her pointed toes on the familiar cloud of snow.

Sasha's eyes glazed over as she allowed herself to feel the triumphant spinning energy of a *fouetté rond de jambe en tournant*: one foot flat on the floor, arms extended to the sides, then *up* on her toe as she drew her arms into a circle in front of her, free leg whipping momentum, her head spotting the turns. This was the first time since the accident she'd allowed herself to feel—to relive, even in her imagination—the full thirty-two continuous *fouettés* she'd thrice performed in the coda of the "Black Swan" *pas de deux* from *Swan Lake.*

Thirty-two turns. Thirty-two years. Such a long time, yet too short a time for so many spinning highs and lows.

Since the year she left for Juilliard, every year on her birthday, her mother had asked if she still had the snowglobe. "Of course I do, Mom! I still remember to keep my eye on the smiling ballerina." And she meant it.

When she'd first arrived at Juilliard and unpacked her dance bag, she wept a mixed emotion of tears: Her mother had surprised her and wrapped the globe in the pink baby blanket. Sasha hadn't seen the treasure since she'd relinquished it in trade for the snowglobe.

How did Mom ever part with it? she wondered, as she fingered the satin trim on her ever-present shawl.

Sasha had kept the globe front and center on her desk at Juilliard. Before heading to her first big recital, she wrapped the globe in the pink blanket she kept tucked in her pillowcase and packed the precious parcel in her dance bag. Before she went on stage, she wiggled her fingers through the blanket until she could see the dancer through the glass, which she tapped.

"May I dance as well as you," she whispered.

It was the first time she'd touched the globe while wearing her pointe shoes. Instantly, her feet felt electrified and an exhilarating power swept throughout her body. She danced with precision, confidence, and a lightness she'd never before experienced.

At the end of the program, her teacher hugged her. "Now that," she said, whispering into Sasha's ear, "was exquisite. It was a performance by a dancer filled with endless and great possibilities."

Before she even graduated, Sasha landed her first job in the San Jose Cleveland Ballet. She quickly moved through the ranks, catching everyone's attention. The artistic director and choreographer were wowed by her unique ability to mesmerize and charm. With lightning speed, she was selected as a soloist.

After a few wonderful years there, she moved on to the Mid-Central Festival Ballet, where she excelled to principal dancer, which led to opportunities to appear all over the world, not only with her company, but as a starring guest dancer with other companies.

From that first Juilliard performance forward, Sasha never dared break the routine of keeping her eye on her talisman—her guardian, her beautiful and majestic ballerina, the one given to her by her mother via a stranger who knew, without even meeting her, what her destiny would be.

Keep your eye on the ballerina. She will lead you. She never forgot what the man had said. As long as she and the snowglobe were together, everything would be okay. No matter where she appeared, the snowglobe went with her. Just before each performance, her eyes lit on the ballerina, her fingers touched the glass, and oh, how she'd dance!

When Donald joined the company, he immediately captured Sasha's eye. The first time they danced together, he captured her heart. He also noticed her globe-tapping routine. When he inquired, she told him the whole story, which until then she'd never told a soul, not even her mother.

After they married, every day before leaving for a performance, he'd ask, "Is Our Lady of Dance all packed and ready?" He'd fondly taken to calling the snowglobe ballerina that saintly name, not a hint of sarcasm in his voice, just sweet private sentiment. And he, too, had joined in the globe-tapping ritual.

"Absolutely!" Sasha would say, patting her bag.

The routine never changed. Until shortly after her thirty-sixth birthday, when she suffered her second bout of what felt like a giant fish flopping around under her sternum. Both times, without warning, the odd sensation blindsided her. She became lightheaded and developed an instant headache, which dissipated the moment the episode, for lack of a better word, subsided. The second bout lasted longer than the first, which was unsettling.

The symptoms went away, but the lightheadedness frightened her. What if either of those episodes had happened while she was performing or struck again in the future? Without telling Donald, who was gone for two days talking to the Pittsburgh Ballet Company about a guest role in *Prodigal Son*, she went to see a doctor, one unrelated to her dance company.

"That was the first of many selfish, very wrong, very cowardly choices," she said to the dancer in the globe, rocking in her chair a few times, the shame of the memory rattling her nerves. "But then, you knew that, didn't you?"

Back then, it would have been the brave thing to admit that something serious might be wrong with her. Those who depended on her had a right to know.

The doctor had listened to her heart, tilted his head. "Hmm. I'm hearing an unusual sound there. Let's take a few tests, see what we've got."

"It isn't anything serious, is it?" Sasha asked, a growing sense of unease spiking her adrenaline.

"Let's wait and see what we find," the doctor said. He told her to stay in the room, that the nurse would be back in with orders for the tests. The number to call for an appointment would be at the top of the cover page, along with pretest instructions.

All that week, during classes and rehearsals for the upcoming premiere of the spring repertory, she was fine. So fine, she did not schedule the appointments for her tests. She convinced herself the strange events had likely been a fluke, so she buried any ominous possibilities and moved on. She didn't need to "bench" herself over nothing. In fact, she'd never felt better. Donald returned. He'd made an agreement for the role. All was too triumphant and well to spoil it over perhaps nothing.

The next Friday, opening night, when she went

to pat Our Lady of Dance, she was horrified to discover the dancer's left arm detached from its body. It lay at a peculiar angle in the snow. For a moment, Sasha thought she might be ill, the sight was so awful. She almost felt as if she herself had suffered a severed limb.

She quickly rotated the globe to see if she might somehow latch it back on. The clock was ticking; the stage director held up his finger, ready to cue her. In dark backstage lighting, she frantically fumbled with the snowglobe. As she worked, the sight of the arm swirling around in the water caused her to break out in beads of perspiration. She wished Donald, who hadn't looked at the globe but merely tapped the top of it before scooting backstage to wait in the wings on the opposite side of the stage, could take a peek. Maybe he could figure it out, put her back together again. But it was nearly time to go on.

With nothing left to do, Sasha gently cradled the wounded dancer in the blanket and stuffed her down in the bag.

At the beginning of the performance, she had to push her way through a slight hesitancy, a dangerous place from which to dance. A dancer must trust. Luckily, it was a routine that quickly partnered her with Donald. The moment his hands wrapped around her waist, she forgot all about the broken body in the snowglobe—at least while they performed.

She didn't tell Donald about the poor ballerina until they arrived home that evening. First, he said he thought a coupling piece must have broken off, but it had nowhere to go, other than the globe. After more careful inspection, he could find no such piece floating around. He got out a magnifying glass and studied the joint of the other arm. No connector piece there either, just two interlocking loops. And the broken arm? Both the shoulder and arm loops were still closed.

"I don't get it," he said. He set the globe on the kitchen table, stared at it for a moment, then smiled and took his wife's hand. "I know how distressing this is for you, but remember, *you* are the dancer. *You* are the one with years of training and credits. You are no longer the young woman with a dream who needs a lucky charm to make it come true. You are the dancer who put in the decades of hard work. You are now living that dream, just like you did this evening."

Sasha tossed and turned that night. She knew Donald was right, but still . . .

Early the next morning, she called her mother. She needed to hear her voice, hear again the assurance that she was a capable ballerina *without* the aid of a good luck piece.

Her mother expressed her sorrow, said she knew how much the globe meant to her, but that she also knew it wasn't Sasha's fault. "Things break. It's old. And you still have the blanket, right? Maybe *that's* what really matters!" she said, adding a soft chuckle. "But I agree with Donald: You don't need anything to make you a great dancer, honey. You already are."

The next day, Sasha left the snowglobe at home, but she packed the blanket in her bag, which felt strangely light without the snowglobe's weight. Every step of the way to the theater, she was aware of the snowglobe's absence. *This isn't right!* With no other choice left, she fondled the blanket before going on stage. What else was there for her to do? Although she danced well, her mind occupied while on stage, as soon as she came offstage, her feeling of unease returned.

Late that night, Sasha and Donald arrived home to a message on their answering machine. Her mother was nearly giddy; she'd just watched a piece on television about a snowglobe repairman, and he was right there in Minnesota, not two hours away from Wanonishaw!

Sasha fired up her computer, Googled the news channel, and followed a link to his name. The next day, she contacted the gentleman, carefully packed up her snowglobe and sent it off. Within ten days (due to the remarkable story she'd told him and her performance schedule, he gave it his earliest attention), her snowglobe was repaired and returned, although he too wondered how it came apart.

With great joy, Sasha went back to her usual

ritual, relief and security once again flowing through her veins.

Four months later, she was in the shower, washing her long hair, when she experienced another heart fluttering episode. It didn't last long, but it was unmistakable. The very next day, when she went to pack the snowglobe in her dance bag, the dancer's right leg lay detached in the snow. The scene made her gasp.

Her husband was gathering his belongings in the bedroom. "Donald! Look!" she yelled, her heart thumping.

"What is it?" He quickly appeared, the tone in her voice igniting alarm.

Head turned aside, she jutted the globe straight out in front of her. She couldn't stand to look at it. Donald took the globe from her.

"Whoa. That's odd. You know, maybe after all these years, the metal is just wearing out."

"No! The repairman said it was fine!" Her bottom lip quivered.

"Well," Donald said, "at least we know where to send it this time, right?" He smiled, then patted her arm.

She chewed her bottom lip and stared at him. The timing of both episodes coinciding with her heart palpitations niggled her conscience.

Keep your eye on the ballerina. She will lead you. The words came alive, murmured within her.

And still, she said nothing.

"Come on, Sasha. We have to go."

Repair number two ensued.

Then her mother died. A sudden stroke, and she was gone. It was all Sasha could do to keep moving, to keep dancing. The focus of classes and performances was the only thing that brought respite from her terrible grief. Dance she must, for stopping was simply too emotionally painful.

Twice after her mother's death, each time after she suffered a bout of heart fluttering—thankfully, never while dancing—one of the legs fell off the body. By then, there was no doubt in her mind that the two were connected.

The snowglobe, four times fixed, had morphed into a complex presence of unending conflict. Now that her mother was gone, it meant even more to Sasha to keep the globe with her, to touch the icon of the career her mother launched for her not only by giving her those first dance lessons but by giving her life itself—which her mother had now lost. However, since she'd connected the heart episodes with the failing of the dancer's body, there was something more ominous about the snowglobe.

Before going on stage, when she tapped the top of the globe, yes, her feet felt electrified, and then oh, how she danced! Reviews were never better. Her jumps felt higher, her balance impeccable. Even Donald couldn't get over an inexplicable lightness about her body, inquiring if she'd lost weight, which she had not. And yet . . . there was this utter terror before each tap that when she did so, the dancer's body would self-destruct, as would she. When the snowglobe was off being repaired, she felt some relief from those angst-filled moments, but a growing anxiety to get it back threatened to derail her mind.

It seemed to be all or nothing: she could tap the globe and either dance her best or possibly dismember herself. Or she could be without the globe and fret herself to pieces in its absence.

Still, she did not breathe a word of her symptoms or the doctor's orders she flagrantly ignored to anyone, including Donald.

Why did I continue to play such odds? It's like the dancer was doing just what the man said, giving me a vision of what was to come if I didn't take care of myself! Sasha closed her eyes and cradled the globe in her hands as she continued to surf through the events that led her to the very rocking chair in which she now spent her days.

After the last episode—after she dropped the snowglobe off at the post office to be mailed away for repair—during a rare afternoon off, she at least mustered enough courage to Google her symptoms. The results were endless. After chasing a dozen links that led to another several dozen each, she didn't know what to think. Heart palpitations, or arrhythmia—or whatever words and scientific descriptions doctors and other Internet forum people used to describe exactly what she felt—ranged from harmless perimenopausal symptoms to dangerous conditions involving holes in the heart, congenital abnormalities of the heart, and bad heart valves. One page even led to trouble with the kidneys! She was either involved with nothing (hormonal shenanigans, maybe?), or she was a walking time bomb.

She just had to tell Donald.

But tell him what? Plus, she was currently performing as the lead in *Giselle*, always a favored role, and likely her last chance before retirement to dance it.

She tried to talk herself into believing she was one of those rare folks who suffered with arrhythmia of unknown causes and no damage was occurring during the bouts. But when she looked at the snowglobe—when she thought about even benign dizziness during a performance—she knew better than to think she could keep ignoring her spells. She promised herself that when the current show closed, she would deal with the situation head on. She would contact the doctor most of the corps de ballet used, let him have a listen, and see if he suggested the same tests. They would take it from there.

But before her one sensible decision took effect, at the top of the lift during the *pas de deux* in act 2, she momentarily fainted. Donald was of course not prepared for her sudden dead weight, and as a result of him unsuccessfully trying to break her fall, they both crashed to the floor, she landing first, he toppling onto her.

The front curtain closed and the show stopped while medics assessed, then loaded them into ambulances. By the time she was released from her six-week stay in the hospital, she'd endured many tests on her heart, two surgeries to her sacrum area, and a simultaneous repair to a fractured leg. She'd been given the news that the fractured coccyx might cause her the longest lasting pain and slowest recovery. Only time and her body would dictate her final outcome. And her heart? Trial medications to stop her arrhythmia ensued.

Sasha carefully set the snowglobe back on the side table. Since her hospitalization, the ballerina had remained intact.

Some days, she thought about throwing the thing in the garbage.

But other days, when she was in her right senses, Sasha knew Our Lady of Dance was her only reminder of the bright, happy, and gifted self she knew before she hit the floor.

Seven

While waiting for Ms. Davis, Evelyn sat in one of the grand lobbies at Mayo Clinic, reading a library book about wild horses. She was so absorbed that when she raised her head to rub an eyelash out of her eye, she was surprised not to find herself in the middle of a dust storm left in the aftermath of stampeding hooves. Instead, countless people scurried across the immaculate, shining floors, although some did sport a rather wild look in their eyes, a comparison which first made her smile, then grimace.

So many stories. So many problems. It made her grateful for her health and the health of her family. It brought home how uncertain and scary life must feel for Ms. Davis. Evelyn shot up a quick prayer, mostly for grace, grace, grace.

She rested the book in her lap and considered her unusual life. It had been two weeks since she'd ridden her bicycle to her grandpa's store in the driving rain. She'd happily worked all day in the butcher shop, glad to converse with so many townsfolk she hadn't seen for a while. The exchanges brought to light how unwittingly out of the Wanonishaw gossip mill she'd grown. Of course word was all over town that she'd moved in with the "reclusive invalid" Sasha Davis. Many customers asked what she was doing in the shop on a weekday, trying to pry into Ms. Davis's business. Evelyn and her grandpa swiftly put the kibosh on inquiries, chalking her presence up as "a gift from Ms. Davis, a golden opportunity for *us* to spend time together!"

Since Gramps made her remove her ring to work in the shop (too many ways to catch jewelry in machinery and accidentally slice off a digit), some wanted to know if she was still engaged to "that Jorden McFinn" who moved into town with his folks a year or so ago. Why, yes, of *course* she was! It was odd, the way some people responded to her good news with nothing more than a raised eyebrow.

When the shop closed, Gramps invited her over for dinner, an offer she gratefully accepted. Before they left, he let her pick out a few choice pork chops for their dinner. In exchange, she helped him and Betty cook.

It was always fun to watch Gramps and Betty together, the two of them still practically newly-weds. She hoped after she and Jorden were married for a year, they'd look as happy too— although sometimes Betty could be a bit stiff.

Betty still worked part time at her factory job, saying that after all her years taking care of herself, she just couldn't suddenly allow herself to become a kept woman. Evelyn had busted out laughing at the comment, but Betty pursed her lips. She was nice enough, but a ball of humor— no.

A couple of times Jorden had mentioned he'd said hello to Betty when he worked the day shift. When Evelyn brought their meeting up to Betty, she gave a halfhearted smile and said, "Yes. I've seen Jorden at work."

Evelyn had hoped for a more . . . positive response, but then, oozing compliments wasn't Betty's style either.

By the time they cleared the dishes and played a few rounds of cribbage, it was after dark. Since it was still raining, Gramps insisted on tossing Evelyn's bike into the bed of his pickup and giving her a ride home. He sat in the driveway, headlights shining through the torrents into the garage, until her bike was safely put away and she disappeared inside the back door of the house.

Although Ms. Davis had left both the front and back porch lights on, which was unusual, when Evelyn got inside, she was relieved to find the sitting room empty.

Evelyn feared she might find a note saying, "Pack your bags tomorrow," but after searching Ms. Davis's side table and the kitchen table, she found no such thing. At first she felt relieved, then gave herself an inner talking-to about letting herself slide into such negative thoughts. One downbeat thinker in the house was enough.

Then she got worried. Ms. Davis had been in quite a state when she left, and Evelyn sometimes fretted about Ms. Davis's flash temper, constant negativity, and gloom. Could they lead the temporarily disabled woman to something . . . worse? Evelyn had read enough psychology books to understand that depression was a snaky devil. She was tempted to peek into Ms. Davis's bedroom, just to make sure she was all right, but in light of earlier events, she also didn't want to wake her and create another uncomfortable situation.

She quietly snuck up the stairs and tumbled into bed, exhausted from the drama as much as the good times with Gramps. She fell to sleep in the middle of her prayers.

Bright and early the next morning, over the leftovers of a full English breakfast (Evelyn didn't notice anything missing from the fridge, then worried Ms. Davis hadn't eaten since she left yesterday), a small miracle took place. Ms. Davis admitted to Evelyn that she had been right: it *was* time to scout out a little music.

Thereafter, every morning at ten, Ms. Davis asked Evelyn to select an album and put it on the turntable. As Evelyn guessed, the turntable was located in the top of the old radio. "Not too loud," Ms. Davis always cautioned. Nonetheless, for the duration of that day's album, there was music in the house.

How did either of us survive so long without music, Evelyn wondered as she folded her hands atop her book on wild horses and shook her head, bringing herself back into the bustling world of Mayo Clinic.

Evelyn's eyes locked on a woman rolling a large harp into the lobby. She was one of several musicians and singers sprinkled throughout the clinic. Evelyn recognized the harpist as one she'd enjoyed the last time they'd come to Mayo. Before she settled in to listen, she checked her wristwatch and Ms. Davis's printed clinic schedule for the day, which caused her to ponder the shocker in their abode on Fourth Street that was even bigger than the presence of music. The same morning as Ms. Davis's apology about the music, she asked Evelyn to do whatever she needed to get the house set up for the Internet. "It's ridiculous that I require you to handle all these things for me," she said, "and you have to go elsewhere to accomplish half of them. I don't know what I've been thinking."

Remarkably, she'd also instructed Evelyn to buy a good color printer and gave her a signed blank check to cover all the expenses.

Two days later, she and Jorden and Jorden's techno-wizard friend Rocky had everything in place. Evelyn could take dictation, edit whatever, then print it right out. Just this morning, she'd printed out the day's clinic appointment schedule and told Ms. Davis, when she waved it in her face, "Thank you for bringing this house into the current century!"

Ms. Davis had even told Evelyn to register a Google e-mail address for her, which she instructed Evelyn to use to sign her up for various things—although oddly, she herself refused to engage with the computer. It was clear, however, that Ms. Davis knew her way around the Internet. This awareness both surprised and confounded Evelyn. Why did Ms. Davis have *her* do all the browsing and e-mailing on her behalf? Wouldn't surfing the net and typing her own letters be a good distraction for Ms. Davis? Or did holding her hands to a keyboard hurt her back?

She kept the question to herself, deciding to concentrate on the positive. Since they'd installed a wireless router, Evelyn could finally stay home and engage with her own private e-mails, too, and research anything from anywhere in the house, which she could even do late into the night from her bedroom. Even the printer tapped into the wireless system.

"Suh-weet," as Jorden put it when they were done with the setup. "It'll be easier to communicate late at night, when I'm off." His family was disinclined to Wi-Fi their house, leaving Jorden stuck in his room with his laptop and a DSL cable that he had to pay for himself. "Maybe now," he said, "when I'm off and you're working,

I can come over here to chillax, cruise the net, maybe even download a few new games or watch some movies. That way we'd get to see each other more often."

"That is a *very* bad idea, Jorden," she'd told him in hushed tones, glad Ms. Davis was in the bathroom when he'd suggested it.

"Why? You two not getting along?"

"Things are quite amenable," she said.

He furrowed his brows. "Please speak English."

"We're getting along fine," she said. Part of the reason for their somewhat less dicey existence together—and it was clear to her and Ms. Davis— was that both were trying harder not to get on the other's nerves. This she kept to herself, as she did all personal matters between the two women. "But I can think of a hundred reasons why you coming here to *chillax,* a word I doubt is yet *in* the English dictionary, is a bad idea. But let me just leave it at this: Ms. Davis wouldn't allow it." What Evelyn didn't say was that *she* didn't think Jorden hang-ing around while she was on duty was a good idea.

He'd groaned. With a saucy kiss, Evelyn let him know she understood his pain. But she also reminded him she was getting paid very well (and that Ms. Davis had paid him and Rocky more than well for their technical services), and that they wouldn't be living apart forever. With that, he could not argue.

The light streaming through one of Mayo's plentiful windows hit her ring, making the diamond sparkle. *I love you so, Jorden.* She waggled her fingers in front of her face, delighted again in their engagement. Life was getting closer to perfect.

Closer.

But even after the arrival of daily bouts of music, the installation of Wi-Fi, and the luxury of an on-the-premises printer, things weren't *all* hunky-dory on Fourth Street. Although somewhat more even keeled, Ms. Davis could still be extremely moody. Then again, if that was the worst thing Evelyn had to put up with, the life experience was worth it.

By the time the harpist moved on, Evelyn had finished reading her book about wild horses, and after reviewing her position in life, she realized she was relatively content with the way things were. Moreover, she realized she was beginning to genuinely like Ms. Davis, to earnestly care about her.

Thank you, God, for grace.

This was the longest day either of the women had ever spent at Mayo. It was time for a major powwow of opinions, so Ms. Davis had appointments with several specialists. As she waited, Evelyn settled deeper into contentment. She felt relaxed, good about her circumstances.

How many other women my age get to spend a day reading? They're either slaving away on the time clock like Jorden or working night and day on college homework, away from girlfriends, boyfriends, fiancés. Blaaach.

After she scanned most of the available brochures in one area, she checked out the assortment of magazines in another. One by one, she flipped through the pages. She didn't care about skin products, fashion, or celebrities. She did jot down a few recipes, then found an interesting article on the brain, which she not only read, but for which she drew a wonderful graphic. One of her favorite pieces was on small engine repair. She wished she could rip it out and take it home. She made a few notes, hoping she could later find the article online.

Then, without warning, a piece on fishing tilted the emotional scales of her contentment.

Field & Stream featured pictures of a small fishing boat that looked just like her dad's. She checked her watch. Four minutes after five. He was likely out on the Mississippi River right now.

Since her parents lived within five blocks of the school, her dad often arrived home earlier than other dads, changed clothes, and headed for the river. He liked fishing around the dams and wing dams, as did she. She couldn't even guess how many times she'd shared that pleasure with him. Sometimes, other than to comment on a good catch or a netting miss, they'd sit in a comfortable silence, listening to nature, watching for eagles and other wildlife along the shoreline, never disappointed.

Other days, when fishing was slow, they'd chatter like magpies, covering everything from the day's global headlines to their favorite moments in vintage movies. They were both pretty good at quoting famous lines and often cracked each other up. "Phone home" when the snacks were gone. "Go ahead, make my day" when they lost a fish boat-side.

Evelyn closed her eyes, imagined she heard the plunk of the heavy metal weights hitting the water when they went bottom fishing. *May the Fishing Force be with you, Dad.*

Last year for the first time ever, Evelyn and her dad, both basketball fans, had rooted for opposing teams in the playoffs. This created no small amount of banter and teasing. But even though she'd always adored Phil Jackson and the Lakers ("Isn't Mr. Jackson cute, Mom? And so spiritual!"), Evelyn had to go with Jorden's pick, the Celtics. ("You're not going to root against your own boyfriend, are you?" Jorden asked, giving her a playful hug.) They'd all watched the game together at her folks' house. Although she acted downtrodden when the Celtics lost, secretly, she was cheering, right along with her dad.

After the game that night, her dad poked his head into her room. "Way to go, Lakers!" he semi-yelled. "I realize that sometimes new love trumps old loyalties, but I have a feeling come next year, when you're off to college, you'll get yourself back on the Laker train where you belong. Good night, sweetie. And may I repeat, *way to go, Lakers!*"

She'd heard him laughing all the way down the hall.

At the time, she thought her dad was just talking about basketball loyalties. But Jorden was a year older than she, out of school and working. The longer they dated—and the more serious they grew—the clearer it became that her dad didn't think *Jorden* was a good match. Although he never stated it in exactly those terms, he especially didn't think Jorden was good enough for her. The more time she and Jorden spent together, the more distance grew between Evelyn and her dad. Sometimes she suspected her dad might be jealous of Jorden, or at least of the time she spent with him.

One Sunday afternoon, when her dad was packing up the boat in the driveway, she came outside to shoot a few hoops. While she was dribbling, her dad called out, "Got your gear packed, sport?" On nice summer Sunday afternoons, they almost always hit the river together for a couple of hours, which was when her mother enjoyed the quiet time (Evelyn and her dad were both big talkers) to catch up on her reading. "We'll stop on the way and pick up some crawlers. Pickings are pretty slim in this last container," he said, holding up the Styrofoam cup.

"Oh! I'm sorry, Dad." Evelyn pulled the ball up under her arm. "I guess I forgot to mention that Jorden and I are going to a matinee. He's been working screwy hours this week, and this afternoon is the only time we have to be together this weekend."

Her dad looked crestfallen. "Come next year, when you're off at college," he said, "you won't have chances like this to get out on the river."

She'd pursed her lips and shrugged. Her dad frowned.

From that day forward, a new friction between them began to build. Sure, they had their disagreements. Evelyn was a chip off her stubborn father's block, as her mom put it. But Evelyn, an only child and a tomboy, was taught by her dad how to hunt, fish, and play ball. He'd even coached her softball team. She was a long-ball hitter, a fearless slider, a superior catcher with a pick-off arm in a league of her own, a daddy's girl and proud of it.

Now, although she'd spoken to her mom on the phone a few times, she hadn't stopped by the house to see her dad for nearly two weeks. *Too much drama.* Still, she missed him.

She put the *Field & Stream* back on the shelf, burying it behind several other magazines. When she looked up, Ms. Davis, pushed in a wheelchair by a volunteer, came barreling down the hall.

When Ms. Davis spied Evelyn, she ordered him to stop for a moment.

"I'm off to my last appointment." Evelyn noticed the relief in Ms. Davis's tired voice. "The doctors, and, I believe, a therapist, are already commiserating about some of today's results. They're likely agreeing"—she paused a moment, gripped the wheelchair's armrests, shifted slightly left in her seat—"that it's time to put together a plan for my therapy." With reserved enthusiasm, she smiled a smile that appeared slightly terrified. "I'll look for you right here when I'm through." She lifted her right arm high enough for the volunteer to see she was waving him forward. As he whisked her away, she tossed over her shoulder, "I don't think I'll be much longer. If I return with good news, maybe we can celebrate with dinner on the way home."

Wow. Did I hear that right? Dinner out? Crazy!

As happy as Evelyn was for news of Ms. Davis's impending therapy, the boat pictures in the article had already created a crack in her otherwise cheery and optimistic resolve. Thus, the news caused her to further deflate and stew. The sooner Ms. Davis was well, the sooner Evelyn would likely be out of a job.

And then what? What would she do? Crank up her business again? She'd have to. Where would she live? Back home? Now that she'd had a taste of being out on her own, she couldn't imagine that. Her old home no longer felt like a respite but a constant battleground. Should she try to rent a room somewhere in town? Perhaps.

Or maybe there was another solution. Maybe she should finally agree to Jorden's escalating requests to marry earlier than they'd originally compromised the day they got engaged. (He'd always wanted *now;* she'd first suggested marrying in four years, after she graduated.) Then they could rent that little trailer . . . The idea felt suddenly tempting, for a number of reasons: not least on her list, the lingering tingles from their juicy kisses.

But if she did marry Jorden now, that might be the end of her relationship with her dad, maybe even her mom. She'd promised them that she and Jorden would wait two years.

But I'm nineteen, legally able to make my own choices. They'd come around if I eloped with the love of my life.

Wouldn't they?

Eight

Donald tossed and turned. It was 2:00 a.m. on August 5, his and Sasha's thirteenth wedding anniversary. He felt tempted—dared himself, really—to pick up the phone and call her. Maybe

106

if he woke her out of a sound sleep, he'd catch her off guard, and she'd talk to him before she realized what she was doing.

Donald was always up at dawn's first glow. He was the one who quietly made the coffee, read the morning papers, and let Sasha sleep in until the last moment. When it was time for her to rouse, he'd turn on the stereo and let the music do the work.

But at the first blush of sunrise on their anniversary, he'd wake her with a series of soft kisses on her long slender neck. He could still picture every detail of her hairline, the way it sensually curved behind her ears. He loved watching her sleep, her thick, long dark mane fanned out on the pillow, as if floating in water. When her heavy-lashed hazel eyes fluttered open, he'd wait a moment, until she was fully alert, then he'd lean down and kiss her nose, each eyelid—which she'd close just so he could—and then her mouth. To the tune of "Happy Birthday," he would softly sing "Happy Anniversary to Us" while he traced the outline of her shoulders with his fingertips.

The longing to touch her skin, feel her body next to his, had not lessened. The desire to dance with her—to partner her, adrenaline flowing, costumes catching the light, the satiny feel of her skin brushing against his arms, their strong bodies well-matched, aesthetically and brilliantly commanding the stage and wide-eyed wonder from the audience—burned inside him like a ball of acid. Sure, both before her presence in his life and since the accident, he'd danced with many able females. But with Sasha, dancing was a unique form of intimacy for which there was no alternative.

Since they worked and lived together, the only times they'd been apart in their marriage were when one or the other contracted as a guest dancer with another company. So while this wasn't their first lengthy separation, on those other occasions, they'd known when the separation would end. They'd talked to each other or e-mailed nearly every day, shared the details of their lives. The need to know how she really was, if she still loved him, threatened to shatter him into a thousand miserable pieces.

Did she even *remember* it was their anniversary?

Did she blame him for what happened? It was a question that would not die. He lay awake at night, dreaming up ways he might have prevented the fall. He should have known something was wrong with her! Maybe if he'd worried less about the pitfall of bulging muscles and pumped more iron, or depended less on her seasoned ability to help launch a lift . . . *something.* Everyone in the tight-knit dance company knew and felt the torment left in the aftermath of the incident and Sasha's departure. Although they were devastated for Donald, they all missed her too. She was well-liked, a genteel woman, yet always so filled with laughter, mischief, and a somewhat self-effacing yet dry wit. He prayed her situation hadn't knocked those playful qualities out of her.

He prayed he'd used divine wisdom when he'd made the choice not to push her further away, to let her have whatever time she needed to come around on her own. He prayed that Janine, one of Sasha's dearest friends, was right. She'd confirmed that he'd made the only decision a strong-headed woman like Sasha allowed for.

He prayed.

If only . . .

When will the what-ifs end? He banged his fist against Sasha's pillow and turned his back to her side of the bed.

It was going on six months since the accident; four months since he'd seen her. The season had just closed, and he had a little time off before rehearsals for the next season kicked in. Dancing was the only thing that had kept him from going mad. Now what?

Maybe, no matter what logic dictated, he'd just get in the car and make an appearance on her doorstep. He had enough time. But then he snapped to his senses. The last thing he wanted to do was cause her more duress. If seeing him incited more pain or pushed her *further* away . . .

Maybe my hesitant thinking is why Sasha didn't tell me about her arrhythmia. Maybe she didn't want to worry me, was trying to protect me. But look what that got her—what that got us.

He'd finally given up trying to reach her by phone, at least for now. The only way he knew she was still alive was because twice in the last month, he'd received a short formal letter on a new letterhead, signed by her prickly assistant and sent to Mr. Donald Major.

The letterhead bore a magnificent new logo. The header incorporated Sasha's name, presented in a distinguished airy font. The letters were surrounded by what appeared to be original artwork, a superb free-form watercolor with darker and lighter spots throughout, some spots appearing lit from within. The multicolor design flowed around the top left-hand side of her name, lending a distinguished soft and feminine appearance to the paper corner. No address; just a business number that could be used to contact her "office." Surprisingly, or perhaps more telling about the state of her health, the logo bore no signs of pointe shoes or tutus or anything that indicated she was a dancer. Her previous letterhead had proclaimed:

SASHA DAVIS, PRINCIPAL DANCER WITH
MID-CENTRAL FESTIVAL BALLET

The recent letters were always the same. "Ms. Sasha Davis would like to inform you that she is still on the road to recovery," and some nonsense about wishing him well, which was, in its own

110

way, progress, he guessed. At least he'd graduated from "thank you for your patience" to well wishes. But he wondered if Sasha was even actually the one saying those things. Then again, maybe this was just the same form letter she sent to her thousands of fans.

He gritted his teeth, turned on his back, and interlocked his fingers behind his head, replaying an odd detail that had at first escaped his attention. After three readings, he'd decided the ridiculous "wish you well" comment ticked him off. He'd wadded up the letterhead and tossed it in the garbage. But after a moment, he'd quickly dug it out again. There was something familiar about a portion of the logo. With the side of his hand, he ironed out the wrinkled paper on the table.

Is that free-form design actually replicating a fabric or shawl, of sorts, and if so, could it be the shawl I gave her as a wedding gift? The one she admired when we performed in Brussels? The one with the iridescent beads worked into it? She'd donned it often, saying she always felt wrapped in his love when she draped it around her shoulders.

The more he looked at the design, the more convinced he became that if it wasn't that exact same shawl, it sure was close.

He fantasized that perhaps she'd had the logo designed to send him a secret sign to indicate she still remembered, still cared . . . still loved. That she desired to feel his love still wrapped around her. But the positive speculation soon waned. *How desperate am I to dream up something like* that?

Did "Ms. Evelyn Burt, Sasha Davis's Assistant" even know he was Sasha's husband? After all, Sasha never changed her name when they married. He couldn't imagine that anyone who worked for Sasha would be unfamiliar with the nuances of her career—her life. But then, what did he know about the personal lives of rock 'n' roll stars, in which he took no interest? Or soccer star marriages, or the lives of any other group of people he didn't follow. Life was like that: one person's entire world was another's unknown entity.

Even though he was sure Evelyn Burt was an elderly old prude staunchly acting as his wife's first line of defense, if, by some chance, she *didn't* know they were married, might she serve as an inroad to at least learning a few things about his wife?

Something to consider, he thought, as he tossed and turned some more before softly singing his anniversary wishes to his wife, hoping that somewhere deep in her heart, deep in her spirit, she could hear him.

The home health-care therapist was scheduled to arrive in ten minutes. Sasha didn't know whether to be excited or terrified, so she allowed herself to feel a little of both.

She and Evelyn had prepared everything as

best they could, according to the printed instructions. Yesterday, after a full house assessment, they decided the living room afforded the most open space.

"We'll have to move a few coffee tables, those two lamps, and that one massive chair," Sasha said, pointing. "Gheesh. Don't you just love the way I say *'we'll* have to' move *anything?* As though in one miraculous moment, I'm going to jump up out of this chair and start lugging furniture?" Sarcasm laced her voice. Then a spark of familiar yet long-buried humor flashed into her head. For the briefest of moments, she felt her own eyes twinkle. "But wait! Perhaps the mere suggestion of therapy has healed me!" She gave an exaggerated flourish of enthusiasm. With the authority of Charlton Heston, she commanded herself to "Rise and walk!" She propped her hands on the armrests and acted like she was about to spring up. "Oh, wait. I just remembered some-thing. I don't always listen to myself, especially when it comes to the impossible."

Evelyn giggled, then broke into guffawing laughter. She acted like it was the first time she'd ever heard Sasha crack a joke, which, come to think about it, it might have been—a thought that startled Sasha and made her sad for the happy parts of her she'd let drift away.

Sasha suggested Jorden come help move the massive chair. She told Evelyn it took two men to move that thing. "When my mother engaged in her annual spring cleaning, she used to pay a couple of burly neighbor boys two pans of brownies to deal with the monster. She was *always* warning me about protecting my back. She should see me now," Sasha said, her voice fading as she slowly stood up and settled behind her walker, her previous spark waning.

Evelyn declined the help. She said she'd already calculated a workable plan.

"You're as stubborn as a mule," Sasha said. "If you throw *your* back out, then what will I do for help?"

Evelyn grinned, then told Sasha she'd highly underestimated her ingenuity. "When I ran my own business, I dealt with far bigger and heavier things than this chair."

Such youthful bravado, Sasha thought.

It was obvious that moving the chair turned out to be a bigger struggle than Evelyn imagined. Using a jack she made from a four-inch-diameter fence post and a short two-by-four from the garage, she'd maneuvered and gyrated her body weight to arrange and rearrange a throw rug under the legs, carefully yet laboriously scooting and pushing so as not to scratch the hardwood floor. Eventually she conquered the beast.

The girl was as strong and determined as an ox, which was even stronger than a mule, which was exactly what Sasha told her. Like a teenage boy proud of his bench-pressing muscles, Evelyn stole a play from the book of Sasha's earlier drama. She held up her arm, made a fist, pulled up the sleeve of her T-shirt, and flexed. Then with great dramatic flair, she faked a collapse onto the floor and pronounced it break time.

A genuine "Hah!" escaped Sasha's mouth. The surprise minilaugh, which would go unnoticed by most, felt so good and struck Sasha with such intense and instant relief that she wondered if an invisible fairy godmother might have just waved a wand of respite in her direction.

Evelyn broke out in a huge smile. "Lemonades around!" she declared, then went into the kitchen and whipped up a fresh batch.

But today the spell was broken, the fun and games were over. They both hoped the setup was good enough. Evelyn seemed as nervous as Sasha about the therapist's visit.

Sasha sat on the edge of the straight-backed chair they'd told her to have present in the area, something that wouldn't slide. Evelyn had purchased rubber footings at the hardware store and applied them to the heavy kitchen chair's legs before moving it into the living room. She tested them again and again, all but full-on hurling herself onto the chair, as only Evelyn could. "I should have played tackle football," she said to Sasha after one rather violent landing that seemed to please her.

Sasha didn't really want Evelyn around for her first bout of therapy, in case she embarrassed herself. But in case they needed to move something else—or had to get her up off the floor—Sasha decided to have her stick around, at least this first time. "You can wait in the kitchen. I'll call if you're needed."

Now Sasha waited alone, heart hammering, walker nearby, watching out the front window for the arrival of what she hoped would be a kind, petite female physical therapist who wouldn't manhandle her. She'd heard horror stories about the rigors of therapy; once watched a documentary on TV about athletic comebacks. Before they prescribed her protocol of therapy, a male therapist at Mayo had put her through a few drills to test her balance, thresholds, and range of motion, all of which were abysmal.

Sasha thought he could have used a few lessons in gentleness; the tests just about did her in. She fretted that since her injury, she'd gone soft. But one thing she understood from all her years of dance: no pain, no gain. Push, push, push.

She'd also done as both the doctors and therapists instructed and taken a pain pill forty-five minutes ago. They let her know in no uncertain terms that yes, there would be uncomfortable moments. Twice the doctor warned her, vigorously admonished her, that there was no point in letting pain stop her progress, pain that could be handled with medications.

"Be smart," he counseled. "Prepare your body to endure what it can. Don't forget: the therapist won't push you further than we all know your injuries can handle. Your surgical fix areas are finally looking pretty strong, the bone growth doing its thing. But that coccyx might stay painful, at least for a while—if not awhile longer than that. Nonetheless, it's time to get your muscles and your balance back on track. Don't worry about your heart. Your arrhythmia medications are doing their job."

Don't worry. Right. She stared out the window, gripping the armrests on the chair as if strapped in for electrocution.

To distract herself, she tried to shore herself up by replaying what each of the doctors, nurses, and therapists had told her during her last Mayo visit. The news about her impending physical therapy had been the happier segment of her Mayo day, but on a more invasively personal note, the point doctor had grilled her as to whether or not she'd been taking her antidepressant. She sheepishly responded with a maybe. He asked about her moods, any anger, her disposition, how she was sleeping.

Eventually, she broke down. When she heard herself describe what she knew to be many symptoms of depression—nearly all the ones her original doctor in Boston had talked to her about, tried to hold at bay when he wrote her the prescription (steps which were then repeated by the Mayo doctor)—the look in the doctor's eyes revealed how disappointed he was in her, how concerned he was for her. "It's not us you're hurting with this defiance, you know." He'd read the charts from her lengthy hospital stay in Boston after the accident, where the surgeries took place. He'd talked frankly with her about the nurse's notes, the nosy nurse who'd felt compelled to write down Sasha's every worst, agonized, and fleeting thought uttered in the wee morning hours about how death would have been better than what happened to her.

Sasha ended her appointment with the coordinating doctor by telling him the whole truth: Yes, she *had* been depressed, likely *should* have been taking the pills. But she also shared that the last couple of weeks, she'd started feeling a smidge better. She didn't talk about the music. The tea bags or her full English breakfast. The beautiful birds. The frying pan. Evelyn. But they ran through her mind, as did how quickly she could sink back into her black hole again.

TRUST! The word—the instruction—rang in her head like a fire bell she knew she must not ignore. *Where did that come from?* She needed to trust that the doctors knew what was best for her, since apparently she did not.

At some point, she must learn to trust that she

would get better, that she was already getting better.

The evaluation therapist at Mayo had said, "We'll start with home therapy, but we believe you'll be surprised how quickly we'll get you up and out and working at an outpatient facility."

That was all well and good, the doctor said. But if she thought she was at *all* depressed, which she'd just admitted she was, and didn't deal with that, she wouldn't do herself, her body, or the therapists any favors by mentally sinking their progress. She would in fact undermine everyone's efforts, including her own.

Since that last Mayo visit, for the first time since her accident, she'd taken her antidepressants with regularity. Who was she kidding? She needed them. At least for now.

Sasha pulled back the living room curtain, then checked her watch again. An older couple walked by, chatting as their feet, rhythmic and in sync, struck the sidewalk. They must have caught sight of her in the window, for they nearly tripped over each other glancing sideways. She let the curtain fall back into place, removing herself from their view.

Thoughts of the debilitated Jimmy Stewart sitting in his chair in *Rear Window* suddenly raced through her mind. She tried to smile but grimaced instead. No one could see her when she spent her days in her rocking chair by the back window. And the view from there . . . The birds were so beautiful, so distracting. A new one had shown up early this morning. Tiny and brown, with a mohawk hairdo. She could use a dose of their distracting antics right now.

Finally, through the crack at the edge of the curtain, Sasha viewed a small white car parking in front of the house. A tiny woman, barely larger than herself, popped out. She opened the back door and extracted a pair of crutches, which startled Sasha. Surely they weren't planning on taking the stability of her walker away already! Next the woman unloaded a rather large gym bag. Up the front steps she jogged, carrying crutches and bag as if they weighed nothing.

When the doorbell rang, Evelyn hollered from the kitchen, "Want me to get that, Ms. Davis?"

"Yes, please," Sasha said, suddenly feeling shaky. Afraid. Apprehensive. Like a child seeking comfort in her blanket, she pulled her shawl up around her neck, rubbed her thumb across its satin edge.

She heard Evelyn stomping through the house, then greeting the therapist with a too loud, "Hi! I'm Evelyn, Ms. Davis's *assistant.*"

Anne. The therapist's name was Anne, "with an *e* on the end," she heard a cheery voice say.

"Ms. Davis is right in here," Evelyn said. "We hope this setup works okay. If not, just let me know and I'll rearrange."

When Anne entered the room, Sasha noted Evelyn had already taken the crutches and bag from her. *Always helpful Evelyn.*

"Where would you like me to put these, Anne with an *e* on the end?" Evelyn chirped.

"Hello," Anne said to Sasha, extending her hand. "I have a feeling you already know who I am." She smiled, turned to Evelyn, and told her to prop the crutches anywhere out of the way, maybe in the entryway, and to bring the bag to her.

When Evelyn was done with her placements, Sasha let her know that would do for now. Evelyn disappeared back into the kitchen. She'd taken her laptop and a stack of books to the table earlier. Sasha imagined she was eavesdropping though.

"Well," Anne said, looking around, "you've done a great job here." She studied the rubber grips on the chair legs. "Perfect!" She dug into her giant bag and pulled out a clipboard. "Let me just check a few things, then we'll get right to it. By the way, do you happen to have Wi-Fi in your house?"

"Yes," Sasha said, finding it an odd question.

"Good! When we're done, I'll take a few minutes to send off my report. I brought my laptop with me."

Sasha's heart felt like it was going to leap out of her chest. "You don't waste any time," she said, trying to sound lighthearted. The tightness in her throat revealed otherwise.

"No need to be nervous," Anne said, looking directly at her. "This is an exciting day for you, for both of us! It's your first day on the official road to helping your body get its strength back. You'll be surprised how quickly one's own body responds to good effort, once it's allowed to have at it."

"I'm quite familiar with the rewards of hard work," Sasha said, her voice shifting from hesitant to verging on sharp. She silently admonished herself and quickly tried to right the first impression she might have left. "I'm willing to do whatever it takes."

"I heard you are a dancer," Anne said.

"*Was. Was* a dancer." Rather than validate what she believed true about her life, that she was a cripple, Sasha simply said, "I'm retired now. Professional dancers don't enjoy very long careers."

It was a line, a reframing thought, Evelyn had delivered one day when Sasha was down. Although at the time the word *retired* irritated Sasha ("What can you *possibly* know about *any* of this?" she'd snapped back at Evelyn), the thought stuck with Sasha, worked on her, into her. Saying —coming to grips with the fact—that she was a retired dancer sounded better than repeating that she was, as a result of her own stubborn pride, a crippled ex-dancer.

"Well, all right then, Ms. Retired Dancer," Anne said, smiling. "Let's see what we can do to at least

122

get you back sashaying around the dance floor again."

The statement let Sasha know the woman had no idea the caliber of dancer she was. Who she used to be. The realization came as both a gut punch and a relief. Sasha found no reason to correct her.

Anne stepped back from Sasha, clipboard in hand. "How about you get yourself up on your feet, Sasha, so I can see what we've got. It's okay if I call you Sasha, right?"

The doctors, all familiar with her reputation as a professional dancer, had called her Ms. Davis. Sasha wasn't used to strangers and her legions of adoring fans taking such liberties when they greeted her. They wouldn't have dared. But those days were behind her. Today, she was no more or no less than one more therapy stop on Anne's agenda. She let out a little puff of breath she'd been holding. "Of course."

"Up we go, then," Anne said, folding her arms across her chest, letting the clipboard dangle from her right hand. "Let me see how you get yourself standing."

Sasha carefully slipped off her shawl and arranged it on the back of the chair.

"Nice shawl," Anne said. "I noticed it the moment I walked in. Did you make it?"

"Thank you, but no," she said, leaning forward to pull the walker into position. She simply couldn't let herself go any deeper into that

123

conversation, not now—not today. She'd already expended too much energy trying to forget about her anniversary. She put her hands on the arms of the chair and pushed off with such determination she momentarily feared she might overshoot her target. Instead, she hit it just right.

"Okay, good. Let's see you do a few laps."

"Laps?"

"Just to the end of the room and back. Figure of speech. Cruise at your usual pace."

My usual pace. Sasha pictured an *arabesque en pointe* leading into an intricate *pas*, where she would settle, for the briefest of moments, in second position, just before a small *sauté* toward Donald.

"Go ahead, Sasha," Anne said, breaking through Sasha's momentary departure from reality. Instead of leaping, Sasha shuffled forward in tiny steps, nothing like the *bourrées*, infinitesimal steps in a crossed fifth position, she'd performed in *Les Sylphides* as a corps dancer so many, many years ago.

"Good," Anne said.

What does she know? She's never seen me fly.

Nine

"Hey, babe," Jorden said to Evelyn after the waitress dropped the check at their table, "would you mind getting this one?"

Jorden didn't call her *babe* very often, but when he did, the word came out low and breathy in a tone that made her tingle. Evelyn never tired of hearing his special term of endearment for her. Even though she was a contemporary, self-sufficient, mostly feminist, kick-butt woman, this was the first time in her life anyone had called her by a nickname that smacked of hot-chick adoration.

Before she had a chance to respond to his "babe"-laced question, he scooted the green ticket across the table toward her. "I just paid my cable bill and my folks are hounding me for my share of the rent. I'm coming up a little short this week."

Evelyn left the bill on the table but twirled it toward her with her index finger. Sixteen dollars and nineteen cents including tax. The words *Come again soon* were scribbled across the top, followed by a hand-drawn smiley face with stars for eyes, signed by the ever perky and petite Christi.

"I thought you paid the rent last week," Evelyn said.

"I did, but I'm a month behind. The used Xbox I nabbed on eBay pretty much tapped me out. Besides, I bought last time."

When they'd first started dating, Evelyn insisted she pay her own way. Jorden said that felt demeaning to his manhood. The compromise, which Jorden quickly agreed to, was that they'd take turns.

Evelyn thought for a moment. "You know I don't have a problem paying, but just to set the record straight, no, you did not pay the last time we ate together. I made the sandwiches and lemonade for our picnic. Remember? We sat under that big tree down by the park? I baked coconut chocolate chip cookies for dessert?"

Jorden squinted. "Ms. Davis pays for all your food, so that doesn't count. Besides, I bet you get free lunch meat from your grandpa."

"Room and board is part of my pay from Ms. Davis, which means I work for my food," Evelyn said, straightening her spine. "So, yes it does too count. And Gramps doesn't give Ms. Davis a discount just because I work for her. Business is business. I even bought a few extra cold cuts and cheeses for that picnic. And not that I really care, but I bought the last time we ate at a restaurant too."

"Where? When?" Jorden asked, a note of disbelief in his voice.

"Three weeks ago last Tuesday. We came here. You ordered a spaghetti dinner and a side salad. Oh, and an order of garlic bread. I had the day's special, which was a barbeque sandwich that came with fries."

"Not that you're memorizing or counting or anything," he said, sounding put out.

"I can't help that I have a good memory. And I'm not counting. It's just that . . . Oh, never mind," Evelyn said. "Who cares? We're in this together."

She retrieved her wallet and put two tens on top of the check. When Christi bounced over to retrieve the payment, Jorden scooped up the pile and handed it to her.

"I'll be back with your change," Christi said, speaking directly to the man who'd handed her the money.

"No need," Jorden said, flagging her off with his fingers. "It's all yours."

Evelyn would have made the same decision about the change, which Jorden knew. One more thing to love about him, she thought: he paid attention.

"Thanks!" Christi said, giving Jorden a wink, then tossing a pasted-on cheerleader smile toward Evelyn.

Evelyn watched Christi sashay away, as did Jorden. *Nobody's backside naturally moves like that.* Over Jorden's shoulder, Evelyn watched

Christi wait on an older woman in the corner booth. No, Christi did not sway her fanny the same way for old women.

It would be easy to get jealous over the way girls, and even some grown women, often acted in front of Jorden, which was downright silly, really. But there was no denying or escaping it: the ladies liked him. The fawning began the day his family moved into town.

"Oh, that black curly hair, those bedroom eyes, his über-buff bod. What *is* it about bad boys?" Danielle, Evelyn's neighbor friend, wanted to know as she watched him carry boxes out of the rental truck and into the rental house, biceps bulging in his sleeveless T-shirt. The two of them were on their way home from the library, and Danielle all but stopped dead in her tracks and drooled.

"Get a grip on yourself!" Evelyn said as she poked Danielle with her elbow.

But even Evelyn couldn't help responding to the crooked grin he fired at them, the way his thick wavy hair moved on his forehead when he tossed them a nod.

"What makes you think he's a bad boy?" Evelyn had asked. "Just because he's wearing black? I thought you knew better than to judge a book by its cover or a person by his attire," she said, looking down at her own clunky, worn-just-right sneakers.

Now Evelyn stared across the table at Jorden, who looked out the window. He couldn't help his good looks. He couldn't be held responsible for women's responses to him any more than she could fault herself for her size nine-and-a-half feet.

Early on in their dating, Jorden said one of the things he liked most about Evelyn was that she didn't rag on him the way most of his previous girlfriends had, and that she didn't seem to have a jealous bone in her body. But why should she? She wasn't the boss of him, didn't want to be the boss of him, she told him. And now, she was his fiancée, and the marriage couldn't happen soon enough for him.

What's to be jealous about that? Evelyn asked herself when Christi came over and dropped off two mints, both on Jorden's side of the table.

Jorden looked at his watch, then turned to her. "How about going to the drive-in tonight? We'd just have time to make popcorn. Maybe I'll pack a special something-something in the thermos," he said with a wink.

Evelyn blushed. Thoughts of their last drive-in movie encounter, which was also her first dating drive-in experience, played in her mind. The uncomfortable evening took place before they were engaged, before she worked for Ms. Davis.

Ron Mack, one of Jorden's good buddies, and his girlfriend, Shari Matson, were parked in the car next to them. Shari was a girl with a "reputation." She was also Jorden's first girlfriend after he moved into town. For the first half hour of the movie, it was all Evelyn could do to keep from craning her neck to catch a look at their rabid clutches.

Before long, they disappeared into the backseat, which was when Jorden drew Evelyn even closer and whispered something startling in her ear, ending with a breathy "babe," which was the first time he'd uttered the spine-tingling term of endearment to her.

Jorden was only the second guy she'd dated. Phillip, her first boyfriend, an incredibly shy guy one year her junior, had treated her more like a sister, only once even taking her hand. Although her resolve was long ago set on celibacy, when it came to actually handling the shockingly powerful lure of the body's response to breathy words and the power of touch, she had no experience from which to draw.

The drive-in evening turned into more of a wrestling match of wills between Evelyn and Jorden and, much to her shock, Evelyn and herself. The mesmerizing flickering light from the film illuminating the front seat and the sounds of the moaning couple parked next to them made their heated embraces feel surreal, spinning, intoxicating . . . with *anything* perhaps zingingly possible. Jorden, a sudden octopus of hands and lips, kept whispering in her ear, causing her cheeks to burn. Evelyn, hands on his chest, reminded him what she always reminded him. He said he knew, he remembered, but it didn't stop him from whispering into her ear her how much he wanted to . . .

Even thinking about it still made Evelyn blush and go weak in the knees.

The date had abruptly ended in the middle of the second movie.

"You ready to go?" Jorden asked, after he finally gave up getting anywhere with intimacies, put both hands on the steering wheel, and sulked. "This movie sucks."

Evelyn scooted closer to him, glided her fingertips across the top of his forearm.

He shucked her hand off. "Don't tease me, Evelyn," he said, not even glancing sideways at her.

"I don't mean to tease you, Jorden. It's just that I don't know how to play this game," she said.

"Sex isn't a game, Evelyn." He turned and looked at her. "It's natural, the way life is supposed to roll."

"For married people."

"Yes. So you've told me a thousand and one times."

"Look," she said, setting her jaw, "if that's something you're going to need, or start insisting on, then I think you should find yourself another girlfriend." She scooted back to her side of the car and buckled her seat belt. "And you are right: this movie stinks."

Jorden put the speaker back on the rack and started the engine. Ron poked his head out the back window and laughed, which made Jorden sulk even more. Neither spoke during the drive to her house. When he pulled up to the curb, Evelyn's father, who usually went to bed early, was visible through the front window. He was watching television, curtains uncustomarily wide open.

"Thank you," Evelyn said, as she unbuckled her seat belt, and she sincerely meant it. Although at Jorden's smart request she'd made a large container of buttered popcorn ("They just rip people off with those ridiculous popcorn prices!"), he had paid for everything else, including their tickets, two giant drinks, and a large box of Milk Duds.

"Uh-huh," he said, barely glancing her way. They sat in silence for a long moment.

"Look," Evelyn said, "if I don't see you again —well, I'll of course run into you around town, but you know what I mean—I'll understand." The rush of words escaped her mouth so quickly, she wasn't even sure if they came out in the right order.

Jorden gunned the engine twice, then shut it off. He turned in his seat to partially face her.

"Evelyn, believe me when I tell you that I have never dated a girl like you before. Never. I've never even known a girl slightly like you. And the truth is, I don't know what to do about you."

Evelyn had no idea how she was supposed to respond. After a long silence, she reached for the door handle. "I'll go in then. I see Dad's waiting up for me, this being my first drive-in-theater experience and all."

"You have got to be kidding!" Jorden said, grabbing her hand to stop her exit.

She stared at him. She wasn't sure which had shocked him most: that she'd never been to a drive-in or that her dad was waiting up. Maybe both. She shook her head and looked down, feeling suddenly ashamed of her lack of experience.

"Evelyn, I'm just . . . frustrated, is all. Let me think on this, and I'll give you a call in a couple days."

"Okay," she said, slipping her hand out of his. "Take your time. I'll be here." She emitted a nervous chuckle. "Where else would I be?"

She slid out of the car and gave a wave as he thundered off, laying a patch of rubber a foot long, which her dad would point out to her the next day as he gave her a lecture about careless drivers—and careless people.

She stood on the front porch until she had at least partially collected herself. When she entered the house, although her dad looked like he wanted to ask her something, he just said, "Hey, sport. There's still some ice cream left in the freezer, if you're interested." He scraped the bottom of his empty bowl with his spoon and licked it.

"No. I'm full up from popcorn and Milk Duds." She was aware that while she spoke, he assessed the look on her face, her clothes, attempted to read between some kind of lines, no doubt. "And by the way, I'm *fine, * Dad."

That was all she felt like sharing.

She went to bed that night feeling sure of one thing: she most certainly was not fine.

The very next evening, Jorden phoned. She couldn't have been more shocked. "Hey," he said, the mere sound of his voice causing goose bumps to run up her arm. "I've finally figured out what to do about you."

He sounded so businesslike. Her heart tanked. "Oh?"

"I'll tell you about it tomorrow. Meet me in the park, near the swing set, about four."

"I've got five jobs lined up tomorrow. I'm not sure if I'll be done by four."

"Doesn't matter. I'll be waiting in the park. If you're done, just show up. Otherwise, give me a call when you get home, and we'll figure out another time."

At 4:35 the next day, even though she was pretty sure she did not want to hear what Jorden had to say, Evelyn raced her bicycle toward the park.

134

When she was a block away, she saw him get up off a swing and head toward his car in the parking lot. She pedaled as fast she could and careened her bike across the grass, cutting him off just before he reached the cement.

"Hey!" she said to his back. "Sorry I'm late, but I'm glad I caught you." She simply could not agonize one more day, waiting to hear how he was cutting her loose. She needed this over with.

He rested his left hand on top of her right hand, which was still on her handlebar. "I've got one question for you."

All she could think about was how good and right his hand felt on hers, how she never wanted to forget the feel of it. She closed her eyes for a moment just to take it in, just so she could remember once he was gone. Then she braced herself for the bad news. "Shoot," she said.

With his right hand, he reached inside his jeans pocket and withdrew something in his closed fist. "Pick a hand." He shot her a nervous smile.

"Um, that one," she said, after acting like she'd earnestly debated.

"Evelyn Burt, will you marry me?" He opened his fist to reveal a ring, smack in the middle of his palm.

Evelyn stared in disbelief. The adrenaline that pumped through her left her breathless. It was a bazillion times the charge she felt the first time he'd asked her out.

Back then, two days in the same week, they'd happened to stand in line next to each other at the Dairy Queen. Evelyn watched the girls in front of her primp and vie for his attention. *What goofballs. Do they have any idea how obvious they look?*

"I think this is a sign," he'd said the third time they ended up next to each other. "You intrigue me. Wanna meet here again tomorrow? As in on purpose, because I asked? Like as in a date?"

Evelyn had almost fainted, but after sputtering for a while, surprised herself by agreeing. Jorden was persistent and convincing. Ice cream the next day, dinner the next week, and much to everyone's surprise, onward their dating progressed.

Several months later, in the parking lot at the park, Evelyn stood before that same man with a ring in his hand and said, "You can't be serious! This is a joke, right?" It was the same two statements with which she'd first responded at the DQ.

"No joke and dead serious, babe." Then that killer grin.

"Tell me that's not a real ring!" Her knees felt like overcooked noodles.

"Can't. It is." He removed his left hand from atop hers, still on the handlebar.

She quickly clasped her hands together to keep them from shaking. *This seriously cannot be happening!*

Jorden peeled her clasped hands apart and took

her left hand in his. "I'll ask you one more time, and one more time only," he said, holding the diamond ring just off the end of her ring finger. "Will you marry me?"

A thousand thoughts, emotions, and reasons why this was wrong simultaneously whisked through her mind, but only one irrational word came out of her mouth.

"Yes."

And just like that, Evelyn Burt, the most unlikely match for that hottie bad boy Jorden McFinn, became his fiancée, news that just about did her family in—not to mention a dozen or more dumbfounded and disappointed females throughout Wanonishaw. The very next day, she revised the graphics on her business cards by adding a ring to her hand.

And now, he sat across the table from her in the restaurant and asked her to make her second visit to the drive-in theater. And now, they were *engaged.*

"Babe," Jorden said, reaching for her hand across the table in the restaurant, "you still on the planet? You look like you're about to faint or something. Why are your cheeks so red? I asked if you wanted to go to the double feature out at the Starlight."

Evelyn needed time to think about the weight and implications of her answer—her choice. There was something about being around him

137

that made her brain stop working. The words "special something-something" flicked through her mind. *Stall,* she said to herself. *THINK!*

"Too full from dinner, I guess. Brain's a little sluggish. Just thinking about my schedule." She pursed her lips, forced a look of contemplation on her face, although consternation was more her reality. If she said yes, did that imply something, especially now that they were engaged? If she said no, what would be her excuse?

How long would Jorden really wait?

No matter. She knew what she had to do.

"As much as I'd love to go," she said, feeling fairly confident that statement would make some points, "Ms. Davis was pretty exhausted and sore after her therapy yesterday. Anne was just starting with her when I left for our dinner tonight."

"I thought Anne with an *e* came in the mornings."

"Sometimes. But our appointments vary. Today's was late."

"Our? Evelyn," he said, shaking his head, "sometimes I think you care more about that woman than you do me."

He went all sulky again. She hated it when she made him feel that way, but also couldn't blame him for doing so. It was true she sometimes had to decline Jorden's invites because of Ms. Davis. But Ms. Davis was her boss; she lived in her house. Their working agreement was that she be available as scheduled and only off when agreed ahead of time.

Evelyn dragged her chair around to Jorden's side of the table and cuddled up close. "You know that's not true," she said, kissing his cheek. "Nobody is more important to me than you." She kissed his cheek again. "It's just that Ms. Davis is almost ready to graduate to an outpatient basis, which means I'll be driving her to her appointments. I'm not yet sure which town we'll go to, or what time of day her therapy will take place. Maybe it'll switch up like the home therapy. But I think we might start with it as soon as tomorrow. I better get on home tonight."

"Can't you just call her?"

"Yes, I could. But if she's still in therapy, she won't answer. And if she's done, she might be napping already, which is what she does as soon as they're through."

He pushed back his chair and stood. "Well, I guess I'm cut loose for the evening then." He smiled at Christi.

"Hey!" Evelyn said, looking at her wristwatch. "No need to rush right off. I can still take a little time. How about for old time's sake we go to DQ for a cone? We've barely gone back since we started dating!"

"I was just there last night."

"Since when has that stopped you? And wait a

minute: I thought you were helping Rocky work on somebody's computer last night."

He hesitated a moment before responding. "I was. We grabbed a cone at the drive-through when we were done."

"So you can't have ice cream two nights in a row? You used to, you know."

"Gotta watch my waistline," he said, sarcasm lacing his voice as he thumped his palm against his six-pack abs.

"I'll buy! I see a large hot fudge sundae landing just about here." She rested her palm on his upper chest, the touch of his warm skin through his shirt causing her heart to feel all flip-floppy.

Jorden placed his hand on top of hers, then curled his fingers around it. He smelled good. She could feel his heart beating beneath her palm. "Evelyn, it sounds like your boss lady is well on the road to recovery, which means she might be done with you sooner than later. I've asked before, and now I'm asking again: when that happens—when you are out of her house—why don't we just tie the knot? You can get back to your own business; I've got my factory job; we could pool our money and find a little place of our own." He nibbled her ear. "I don't get what we're waiting for, babe."

Her body turned to jelly. She answered in barely a whisper. "I've been thinking about that same thing. But I don't want to make a promise I can't keep. We need to take this one step at a time . . ."

He interrupted her statement with an amazing kiss, his large warm hands framing each side of her head.

"Step one. Check," he said, a devilish grin on his face.

Evelyn felt like her entire body was on fire. She backed away and looked around the restaurant. Christi and the older people in two other booths were staring at them. She was utterly embarrassed.

"Look, I've got to go," she said, pulling herself together. "Call me tomorrow."

"What about the ice cream?"

She glanced at her watch. "It's later than I thought. Sorry about that. I owe you a hot fudge sundae."

And out the door she went.

Ten

Evelyn turned Sasha's mother's giant 1991 Buick LeSabre onto Interstate 90. The boat of a car wasn't the ride either of them was used to, one preferring two wheels and the other a taxi or limo, but they were both grateful for the old car's availability.

"It's a beautiful day for a drive," Evelyn said

to Ms. Davis. Even though the sun was shining, as soon as the familiar words left her mouth, her heart sank a little.

Nearly every weekend before her teen years, when part-time jobs and club activities began to interfere (and father-daughter fishing took over), she'd heard her dad say exactly those words. *It's a beautiful day for a drive.* She could see his smile, knew her own head always nodded in agreement. It didn't matter the weather; it was always a beautiful day for a drive, which really meant it was a good opportunity for them to spend time with each other. She and her folks would pile into the car and head for "places unknown" in search of any number of treasures: a fishing hole, the just-right Christmas tree, a perfect picnic table at the park, a leisurely route across the river to buy fresh cheese curds, a fresh stack of books at the library, or the newest sundae at the Dairy Queen— a memory that made Evelyn's heart sink further.

It had been a week since she'd pulled the plug on Jorden's drive-in invitation, then bailed on her own enticement to buy him a sundae—something he reminded her about the one time they'd since gotten together, at his house. His folks had been home, for which Evelyn was grateful—mostly. Although they were cordial enough, she didn't get the feeling they cared one way or the other about her being their son's fiancée. For that matter, they didn't seem to care that much about him. Nonetheless, she was glad for their presence, even though all they did was sit in the kitchen and sip "evening happy hour cocktails," which she'd declined upon their offer. Being alone with Jorden was getting more and more uncomfortable, since each time it took her longer to pull herself away. She knew her cheeks flared red just thinking about their clutches.

Evelyn sat up straighter, shook her head, burned her eye onto the road, then snapped her thoughts away from Jorden. Better to stick with childhood memories during the silence. Ms. Davis was busy fussing with her cell phone anyway. Evelyn was free to let her mind roam wherever she wished. Just not back to Jorden's muscles.

When Evelyn's mom came along on their "places unknown" family expeditions, she always brought a book, just in case. That was what started Evelyn on the habit. *Life was so much simpler then.*

She quickly checked the backseat for her book-laden backpack. Although Ms. Davis was getting good with her crutches, things sometimes still took her longer than they'd allowed for. When they finally backed out of the driveway today, they realized they were starting out later than planned. Evelyn fretted she might have left her backpack behind, maybe even on the garage floor, where she'd set it when she helped Ms. Davis get her crutches into the backseat. She was glad to spy the top of the shoulder straps. Her familiar backpack, always filled with new information, served as a touchstone to her core self, the self she'd always known she could rely on.

Lately though, she sometimes wasn't sure *who* she was—or was becoming.

She and Ms. Davis were on their way to La Crosse, Wisconsin, for Ms. Davis's first outpatient therapy session. Ms. Davis had had Evelyn conduct an Internet search for physical-therapy centers covered by her insurance company. Even though Ms. Davis hadn't seen her surgeon for months now, she'd also asked Evelyn to contact his office in Boston to see if they had any PT recommendations in her area. They deferred to Mayo's Clinic's lead, which was a little disappointing. Ms. Davis had hoped to hear the same name surface twice: once from her original surgeon and once from Mayo, but no such luck. Although the clinic itself offered PT opportunities, the drive to La Crosse was shorter, which, since Ms. Davis was scheduled to go three times a week, seemed more prudent. Evelyn's grandpa had asked around and garnered a couple of strong firsthand recommendations for the La Crosse facility too. Several of his customers were happy to laud their praises, one even breaking out in a box step waltz to show how well her new knees worked.

"Nervous?" Evelyn asked Ms. Davis after she put her phone away.

"Not really nervous. I'd say *anxious* is more accurate. Anxious to get this slow-moving freight train of a body back on the right track before it's declared permanently derailed. Anxious to push myself to the limits and learn firsthand, that no, I won't fall to pieces just because a therapist says, 'Give me twenty reps. Or forty.'" Ms. Davis wrung her hands. "Okay, perhaps I am nervous."

"Can't blame you. But aren't you excited too? I'm excited for you!"

"You are?"

"Of course! I feel lucky *and* blessed."

"Lucky and blessed to be shuttling a cranky and broken ballerina to her first round of torture?" She shot Evelyn a sly smile.

"Torture? Aren't we dramatic today! But *yes*. I *do* feel blessed. It's like I'm getting to help a friend find her way back into the world again."

The moment it was out of her mouth, even though it was true, Evelyn realized how sappy that sounded. She hoped it wasn't insulting. It seemed a little presumptuous to put herself, a hired hand, in the friend category with a world-class dancer. Ms. Davis said nothing in response to the state-ment, causing her further regret. *Think before you speak, Evelyn. Think!*

They drove fifteen miles before either of them uttered another word. The silence was torturous. Evelyn finally couldn't take it anymore. Even though she remembered, she asked Ms. Davis to check the exit number for her on the MapQuest sheet she'd printed out.

By the time they pulled into the parking lot and Ms. Davis crutched her way into the facility, she had just enough time to fill out the paperwork before they called her in. "You can leave your handbag with me," Evelyn said. "No sense trying to drag that around with you."

"Thank you," Ms. Davis said, surrendering her bag. "Just so you know, I have my cell phone set to vibrate, and it's in that front zipper compartment. Don't want you to think there's something alive in there should someone try to phone." She chuckled, something she did more often lately. It was a happy sound. "Feel free to answer it. You know the drill. I'm expecting a call from the insurance company. I put your name on their records so you can take messages for me," she said. Then she disappeared behind the door the therapist held open for her.

Evelyn set the purse on the floor and stuck her leg through one of the straps, a security method she'd once invented at a concert. To get away with the bag, a bad guy would have to drag her too. Evelyn, not exactly a lightweight, figured she'd win that contest.

She rested her backpack on her lap and extracted a book on the history of coal mining. While trawling the library, she'd run across the title and checked out three books on the topic. She remembered hearing about black lung from her grandpa, who'd lost a distant relative to the disease, which meant that so had she. She wondered if such maladies still existed, or if coal mining safety had progressed since subjecting workers to the disease. She knew coal mining accidents like cave-ins and explosions still occurred. They'd captured their share of terrible news earlier in the year, which not only fed her curiosity, but also caused her to send up many prayers during the horrid waiting. One night she'd dozed off while firing up pleas to God as she tried to extinguish thoughts of how scary it must be for those trapped and those waiting. *Grace, Lord, grace to all. And hope. And peace in the darkest places.*

She was on the fourth chapter of the first book when she felt Ms. Davis's cell phone vibrate against her foot. Due to her odd encampment, she had to scramble to get to it. "Hello! Ms. Davis's phone!" she yelled in a high-pitched voice, breaking formal protocol, afraid whoever it was would hang up before hearing her.

A silence just long enough to make her think she had missed the call ensued, but she gave it one final loud hello, just in case. The man sitting across from her rattled his newspaper and glared at her.

A male voice on the phone responded. "Who is this?"

Evelyn's book started to slide off her lap

("Never let library books hit the floor," her mom had taught her early on), then her backpack. By the time she grabbed them and resettled the phone to her ear, she was more than a tad discombobulated. "I'm sorry, who did you say is calling?"

"Donald Major. And who did you say you are, please?"

Oh, it's him. Evelyn gathered herself and put on her business voice. "This is Evelyn Burt, Ms. Davis's assistant. How can I help you?"

"I'm sorry, Ms. Burt. It didn't sound like you."

"You caught me at a . . . strange moment." She opened her mouth to describe the scenario, then felt proud of herself for not doing so. "What can I do for you, Mr. Major?"

"Is Sasha there?"

"Sir, Ms. Davis is not present."

"I realize she won't talk to me, but I'm wondering if right this moment she is within earshot and you are, as usual, shielding her. Or is she indeed not there?"

Whoa. Here's a new tactic. It wasn't in Evelyn to outright lie to him, or to anyone for that matter. She'd already pushed her moral envelope with Jorden and the ice cream cop-out—although she *had* wanted to check on Ms. Davis. Just not right that minute. She needed to guard against making stretching the truth a habit. "At the moment, she is not here with me."

"Good. It's you I want to speak with."

"Sir?" Evelyn cocked her head. A strong unease began to rumble within her.

"Are you aware, Ms. Burt, that I am Sasha's husband?"

What? Evelyn raced through everything she knew about Ms. Davis. She wore no wedding ring. She did not speak of a husband. Although everyone in town inquired about Ms. Davis, nobody, not even her grandpa, bothered to ask about a *husband.* This was creepy. Ms. Davis had, early on, given her strict orders never, but never, to hand her the phone if and when a Donald Major called. Was he a known stalker, perhaps a dangerous one?

She finally answered with the only thing she could think of.

"Sir, I do not engage in personal conversations about Ms. Davis. She does not wish to speak with you. We hope you've received her mailings."
Where did we send those? To Boston, right? She grabbed a pen and tablet out of her backpack and wrote the caller ID number down, one she would have recognized if she'd had time to look before answering.

"Right. The *mailings,*" he said, a note of mixed anger and sarcasm lacing his voice. "Yes, I've received them. I'm sure everyone on her fan list has."

Now that Evelyn thought about it, Ms. Davis

did once slightly alter the wording in the letter to Mr. Major from those on the rest of her list. That was something he didn't need to know though. "Good. I'm glad you've received them."

"Good? You think anything about this is good? A wife shutting out her husband is not *good!* I don't even know if my wife can walk! It's bad enough I was dancing with her when this terrible thing happened. But to be shunned like this . . ." His voice cracked. "Look, Ms. Burt," he said, with what sounded like an attempt to pull himself together, "I'm sorry for raising my voice. This is not your fault; I'm sure you're just acting on her behalf and under her strict instruction. Believe me, I know how convincing she can be. I'm just so . . . frustrated and worried, I feel nearly insane. I thought about arriving on her doorstep and—"

Evelyn cut him off. "You know where she lives?" Her throat constricted. Was this guy unbalanced?

"Of *course* I know where she lives!" He stated the address and the color of the house. He described the stained glass window in the front door. Her heart felt like it was about to bang out of her chest. "We traveled a lot and lived far away. There is no choice in our profession, which sadly means neither of us was around Wanonishaw much, especially me. Still, you're not married to someone for thirteen years without at least once or twice visiting her hometown. Genevieve Davis was my mother-in-law. I adored her. Sasha and I stayed in her house when we visited, in the upstairs bedroom, to the right at the top of the stairs. Sasha's bedroom when she was a child. It's painted blue. See for yourself. How else would I know this? There's a picture of us hanging on the wall in that room—at least there used to be. I tell you, Sasha is my *wife*."

And then he began to cry.

In her entire life, Evelyn had only seen or heard grown men cry twice. Both incidents took place at her Grandma Burt's funeral, when her father and grandpa hugged each other in front of the casket. She couldn't imagine Jorden crying, although he told her he'd cried when his dog died a couple of years ago, an intimate detail that endeared him to her all the more, for she, too, had cried when they had to put down Bess, their thirteen-year-old collie.

She chewed on her knuckle and stared at the door through which Ms. Davis had disappeared. How long had it been? She might reappear at any moment. The last thing Evelyn needed was for Ms. Davis to discover her talking to Donald Major, whoever he was.

"Look, sir," she said, softening her voice, disarmed by his tears, "like I said before, it is not my business to discuss Ms. Davis's personal life. I have to go now."

"Please! *Please,*" he said, sniffing. "Just tell me

if she's okay. Is she in pain? Is she walking? Dancing at all? Do you think she might be ready to see me now, if I surprised her?"

Evelyn swallowed. She scrambled to put together any pieces that might make this remarkable story true. But even if it were true, it was not hers to either question or to intervene. Ms. Davis was doing so well lately. She was happier and progressing. She'd even cracked a few jokes. The last thing she needed right now was for this man—a man Ms. Davis made it clear she did not wish to speak with—to show up.

"Mr. Major . . ." Just then, the door opened and she gasped. She could not yet see who was coming, but she spoke quickly. "Sir, all I can say is that Ms. Davis does not wish to speak with you, and I have to hang up right now!"

"Please!" she heard him say as she started to close the phone. "Tell her I love her. Tell her I miss her. Tell her—"

Evelyn finished closing the warm phone and quickly slipped it back into Ms. Davis's bag, just before first a pair of crutches, then Ms. Davis appeared.

When Ms. Davis reached her, Evelyn's heart was still racing. Even though she had done nothing wrong, she was afraid she looked guilty, so she pasted on a smile and said, "How'd it go?" She barely recognized her own voice.

Although Ms. Davis smiled while she talked,

Evelyn had no idea what she said. Her mind was too preoccupied.

If Donald Major really is *your husband, then why isn't he with you now instead of me? Why hasn't he come to see you, even if you profess you don't want to talk to him? Why didn't he come here from the beginning to take care of you? Did you run away from him? Was he mean to you? Is your condition his fault? Or is that why you don't want to talk to him, because he* wouldn't *take care of you? Isn't that a husband's job? To keep you safe? To be with you? To honor and protect you, in sickness and in health? To give you tingles from this day forward?*

On the ride home, Ms. Davis was chattier than ever. Although she said she was exhausted, she had a hopeful spark in her eye, one Evelyn had not before seen. Evelyn imagined Ms. Davis looked closer to what she must have looked like before the accident took its toll. Her smile came easily today. Evelyn kept looking her way and nodding, but she could still barely process a word Ms. Davis said, which was something about finally getting to rid herself of the therapeutic air bed.

All Evelyn could think about was how she would ever keep from asking Ms. Davis about Donald Major and how she could find out the truth. She couldn't ask anyone else in town for fear of sounding like she was either ignorant or gossiping. She wasn't even sure if she should bring it up with her grandpa, who seemed to hear everything.

One thing she could do was take a look in that room to the right at the top of the stairs. But how and when? And what if she got caught? She knew how Ms. Davis felt about privacy and snoops.

What if Donald Major suddenly rings our doorbell? Should I call the police? Let him in? What if he mentions he called and Ms. Davis gets mad I didn't tell her?

"Evelyn, are you listening to me?" Ms. Davis said, tapping her on the arm.

"I'm sorry. No, I'm afraid I missed the last thing you said. Traffic is really something today."

Ms. Davis looked around and saw what Evelyn saw: there were only two cars within half a mile of them. Evelyn felt like a dolt. *Stretching the truth again, Evelyn. Shame on you!*

Lord, I receive your grace for my shortcomings. Now, can you please do something about my mouth? My awkward position with a possible Mr. Davis?

My tingly self when I'm with the man I love? HELP!

Eleven

The next day, Evelyn asked Ms. Davis for a couple hours of personal time, which she gladly granted. An undying curiosity about Donald Major drove Evelyn straight to her folks' house.

The timing was perfect. Evelyn's Dad would be out on his Saturday morning drill, which included stops at the hardware store, the meat market, the bait shop, and the donut shop. Evelyn had run the route with him countless times. The Saturday morning ritual was kind of a joke in their family. Although she missed her dad something fierce, she still wasn't ready to talk to him. Not until he came around about Jorden. *The more he talks against Jorden, the unfairness of it drives me further toward Jorden, makes me choose between them. Why can't he see that?* she thought as she sped along on her bicycle.

Her mom, whom Evelyn decided would be the person most likely to have heard about a husband if Ms. Davis really had one, would be home cleaning and doing laundry. Theirs was a family of routine.

Evelyn spent the bicycle ride trying to figure out how to casually work the question into a conversation without raising inappropriate flags. By the time she pulled into her folks' drive, she'd decided to just let the opportunity find its own way in. Any other plan would sound contrived. She wasn't good at sneaky.

Not wanting to just walk in and scare her mom, she knocked. When the door swung open, there stood her dad, a can of Pledge in one hand and a dust rag in the other.

Evelyn blinked, grabbed hold of her ponytail and gave it a twirl, then looked at her wristwatch. "What? No route today?" she said with a weak smile. Their last encounter had been so bad that the aftermath still hung thick in the air between them.

"Your mom's been under the weather the last few days. I told her to sleep in, that I'd get a head start on the cleaning for her."

"Oh." *Awkward. Now what?* "Nothing serious, I hope."

"Just a cold. But she hasn't been sleeping well for all the coughing." He stepped back. "Come on in. This is still your home too, you know." She detected a slight note of sarcasm in his voice, one she could tell he was trying to hold at bay. "Is Jorden with you?" He craned his neck toward the street.

"Nope. Just me."

He looked relieved. "I was about to stop for a coffee break. Come on back to the kitchen." He lowered his voice. "As much as I know your mom would like to see you, I think it's best we let her sleep."

They settled at the kitchen table, the family's usual chat spot. Her dad stared at her, a slight frown lacing the corners of his mouth.

"So, how are things going?" he asked.

"Great!" *Way too enthusiastic. Don't try so hard.*

"I heard you were out at the Sunrise for dinner a week or so ago."

"Oh?" She thought a moment, then recalled her dinner with Jorden, the sway of the waitress's backside, Jorden's invitation to the drive-in. Her cheeks flushed. "Who told you we were there?"

"Doesn't matter. Just someone who said you and Jorden seemed to be . . . quite comfortable with each other." Although the statement was casual enough, the tone in his voice told her differently.

She thought back, remembered kissing Jorden a couple of times, then recalled the way he'd kissed her. Her cheeks flamed. *So that's what he's snarking about.* The thought that her dad was implying something inappropriate took place made her bristle.

"Yes, we do enjoy each other's company. That's a good thing, Dad."

"I heard you might have been a little too comfortable with each other, especially in a public place in a small town like Wanonishaw. Word gets around, you know."

"Gads, dad!" She shook her head. "Have you no

157

trust in me at *all* anymore? It was nothing, just a couple quick kisses. With my *fiancé*." She realized her voice had escalated, then remembered her sleeping mom. "It was *nothing,*" she said, nearly beneath her breath. "Some old busybody's looking to start trouble is what it sounds like to me. Have you completely forgotten what it feels like to be young and in love, Dad? And may I remind you that I'm nineteen, not twelve?"

"Evelyn, it's not you I don't trust." There was a slight pause. He swallowed. "I'm going to be perfectly honest with you here, sport. I've been kicking myself for not bringing this up sooner, before you were . . . I'm worried you're in over your head with this guy. You're . . . vulnerable, Evelyn. You're as smart as a whip, but I just don't believe you have enough experience to handle a player like Jorden. I know his type, always pushing, always wanting more." A red rash spread up his neck, revealing the depth of his emotion.

Evelyn stood up and paced, then whirled on her heels. "Player? Why can't you just leave this alone, Dad? Why can't you just be *happy* for me? Is it so hard to think someone might love me?" A thought sprang into her head, one she knew she should keep to herself, and yet her mouth opened. "And by a 'player' like Jorden," she said, drawing air quotes around the phrase, "do you mean the kind of guy *you* were, who caused you and mom to have to get married?"

Her dad's head snapped back. She might as well have slapped him in the face. The thus far unspoken family truth had rendered him speechless. *Well good.*

"Do you think I can't count, Dad? Do you think I can't read between the lines?"

"Evelyn, I . . ."

"I am not you. I am not Mom. *Jorden* is not you, nor is he the enemy here. You don't even *know* him, Dad. You've never once given him a chance."

Her dad stood. "I know him well enough to know he's not going to college. Where's his ambition, Evelyn? Where's his common sense? The guy laid a patch of rubber in front of our house! That's something immature hotheads do, not grown men with good intentions."

"Back to the patch of rubber again? Do you ever let anything go? You have no *idea* about his intentions," she all but spat. "He's a hard worker, Dad. Why is that not commendable? Has it ever occurred to you that maybe, just maybe, Jorden McFinn has *my* best interests at heart? That he really does love me and knows what's best for me, maybe better than you do?" Her voice had gone up in pitch nearly a whole octave.

"What on earth are you two yelling about?" her mom said. She stood in the doorway with messy hair, a red nose, and a tissue in her hand.

"What do you think?" Evelyn said, disgusted. "The same thing we always argue about these days." She moved toward her mom. "I'm sorry you're sick," she said giving her a quick hug. "I'm sorry we woke you. I hope you feel better soon. But I've got to get out of here before I say something *else* I regret."

It struck her that any implication about her dad and a shotgun wedding also spoke poorly of her mother. She loved her folks; talking trash about them wasn't her intention. Yet there was a basic truth there: her mom was pregnant before they got married. Although theirs was not an outwardly passionate marriage, it ended up comfortable enough. Until Jorden happened, Evelyn had never felt anything from them but love, even though she'd known for a long, long time that her conception was the catalyst for their marriage.

"Something else?" her mom said, holding the tissue to her nose, flashing her eyes between Evelyn and her husband.

"Ask Dad," Evelyn said over her shoulder on the way to the door. "I'm not as dumb as he thinks I am."

Sasha was a little more than two weeks into her outpatient therapy in La Crosse. Some things were changing; some stayed the same.

She closed the bird book Evelyn had given her and set it next to the snowglobe. The tiny feathered visitor would have to come another time and stay longer, when she could give him a better study. There were too many pictures of similar birds in the book to be sure of his identification. What color *had* his beak been, or how, exactly, did his tail slant? It was so easy to miss the details when one was lost in the overall beauty, the fragileness, the performances—the certainty that the same little bird *would* return for another show.

On a sadder note, Evelyn had reported she'd found a dead sparrow in the driveway the other day. Sasha was glad Evelyn had buried it in the backyard before she'd told her about it.

Here, gone . . . suddenly injured.

Life.

In the midst of everything that was wrong, Sasha began to realize how important it was to pay attention while one could, to remember to be thankful for small things. Thankful for growing health and the people who came alongside you.

Baby steps in the right direction.

She smiled as she felt a slight shifting of purpose within her, caught a glimpse of expectancy, which surprised and comforted her. She tucked the small epiphany away, hoped to remember its brightness the next time defeat, no matter how small, threatened to knock her down again.

She hoped the bird returned soon. More details could help her positively ID him. Same as humans, she mused. *It's the details in each of us that set us apart, really. That and our stories. How self-absorbed have I been to have missed*

161

that? Next time the little guy showed up, she'd hone in on one thing, like the color and shape of his beak, which she guessed served as a combination mouth and nose. *Maybe I should have Evelyn pick me up a book on bird anatomy!* She chuckled. The reality that she'd traded playing the lead in *Swan Lake* for excitement about a book on bird anatomy struck her as funny. She shook her head, then decided to celebrate her newfound daftness by making her way to the kitchen for some peanut butter crackers.

While she rinsed the knife, she watched a flock of birds fly high above. It occurred to her how the corps de ballet was kind of like a flock of birds: so many comparably shaped bodies. As opposed to the birds' chaotic actions, though, the corps often lined up in rows, moved together as one, wore costumes and headpieces of the same design. Uniform bodies were important. From a distance, it could be difficult to tell the dancers apart.

On her way back to her chair, crackers wrapped in a paper towel and tucked in her pocket, Sasha thought of Janine Selby again. She'd been thinking about her just this morning. In a line of ballet dancers, Janine's nose would be the thing that most set her apart. Janine would be the first to admit it. She had a wonderful nose, a full-throttle Roman nose, Janine called it. Aside from Donald, Janine was the next closest friend Sasha had. *The only intimate friend I used to have.*

A month before Sasha's accident, Janine received an invitation to join a company in San Jose as principal dancer. As soon as Mid-Central Festival Ballet's current show closed, she'd be off, she'd said. Sasha, Donald, and Janine toasted with champagne, then cried and made promises to always stay in touch.

Then came Sasha's injury. Janine moved while Sasha was still in the hospital. That was the nature of the profession. The dancer must go when and where the work and the opportunities arose.

Sasha bit into one of the salty crackers, let the taste of the peanut butter spread throughout her mouth. She missed Janine and was sure Donald did too. The three of them had been pretty tight. Since their separation, Janine had once phoned Sasha's cell number. She'd left a brief message saying she understood why Sasha needed to be alone, at least for a time, and that she didn't wish to bug her, but that she should *please* let them all know how she was doing. "If you don't want to answer your e-mails, fine. But at least do *something,* give us *some* word, that says, 'Don't worry!' Or 'pray harder'—which I'm doing anyway!"

To have called Janine back would have opened the door on a world of devastating hurt and longing. Too much time had passed. Too much sorrow. Too much explaining to do now—or worse yet, maybe even second-guessing her choices to begin with.

No, it would simply be too difficult, too complicated. What would they even have to talk about anyway, now that Janine was dancing leads and Sasha was shuffling one foot in front of the other?

All the worry she'd caused so many. Such terrible guilt.

A part of Sasha knew her decision to leave them all behind was brutal, yet she would not reach out to either of them, for reasons far beyond her own discomfort. She earnestly did not wish them to miss a single moment of their dancing lives grieving for the loss of hers. What could they really do anyway, besides be sad?

It was difficult for a dancer to be around a dancer who was laid up, or worse yet, had her career ended in such a tragic and stupid way. She was too much of a reminder of how fragile the profession really was. She'd gone over this a million times in her head: Dancers need to dance with control and trust, not fear and hesitation—the biggest reason she knew she should never dance with Donald again, even if she could. He would be too protective, too careful, too worried about her heart.

Her heart that was broken into a million more pieces than her body.

She wiped her mouth with the napkin, then picked up the bird book and fanned through it again, as if the breeze might shoo away the memories and sorrow. Forcing herself to change gears, she began to slowly thumb through the pages, which served as a sort of diary for her new bird-watching hobby and the swift passing of days. When she felt sure she'd identified a bird correctly (and after double-checking her prediction with Evelyn), at Evelyn's suggestion, she'd written the date next to the picture. She was surprised at how quickly the entries racked up, how many pages already sported check marks.

Now that she was more mobile and gratefully spent less time in her chair and more time doing her "homework therapy," as Evelyn called it, entries came slower. She'd even undertaken a few minimal household chores, such as dusting pieces of furniture for which she didn't have to bend over too far, like the top of the old radio. It was great to feel useful.

Sadly, not until she was wholly laid up did she realize what a gift it had been to be able to wash a dish, clean a toilet, or make her own bed; she still couldn't do the second two. All her life, her body had been so strong, so worked, so agile and solid. She felt like Humpty Dumpty, slowly putting herself back together again—at least until all the king's horses and all the king's men realized *they* couldn't completely put her back together again either. Not well enough to take the stage.

Her life as she knew it was over. It was time to come to solid grips with that fact and find a way to move forward gracefully, a way to glean satisfaction and purpose in a simpler life. She had to learn how to let go of consuming bitterness, guilt, and regret. But how? That was the question.

She set the bird book aside and stared with longing at the dancer in the snowglobe. Resting her left palm on top of the globe, she leaned her head back, closed her eyes, and let her mind drift to happier times. She'd love to be able to get up the stairs to her mom's sewing room right now, enjoy the piles of colorful fabric her mom hadn't been able to stop herself from collecting. An avid seamstress and quilter, her mother delighted in selecting unique fabrics as much as Sasha loved dancing and donning her mother's handmade costumes.

As a child, every week, Sasha would put on at least one show, complete with a stage curtain her mom quilted special for that purpose. She'd sewn large iridescent sequins into it, same as she'd done for many of Sasha's costumes. Standing on a chair, her mom would hang the curtain on a removable tension rod in the doorway between the kitchen and the sitting room.

Sasha opened her eyes. There, through a hazy blur like a gentle snow, was the curtain! It hung right where it always had when she was young. Sasha removed the shade from the lamp on her end table so the light from the bare bulb would better catch in the sequins.

In a jiffy, she disappeared into her mother's bedroom and selected her wardrobe from the giant costume chest. Today she would wear the peacock blue skirt and top, the one that rustled when she moved. Underneath, she added two layers of her mother's crinolines, rolled at the waist until they fit snuggly and were the right length.

While she prepared, her mom selected an album. Sasha waited until the music began, the volume rose, and her mother had enough time to seat herself in her rocker, excited for the performance to begin.

At the music's crescendo, with great *ta-da!* fanfare, as she'd done countless times during her childhood, Sasha extended her long leg and pointed toe through the side of the curtain. She delighted in the sensuous feel of the rich curtain fabric brushing against her leg, in hearing the rustle of the crinolines. Then she slipped her right arm through the curtain. She held her fingertips pointing upward, as if surrounding the bowl of a chalice, its golden stem between her pointer and middle finger. When she heard her mother's applause, she slid the curtain back, let loose her brightest smile, and began her spontaneous and gloriously free choreography.

A leap, a *plié*, a *glissade*, a *jeté*, a perfect *arabesque*, then a twirl, a leap, leap . . . *Attitude!* she told herself, snapping the carriage of her head just so. With abandon, on she danced, through the sitting room, into the living room, her mom following and clapping. When the music began to wind down, she worked her way back into the sitting room, where her mother again seated herself in the rocker. In sync with the final notes of the record, in a grand flourish of exaggerated moves, she curtsied, bending nearly to the floor. When her mother finally stopped applauding—after two curtain calls—Sasha burst through the curtain and plunked her lanky breathless self onto her mother's lap.

As Sasha turned her head to look at her mother, she felt a tear stream down her cheek. She gasped, startled to discover herself sitting in the chair, alone, her hand atop the snowglobe. It took her a moment to regain her bearings, remember that her mother was gone and that she herself was a grown woman with crutches next to her chair. And yet, she was breathing heavily, sweating, as if she had just danced through the house. Her body felt alive with the same exhilaration she experienced right after a performance.

She shook her head, rubbed her eyes, grounded herself by removing her hand from the snowglobe and placing her palms on the arms of the same rocker in which her mother had spent so much time: nursing, hand stitching, watching, cheering, praying—resting her hands too.

She longed to wrap herself in her mother's

fabric, search the sewing room closet for her curtain, find a box containing her old costumes, maybe even her first real pair of ballet slippers. Her mom was such a sentimental saver. She was sure to have kept at least some of those things. But Sasha didn't yet trust herself to deal with her crutches on the steep stairway. She'd learned in therapy how to approach stairs, but even though she was getting stronger, the smallest endeavors could still exhaust her. Even just imagining she was dancing left her nearly breathless, for her heart had yet to return to its normal pace. To tackle the stairs and risk a fall when Evelyn wasn't there? Nope. Her shoulders slumped as this new defeat washed through her.

Do not get stuck in defeat, Sasha! Start focusing on your gains again, not your losses!

One of her favorite therapy tricks she'd learned for certain circumstances—like going up the stairs with the aid of the banister or working on a project—was to put both crutches under one arm. Doing so had allowed her to undertake some light cooking, although her fried eggs didn't taste as good as Evelyn's. Or Donald's. But then cooking had never been her forte. *One crutch, two crutches, no crutches—I am not a good cook.* Nonetheless, she was glad to be more mobile than she had been, which certainly helped fight the boredom monster.

"Change your scenery, change your mood."

169

Evelyn had said it several times this week as they shuttled back and forth from La Crosse or when she all but shooed Sasha out of her chair.

Sasha grabbed her crutches. Using the hand-grips for leverage, she rocked forward and stood. *This is how I mark progress: getting out of the chair still takes concentration, but doing so no longer nearly buckles me.* Although the shawl didn't work well with crutches, she thought she might need it, so she tied it around her waist. She smiled. With all the beadwork, the shawl passed as a fancy dance skirt. She made her way to the living room, enjoying the sway and swish of the loose fabric against her slacks as she moved.

So many tactile memories.

Evelyn was off with Jorden for the evening. As Sasha ventured down the hall, she realized anew how much she missed Evelyn when she was gone. But also, what if she fell down or fainted while Evelyn was away? Then what? Evelyn gave her security.

Still, the therapist had warned Sasha not to play it too safe. After her wash of memories about dancing through the house, she was definitely in the mood for music. Tchaikovsky, to be exact. There was no reason she couldn't put some on herself, so she headed to the bookcase.

Using the double-crutch-under-one-arm trick, she stretched as far as she could, up on her toes *(progress!)* until she reached the bottoms of a couple of record albums on the second shelf from the top. She wrangled them partway out. But just when she got them to the tipping point, she no longer had the strength to stay on her toes and started to wobble. She had to let the albums crash to the floor and grab the bookcase for balance. After a heart-racing and steadying moment, she got herself back on both crutches.

Her determined effort to retrieve the music felt ill-advised at best and dangerous at worst. Nonetheless, no matter how ugly, she'd tried. Her therapist would be proud. "Be smart, but don't coddle yourself," she'd said. "And don't let small defeats do you in." A goal Sasha repeated to herself out loud.

She sat in the nearby chair and remained still until her jitters ceased. Using her crutch as an extended arm, she pulled the toppled albums close to her chair. However, try as she might, she could not bend down far enough to pick them up without spiking tailbone pain. The therapists also told her to let the pain be her guide and to pay special attention to sharp pain.

Oh, well, at least the music's selected for tomorrow, she mused. She leaned back in the chair and smiled. *And such a handy place for it, all over the floor like that!* Evelyn would probably scold her for attempting such a thing on her own. Then again, she might applaud. If nothing else, she was a relentless cheerleader.

Evelyn.

For a young woman, Evelyn was old beyond her years. Evelyn, Sasha decided, worried too much about her—although far be it from Sasha to tell her so. Evelyn acted more like a mother hen than an assistant, really. But it was nice to know someone still had her back, a phrase Donald used to use.

Donald.

She pulled the end of the shawl up in her lap and fondled the familiar beads, selected one and brushed it over her lips. When she'd made the decision to pay someone to move her out of the hospital and far away to her mom's house, it seemed her only choice. Why ruin two careers? She knew Donald. He wouldn't think twice about giving it all up to take care of her. She made her decision to cut him loose the day she learned his injuries were healing and he would soon dance again.

And dance he must, dance he now did—for both of them.

No, she could not bear to see his sad eyes looking at her every day, longing for the way things used to be—for both of them.

If it wasn't for Evelyn, Sasha couldn't imagine how dreadful her life would be. Unbearable, likely. Enthusiastic, self-assured, creative Evelyn. If nothing else, Sasha had learned a lot of random things about life just from trying to keep up with

Evelyn's ever-changing library book topics. Who would push her to her limits, bake her cookies, mark her tea bags, handle her correspondence with panache, keep her company, even design her a new letterhead, and keep the frying pan birdbath full, if it weren't for Evelyn?

Thoughts of the frying pan caused a sudden surge of guilt to zing through her. She put her hand over her heart and shook her head. One of these days, and soon, she owed Evelyn a long overdue explanation and apology.

"It's like I'm getting to help a friend find her way back into the world again," Evelyn had said in the car on their way to that first outpatient therapy session a couple of weeks ago. When Sasha heard those words, spoken so sincerely, it was all she could do to keep from weeping. They'd played in her head time and again. Yes, someone *did* have her back. There'd been such an earnest, tender, and genuine enthusiasm in Evelyn's voice. Such care.

Such hope. Of all the gifts Evelyn dispensed, hope for the future was at the top of the list.

Although Sasha would likely never see the dance floor again, she'd closed in on herself so much after the accident that right now, just finding her way back into the world again felt like an even loftier goal, one she was beginning to think might be possible.

It struck her that maybe for the first time ever,

she could learn who she was apart from dance.

Night had crept in before Sasha realized she was sitting in the dark. She switched on the side table lamp. She wasn't wearing a wristwatch, but she guessed it was going on nine. She didn't expect Evelyn back till eleven or so, had no idea where she and her fiancé Jorden were off to. The few times Sasha had met Jorden, it was beyond her what the two of them had in common. But then how would she know? What did she have to compare it to? Dance had occupied so much of her young life, she'd barely had time to make friends in high school, let alone have boyfriends.

Apart from dance, Sasha's high school years had been tough. She didn't really fit in with any crowd—perhaps not too unlike Evelyn. Free time, the little that she'd had, was usually spent with others she'd met in her dance classes, most of whom didn't attend her school. The handful of girls she did hang around with in school were, as she recalled, pretty snooty. Her crowd made fun of clunky, socially backward girls like Evelyn. She cringed at the cruelty and ignorance of youth.

She bet the old-time Wanonishawites, as her mom used to call them, were having a field day with her now. She supposed she'd given them reason. Once she left town, she rarely ever came back. What she and Donald enjoyed most was to get her mom away from the little town. They'd send her airline tickets for a weekend visit, or fly her to different global venues to watch them dance, which her mother reveled in. "Oh, my little bird!" her mom would say after each performance. "I'm the luckiest mother alive to receive such wonderful opportunities!"

No, I was the lucky one, Mom. How many people have the chance to realize their dreams? A bubble of gratefulness swelled within her and erupted in happy tears. She *had* lived her dream. That was something to hold on to.

Sasha shivered. Evelyn had, with great grunting and pounding this morning, opened the windows, a first since Sasha had moved in. Ancient painted windows didn't go up or down easily after long bouts of closure. The fresh air had felt good to both of them, and Sasha couldn't imagine why she hadn't had Evelyn open them earlier. But now, the night air felt damp.

After seeing what Evelyn went through to get the windows open, Sasha wasn't about to attempt closing them. She untied the shawl from around her waist, gingerly removed it from beneath her, and pulled it around her shoulders. She rested her head against the chair back and listened. Somewhere off in the distance, a dog barked. The crickets sang outside the window. A slight breeze tiptoed over her cheeks.

Something brushed her left leg, startling her. When she leaned down to see what it was, to her amazement, TuTu sat by her feet. For unknown reasons, rather than freak her out, Sasha found the company pleasing.

"You chilly too?" she asked. "Or maybe lonesome?"

In answer, TuTu hopped up in her lap and quickly curled up in a ball. Sasha dared to rest her hand on the soft creature's back. It was then the purring began. In silent wonder, Sasha watched as Arabesque—the elusive one, as Evelyn referred to him—appeared and began to weave his way through her legs. With each light stroke of TuTu's back and the vibration of her contented purrs against Sasha's thighs, plus the soft brush of Arabesque winding around her legs—as well as grateful memories and a love-laden shawl wrapped around her shoulders—Sasha felt content for the first time in a long, long while. As much as she'd enjoyed the applause, there was, to be sure, a decadent joy in this simple, delicious, hometown peaceful quietness.

My life, she thought in the stillness of this deep and abiding moment, *isn't what I left behind. My life is here and now. And it is filled with choices.*

Could this, she wondered, be a true insight into Evelyn's "grace"?

Twelve

Evelyn and Jorden had gone for a long walk, then driven to the movie theater—indoor theater, thank goodness. The Dairy Queen finally got their busi-ness afterward. They'd enjoyed a relaxing even-ing, right up until Jorden embraced her in the car in Ms. Davis's driveway at 11:30 p.m. and started pressing her again about marriage. Her mind fired like static electricity, jolting her system and sensibilities.

"Think about it, babe," Jorden said. *Zap!* "Ms. Davis is on the mend, and your job, your living arrangement, will end soon. And I can't believe it, but my folks are talking about moving again." His voice turned forlorn. "This will be our third move in the last two years, not to mention the countless moves before that. I'm sick of packing up and finding new jobs. I like this town, and I love you." He gave her a surprisingly tender kiss, then play-fully tapped the end of her nose with his finger. *Zing!* "I've never had a choice before about moving, but now . . . let's just get hitched, find a place of our own, *now.* My folks can hit the road if they want. I can move in the new place till you're free of this job." He drew her closer, nibbled her ear, ran his fingers through her hair, sprawled them on the back of her head and drew her mouth to his. "Do what we want, when we want," he said, his voice barely audible.

Crackle!

As intoxicating as the moment was, unbidden, thoughts of Donald Major played in the recesses of Evelyn's mind. She wondered if he'd told Ms. Davis the same things before they got married. And where was he now? Was *he* one of those players her dad had referred to?

But then what about Evelyn's own parents? They hadn't waited, and they were still together.

Love was complicated and blindsiding, she guessed. Jorden's lips pressed hot upon hers.

Pop! Sizzle!

She wished they were parked in front of her own house, where she could see her dad through the picture window. He'd be watching out for her. Instead, she and her dad were nearly estranged, which made her incredibly sad. The more time that passed, the more their last horrid exchange bothered her. Yet, the more time she spent with Jorden, the more she knew her dad was dead wrong about him.

She backed away from Jorden, turned her head to look out the window, and stared at her temporary abode on Fourth Street. There was a light on in the living room. Ms. Davis must have left it on for her. *What if* she's *looking out the window?*

"What do you say, babe?" Jorden asked. "Please tell me you're seriously thinking about marriage."

"To be honest," she said, after a great sigh, "it's getting difficult to think of anything else."

She wanted to talk to him about Donald Major, ask Jorden what he would do if something happened to *her*—hear him promise he'd never leave her side. It was on the tip of her tongue to do so. After all, Jorden didn't know any of the townspeople the way the old townies did, so it wouldn't really be gossip now, would it? But something stopped her. If she did ask Jorden how he'd respond should something terrible happen to her, wouldn't he assume she didn't trust him, to ask such a ridiculous question? Wouldn't that be insulting?

"So," he said, running his finger across the back of her neck, down onto her collarbone, "what have you decided?"

Flash fire! Seize the water!

As difficult as it was to do so, she pulled his hand away from her neck and held it between hers. "I think life is complicated right now. I've got a lot on my mind, not the least of which is my folks. I miss my dad, Jorden. In fact, mostly because of us," she said, pointing her finger between them, "Dad and I aren't speaking."

There. She'd said it. Something she'd kept to herself for far too long.

"I wish I could say that about me and my dad,"

Jorden said. A darkness she'd never before witnessed raced across his face.

"Why on earth would you wish that?" She kissed his fingertips.

He stared at her and bit his bottom lip. For a moment, he looked like he might tell her something, something bad, but then decided not to. "It doesn't matter. Nothing I can't handle, haven't handled a thousand times before. Let's just say from what I can tell, your family—especially your dad—is the exact opposite of mine. Enough said."

"There can never be enough said!" She let go of his hand and leaned away from him. "If a couple's going to make it in this world, they need to talk about things. *Every*thing." She thought about Ms. Davis and Mr. Major, a husband and wife—if that was indeed what they were—not only living apart but not talking at all. She recalled—was haunted by—the pleading in Donald Major's voice before she hung up on him at the rehab facility. *Please, tell her I love her. Tell her I miss her. Tell her . . .* Tell her what? Evelyn had wondered since.

"Sometimes talking makes things worse," Jorden said.

She thought about the last time she and her dad had spoken, the way she left her house. Yes, sometimes talking did make things worse.

"I suppose," she said to Jorden, her head drooping. She yawned. "Look, I'm tired. I gotta go in. I promise you," she said, leaning into him, "that I am thinking about getting married. But that's all I can promise you for now. You'll just have to be patient with me."

He shook his head and frowned. But then he grinned that killer grin that made every woman he looked at swoon, including Evelyn. "So I've heard a million times," he said. "And a million more."

He delivered one more tender kiss, after which she scurried into the house.

Evelyn discovered Ms. Davis sound asleep in the giant living room chair—a first. Not even TuTu jumping off her lap when Evelyn entered woke her, which reminded Evelyn of the same scene she'd witnessed awhile back, the day she'd teased Ms. Davis about drooling.

Evelyn stared at Ms. Davis for a long time. Her face appeared uncommonly peaceful. She looked so tiny and vulnerable in that big chair. Evelyn gently nudged Ms. Davis's shoulder twice before she woke.

It was difficult for Ms. Davis to get out of the chair. Her body must have stiffened, perhaps because it was so cool in the house. Due to the deep cushions, it was also a long way up for her to stand. She winced once, something Evelyn hadn't seen her do the last few days. Evelyn encouraged her to take a pain pill before heading to bed, but Ms. Davis declined. She said she felt relaxed and groggy enough that she wasn't worried about getting back to sleep. She walked like she was still half-asleep too, so Evelyn waited in the kitchen till she saw Ms. Davis's light go out.

Ms. Davis didn't need another fall now; Evelyn felt relief knowing she was safely tucked in. She closed most of the windows, turned on the hall light, and headed upstairs.

After midnight, in her pj's, books on her nightstand, Evelyn sat up in bed with her laptop on her lap. She booted up, locked into the home Wi-Fi connection, and opened her Internet browser, then leaned back on her stack of pillows. She was tired, yet too buzzed to sleep. *What a night.*

Zing! Another dose of electrifying energy zapped right through her pajamas as she recalled the scent of Jorden, the feel of his lips, his hand on the back of her head. Even her toes felt like sparklers.

She looked at the time. Twelve thirty-five. With goose bumps racing up her arms, she typed "DONALD MAJOR"+"SASHA DAVIS" into Google and pressed the search button. Hundreds of hits appeared. Without clicking the links, she carefully scanned a few dozen preview texts to gather leads.

So, he is *a dancer!* They'd definitely been in the same dance company. They were listed as guest dancers here and there too. They were on YouTube performing one thing or another. But nothing jumped out that indicated they were actually married.

Dozens of dance blogs and newspaper articles mentioned Ms. Davis's accident. Some noted that Donald Major was partnering her when it happened, which got her attention. In the back of her mind, she filed the question—perhaps the fall *was* his fault? Was he the *reason* Ms. Davis was injured? Right now, that wasn't Evelyn's main interest. She'd follow those trails another day.

She clicked on some photographs of the two of them dancing and downloaded the five largest ones. Using her Adobe Photoshop program, she opened the shot in which their faces were closest together. She wanted to enlarge it so she could see the way they looked at each other—up close and personal. See if they at all resembled the way she and Jorden twinkled into each other's eyes, or the way her mom and dad looked at each other across the dinner table, relaxed yet cordial expressions on their faces.

As she peered at the photo, for a moment, Evelyn thought she actually saw heart-shaped sparks soaring between their eyes.

Whoa.

Donald packed his small travel bag. If he got on the road by sunrise and caught a few hours' sleep in a rest stop, he could make it to Wanonishaw before dusk the next day. He didn't want to show up after dark. His appearance would present enough of a shock. If slow traffic was an issue, he'd stay at a nearby hotel and knock on Sasha's door early the next morning, right after breakfast. In fact, he should probably make a hotel reservation, just in case. It was presumptuous at worst, and hopeful at best, to think she would welcome him into her home, her arms, her bed, which was what he'd been picturing—counting on—for days.

That was, if he could get by Evelyn Burt, who was tough as nails.

For a moment, he thought he might have softened Ms. Burt during that last phone conversation. But if she could hang up on a pleading, crying man, she could—and would—slam the door in his face and call the police. Wouldn't that be something? Getting arrested for trying to see his own wife!

Don't be absurd! Sasha had no formal restraining orders against him, just her own definitive NO, she did not wish to talk to him. She had no legal reasons to deny a visit, which wasn't to say she hadn't ultimately filed the dance incident in her head as abuse of some kind.

You know her better than that! All he'd ever done was love her, then accidentally drop her in front of a theater full of people.

Maybe he didn't know anything at all.

Deciding that yes, he'd better get a hotel reservation, he unzipped his travel bag and fired up the computer. After finding two motels in

Wanonishaw, he opted for a reservation at a chain hotel in La Crosse. The Wanonishaw motels were independently owned and therefore too close to the small-town gossip mill. This was a private matter between a husband and a wife.

For the first time, it occurred to him to wonder what the townies might have speculated about his absence. Then again, he wasn't sure how much either Genevieve, a private person, or his wife had ever shared, if anything, about their relationship, their marriage. For the sake of autonomy as it applied to their career platforms—aside from their company, which highly approved of married couples staying together—their engagement and marriage were kept quiet, confidential affairs. The only people who even attended their wedding, witnessing their marriage in the county building, were Janine and another dancer from the troupe.

Sasha had told Donald that although her mother never admitted so, she knew it broke her mother's heart not to be able to create her only child's wedding gown. The two of them had fantasized and dreamed about it since Sasha was small. But Genevieve said she understood. She was delighted they'd found each other and were equally committed to the same passion in life: dance.

Instead of making her daughter a gown, Genevieve had put her heart and energy into quilting them the most colorful, magnificent, and unique wedding blanket. She designed pockets, complete with button closures, and sewed them into the beautiful creation. "You can tuck your special memories into them," she'd said.

They'd used it as a bedspread for the first seven years of their marriage. Then, afraid it might eventually wear out, they hung it on their bedroom wall as an endearing object of art. Until their parting, they'd made use of the pockets, which were filled with notes. In fact, just last week, Donald had written a prayer and folded it into a pocket on Sasha's side of the bed. *"Please, God, bring us back together."*

Hotel reservation in place, car loaded, reminder map on the front seat, insulated mug filled with hot coffee, heart racing, he headed west. Janine said she could not imagine Sasha turning him away if he made an appearance. However, Janine had also admitted she couldn't imagine Sasha not answering e-mails or calls from them either. And yet, she had not.

Still, Janine's last phone call with Donald had given him the nudge, confidence, and courage he needed to take the leap.

"For both of us," she'd said. "No, for Sasha too. You know how stubborn she can be, Donald. Once she sets her mind, there's no changing it, even if it's a decision that may cause her own destruction."

Fifty miles into his trip, to entertain himself as well as mentally prepare for the possibilities, he began playing through every real, dramatic, and ridiculous scenario as to how he might be received. Of course Evelyn always answered the door.

- He says he's Donald Major. Old lady Evelyn screams, "POLICE!"
- He says he's Donald Major. Evelyn pulls out an Uzi and blows him and half the neighborhood away.
- He says he's Donald Major, and Evelyn's eyes light up. She says to wait right there and disappears into the kitchen. He hears Sasha screaming in the background for him to GO AWAY and that Evelyn is fired for even opening the door.
- He says he's a United States census taker and that he needs to see the owner of the house. Evelyn gives him the squint-eye, then asks for credentials.

"Foiled again," he said aloud to himself with an amused grin, noting another mile marker.

- He says he's with the *National Enquirer* and he is there to do a story on the esteemed Ms. Sasha Davis. Evelyn lets him right in, says she's been a subscriber for fifty years, and asks if she can please be quoted. However, as he heads for the kitchen, she stabs him in the back with a kitchen knife; the whole invitation a ruse to finally get him off both their backs.

"Could you *be* any more dramatic?" he asked himself, turning down the annoying voice of the radio announcer spewing through his car speakers.

- He says he's Donald Major and Evelyn says, "Finally! I thought you'd never come!" Sasha appears in the doorway and falls into his arms. And they all live happily ever after.

But then he pictured Sasha opening the door. She stood before him, dressed in her favorite pair of pressed white linen slacks and the red satin top he gave her for her birthday two years ago. She looked so beautiful that he was momentarily speechless.

- She does a double-take, smacks him in the face, and says, "I told you to stay away from me!" She slams and bolts the door.
- She opens the door, breaks out in tears and says, "Why bother coming now? Where were you when I needed you? You know it's never been my strength to ask for help!"

Yes, dear Sasha, he thought, as another mile marker ticked by. If you have but one fault, that is it.

- She opens the door, says, "I despise you!" and clearly means it. "Now go away."
- She opens the door, then calls Evelyn, who appears behind her with an Uzi.
- She opens the door, then calls Evelyn, who's already let the police in the back door.

They come at him with handcuffs.

- She rushes into his arms and says, "Never again let me lose sight of you!" And they all live happily ever after.

But after another ten miles of driving and mulling, a third batch of scenarios developed that made his heart sink. In each case, he rang the doorbell, and then . . .

- From the inside, Sasha fumbles a long time with the door. Finally, the door opens and there she is, in a wheelchair. She sees who it is, points to her useless legs, and says, "Look what you did to me!"
- She fumbles with the door, barely able to open it from her wheelchair. When she sees it's him, she spits on his shoes and says she hates him.
- He hears someone fumbling with the door handle so long he finally peeks through the stained glass window. First he sees no one. Then he looks down, notices the top of Sasha's head. She's in a wheelchair, withered, all pointy angles and skin and bones. Anger and pain have eaten her broken body from the inside out. She no longer wishes to live and has therefore stopped eating. He dares not be the one she sees if and when she finally opens the door.

At that thought, he shook his head, turned his car around, and headed back toward home.

Just showing up is the selfish thing to do. She obviously needs time to mentally prepare, to physically heal, or to emotionally shore herself up to see me again. Why can't I respect that! He banged the steering wheel with his palms.

Or maybe—he was ashamed to even admit it to himself—he was not strong enough to handle what he might find when he saw her. Maybe she already knew this to be true, which was why she wanted him to stay away.

When he arrived home, he unpacked his bag, crawled into bed, and cried himself to sleep. He didn't even call to cancel his hotel reservation, an unused room for which he'd be charged. And he didn't even care. He was convinced he deserved whatever price he had to pay—for everything.

Thirteen

After only one month of outpatient therapy, by the autumnal equinox, Sasha had gained not only significant strength, but flexibility. At the end of last week, she'd graduated to walking with a cane, something she didn't believe *ever* possible back in early May when Evelyn moved in. She wouldn't break a record for speed walking anytime soon, but she was beginning to hope that within the next couple of months she might be able to walk free and clear. No aids. Maybe with a slight gimp, and carefully, of course, but surely something to shoot for.

Another show of faith in her progress: her therapist had reduced her forthcoming sessions to just twice a week. In doing so, she'd also added yet another page of exercises to Sasha's rigorous homework routine. Although Sasha sometimes became cranky about Evelyn's constant pushing and prodding to make her do her twice-daily therapy on Fourth Street to perfection, Sasha had no doubt that Evelyn played as large a part as anyone in her ongoing recovery. Evelyn was pushing her back into the rigorous disciplines of a dancer, something that used to be part of Sasha's innate grit. Not that she'd ever dance, but the return of discipline and hard work made her feel more herself again.

Life was heading in the right direction.

Sasha sat at the kitchen table eating a small bowl of ice cream, an occasional decadent treat. When she did allow herself the pleasure, she took the teeniest bites to make it last as long as possible. As she slid the third bite into her mouth, the doorbell rang. Evelyn always responded to the doorbell, but after a delay, it rang again. Evelyn must be upstairs with her fan on.

Sasha yelled, "Just a minute!" then made her way through the house.

A UPS man stood at the door, holding a package for Ms. Sasha Davis. Tucked under his arm was a long skinny corrugated box, the right shape to hold a dozen roses.

Sasha leaned on her cane to sign the electronic device with the plastic pencil. She hadn't received a surprise package since she and Donald separated. His gifts had always been extremely extravagant and timely. Her hand began to shake, to the point she barely recognized her own signature. She closed the door and tucked the box under her arm. With every step she took back toward the kitchen to retrieve a knife to open the box, the height of her hope and anticipation welled.

Roses! Oh Donald! She swallowed hard to keep her guarded yet rushing swell of happy emotions from crumbling her to the floor. No matter how much stronger she'd become, she suddenly felt weak in the knees.

Grace? she wondered, forgetting all about her ice cream. *Undeserved grace?*

After she wrestled the box open, her heart beating faster with each pull and tug, she searched for a note. Nothing.

She peeled back the tissue paper and could barely believe her eyes: instead of discovering roses, she found a multicolored, rhinestone-studded, adjustable cane. She laughed with delight until she broke into tears at the perfect thoughtfulness of it. The outreach. The love. The acceptance! And the insanely goofy question: what kind of new life was she leading that a fancy *cane* could make her so deeply and utterly happy?

How did Donald know it would delight her so?

How had he found out?

Why was there no note?

Then a wondrous thought struck her: *Maybe the doorbell will soon ring again and I'll open it and there he'll be . . .*

Interrupting the sudden onset of hope-filled longing, Evelyn walked into the kitchen. Sasha was holding the cane and wiping tears from her face.

"Look what . . . someone sent me!" Sasha said, lifting the cane, her voice froggy from crying.

"Oh, Ms. Davis! I am so sorry!"

So that's how he found out! Sasha never thought she could be so grateful for disobedience!

"When I discovered the cane on the Internet," Evelyn said, "I thought it was fun and frilly. Medicinal gray—as in your walker and the crutches and that old-lady cane—just does not suit your bright self. When I ordered it, I thought it would make you—"

"*You* sent this to me?" Sasha blurted, cutting Evelyn off. *How foolish of me!*

"Yes, ma'am. I put in an express order shortly after we got home from your appointment. You know, to celebrate your graduation off the crutches." Evelyn's posture crumbled. "I'm sure it's returnable though. Again, I'm so sorry, Ms. Davis. I guess it's just one more time I didn't think something through. I thought it would make you happy."

Sasha quickly pulled herself together, away from the ridiculous notion that she could cut Donald off the way she had, then think that after her cruel silence, he'd reward her with a gift—an appearance.

The disappointment on Evelyn's face doubly broke Sasha's heart. She'd obviously waited upstairs so Sasha could be the one to receive her gift directly from the UPS man.

She waggled her finger for Evelyn to move closer. With hesitancy, Evelyn took a small step. "Come *here,* Evelyn. This extraordinary sparkling gift," Sasha said, leaning on the table for balance while holding up the cane in her other hand, "deserves a hug." *And oh, how I need one!*

She waited till Evelyn got close enough to grab hold of, then she threw open her arms just as Evelyn stepped into them. Instantly, tears flowed from Sasha's eyes.

It was the first time they'd hugged. At first Evelyn stood awkward and stiff, obviously attempting to hold Sasha up in case she toppled. A much larger woman than Sasha, Evelyn had to bend her knees and scrunch down to make the hug work. But the longer Sasha held her, the more Evelyn relaxed—the more both of them relaxed—until Evelyn, continuing to maintain balance for them both, finally hugged her back. Sasha leaned into Evelyn, trusting and drawing on her strength and care.

When the women stepped apart, Sasha, with tears still in her eyes, leaned back against the table for stability. "Evelyn," she said, gently reaching out and touching her cheek, "I couldn't be more proud and lucky if you were my own daughter."

To Sasha's surprise, Evelyn erupted in sobs and ran toward the sitting room.

"Evelyn! What is it?" Sasha fumbled with the adjustment on the new cane until she got it to the right height. By the time she reached the sitting room, Evelyn stood against the window with her back toward Sasha, shoulders heaving. "Evelyn, that was a compliment!"

But Evelyn did not speak.

Sasha had no idea how to handle the situation. Had she offended Evelyn? Surely she understood what Sasha had meant by her statement. If Sasha had been blessed with children—had set aside time in her career to even try for children—she couldn't imagine raising a finer, more caring, and smarter daughter than Evelyn. Her folks must be so proud of her.

Sasha grabbed a couple of tissues from the fancy dispenser on the side table and wiped her nose with one of them, then she moved closer to rest her hand on Evelyn's shoulder. "Evelyn," she said quietly, waving the other tissue at the side of Evelyn's head, "please turn around."

Evelyn sniffed while the birds, which had scattered when Evelyn approached the window, began to reappear from their nearby posts. The two women stood in awkward silence. Sasha scrambled to come up with a way to correct whatever wrong she'd committed. The words, *details and attentiveness. It's not all about you,* whispered through her as she noticed the little brown bird was back. He landed on the melted stub of the pan handle. *Such a round little belly.* His beak was brown on the top, longer than shorter, the top bill slightly curved. It looked like he had a sort of beige stripe running just above his eye, like a low eyebrow. How, she wondered, had she spent so much time throughout her decades ignoring so many nuances? Had life always been just about her?

What did she really know about the young woman standing before her, trying to stop her tears? What had she even *tried* to learn since they'd met?

Finally Evelyn turned to face Sasha, once again scattering the birds. Her face was blotchy. "I'm sorry, Ms. Davis. I took your comment as a compliment. It's just that . . ." Tears started to well again. "It's just that . . ." She shook her head and covered her face with her hands.

Sasha grabbed another tissue and stuffed the

end of it between Evelyn's fingers. After a while, Evelyn blew her nose and finally took a deep breath.

"Let's sit down, Evelyn. You take the rocker." Sasha settled into the smaller wheeled chair at the roll-top desk, the one Evelyn usually sat in when she worked with Sasha on correspondence. She waited for Evelyn to calm herself. "Now, what is this all about? Talk to me."

Evelyn studied Sasha's face, chewed on her bottom lip, twiddled with her fingers. "It's not the kind of thing a person should trouble their boss about," she finally said in a quiet voice. "It's personal, really. And complicated."

"If you don't want to talk about it, that's fine. I understand privacy. Believe me, I understand privacy. I just want to make sure I didn't offend you."

"No. Not at all. In fact, far from it." Evelyn chewed on her top lip, heaved a great sigh, appeared to silently wrestle with herself about spilling what was bothering her.

"If there is anything you would like to share with me," Sasha said, leaning slightly toward Evelyn, "something of a personal nature, please feel free. Yes, I am, in the literal sense of the word, your boss. But Evelyn, you've come to mean so much more to me than an employee! That's what I was trying to say before. I don't believe I'd be as well as I am—certainly not as happy as I am—if you

197

hadn't been here with me all this time, nurturing me—tolerating me! You treat me . . . like a family member. You always have. And I, Ms. Evelyn Burt, have not even always treated you kindly."

Sasha couldn't maintain eye contact, she was so ashamed of her confession. Her eyes darted everywhere, including out the window. The little brown bird was back, on the frying pan rim. He hopped in and engaged himself in a raucous bath, splashing water every which way. His unself-conscious abandon nearly made her jealous. *Oh, to move and feel that free to just be me!*

Like the surprise rattling of thunder, her decision to share with Evelyn what was really behind her reaction to the incident with that frying pan boomed into her mind. It felt clear that now was the perfect time.

"Evelyn, how about this? I'll share something personal first, then when I'm done, you can share, if you'd like. There's something I need to tell you anyway, and it has to do with that pan." She nodded toward it. "I'm not going to speak as your boss now, other than to make it clear how *truly* unprofessionally I treated you when the incident happened. I'm talking as one woman to another. I'm confiding now," she said, her voice catching in her throat, "as one friend to another. I'm con-fessing a mistake." Her eyes momentarily dropped to her hands. "Something I've never been good at."

"Oh, Ms. Davis! You don't owe me any—"

"Shush!" Sasha put her finger to Evelyn's lips, cutting her off. "This is important for me to say, Evelyn, to *admit*. Let me move ahead with it while I have the courage, okay? This will be good for both of us."

Evelyn nodded and folded her hands in her lap. She began to quick-rock in the rocker, as though the concentrated momentum might help keep her impulsive mouth shut. Sasha had to stifle a smile. She *was* getting to know the girl pretty well.

"I'm sure you remember the chain of events that led to my screaming meltdown over that pan. However, just for the record—and to help you put my response in perspective—let's walk through the details again. But before I start unfolding the story," Sasha said, allowing a soft smile to shine through, "would you like a cup of tea? You're sitting in the tea chair, you know." A hint of playfulness laced her voice. "And I can carry things now." She quickly scribed a figure eight in the air with her colorful new cane.

Evelyn smiled. "No, ma'am. I'm good. But I'll get you one."

She started to rise, but Sasha lifted her cane and motioned her downward. "Sit," she said, and Evelyn obliged.

"No tea for me either. I'm good too." In light of the situation—so many situations, really—the irony of the statement caused Sasha to laugh, which helped her relax. "We are quite the pair, aren't we? Both *good,* yet both crying." She took a deep breath. Finally, she began.

"Keep in mind that back then, not long after you moved in, I was in a pitiful—no, a pity-party—state of mind. In fact, as I recall, you actually once told me so." She paused and chuckled. Evelyn's face reddened. "And you were exactly right," she said, letting Evelyn know it was nothing for her to feel badly about. "There were so many changes in my life . . ." She slumped slightly, as if the weight of the memories physically pressed her down. "I was suffering from the immense extent of my pain and injuries, of course. But I was unaware that I was also suffering from a pretty intense depression. It wasn't until more recently, after I started therapy and taking the anti-depressants on a regular basis, the way the doctors suggested I do all along, that I realized how deeply my state of mind had sunk, how unable I was to help myself.

"That Sunday afternoon of the frying pan debacle, you asked me if I'd like meat loaf for dinner. Although I can't remember my exact response, I believe I said something like, 'I don't care. Suit yourself.' "

"That is exactly what you said," Evelyn responded, nodding.

"Well, I guess you do remember every detail. No wonder. It was likely one of the most dramatic, tongue-lashing encounters you've experienced in your short life," Sasha said, stopping a moment. "And again, I am truly sorry. After the way I treated you, the fact you even stayed on is a testament to your strong and resilient character."

Evelyn shrugged. Sasha noticed she also blushed again.

"I heard you working in the kitchen . . . Let me stop myself here to be *totally* honest: you working in the kitchen can sometimes cause a bit of a racket"—she smiled, then winked at Evelyn—"that, due to my state of mind back then, I must admit set my teeth on edge. The sounds of your kitchen music, as I've come to think of it, has become a familiar comfort now. But then . . .

"But I digress. Let me stick to the facts. If I'd been thinking clearly—and now in hindsight I know this to be true—I'm the one who should have warned you. It wasn't until I smelled something burning that it occurred to me you might not have looked in the oven before you turned it on, especially since it was the first time you'd used the oven since you arrived."

"I should have—"

"Nonsense!" Sasha said, cutting Evelyn off again. "Evelyn, I just need you to listen, please. The frying pan incident and my response to it were not your fault. What you don't know, because I never had the courage to apologize or share this before, is *why* I reacted so strongly after the smoke started billowing out of the oven and I saw you set the ruined pan on the porch. Rather than commend you for how you heroically donned an oven mitt and carried the pan outside, melting handle, toxic fumes and all, I laid into you!" She shook her head in self-disgust. "Keep in mind, even after you hear the whole story, *nothing was your fault.* Got it?"

Evelyn drew her lips into her mouth and nodded.

"From the time I was a girl, my mom stored that pan, the pan she used on a daily basis, in the oven. I don't know if you've ever noticed, but that old stove has a shallow drawer at the bottom, one made for storing pans. Mom contended the stove must have been designed by someone who never used a kitchen. 'Who wants to have to stand on their head to get a pan?' she asked." Sasha smiled at the memory. "Because she was a single working mom, we lived on a shoestring, although I wasn't much aware of it at the time. After I started dance lessons, our meal pickings were sometimes pretty slim. But Mom put her creative soul to work in the kitchen as well as at her sewing machine, plus she always planted a big garden and did a lot of freezing and canning. While cooking, she often said, 'If it doesn't fit in this pan, we don't need it!' She made the most delicious hodgepodge casseroles, she called them. That pan handle was laden with years of her loving fingerprints.

"Anyway," Sasha said, leaning back in the chair, "the other piece of back story here is that long before I even took dance lessons, I used to drive my mom crazy by using the long horizontal handle on the oven door, which was just the right height, to practice my little girl barre work. I could see a portion of my lower body reflected in the glass in the door. She worried I wouldn't notice that the stove was on, or that I might accidentally knock the hot pan off the stove, especially since it had such a long handle. Or lose my balance, fall away from the stove, and pull off the whole oven door. This is what parents do: they worry. And cheer us on, of course."

Sasha noticed the expression on Evelyn's face suddenly fall. Evelyn bit her bottom lip and quit rocking. Perhaps sharing the significance of the pan was a mistake and would make Evelyn feel guilty. Well, she was already into it now. Determined to set her wrong right, Sasha soldiered on with her story.

"But as much as my mother fretted about me and the stove, she also never banned me from it. She loved watching me practice—loved watching me watch myself. She would sit at the table, snapping beans from her garden or peeling carrots onto a newspaper for the compost pile, and her eyes would shine with pride at her little girl who 'danced like an angel.' " Sasha stopped and swallowed. "So the stove, the oven, that pan, all hold special memories for me, and they're all centered around my mom. I miss her so," she said, her voice nearly a whisper. She fell silent.

After a while, she swallowed and continued. "I should have told you there was a pan in the oven. The melted handle is my fault. It just so happens I've had plenty of time to think lately," she said, smiling again, "and it's *okay* about the melted handle being mostly gone because I realize now that nobody can ever take away the memories. *Any* memories. All you did was turn the oven on to prepare a meal for me. But back then, when I saw the disaster, it washed up *everything* that was wrong. My mother was no longer here to use her favorite pan. Remnants of her fingerprints were melted away. I could barely shuffle to the kitchen, let alone stand there and use the pan myself. Goodness me, I couldn't even bend over far enough to get it out of the oven! And I could no longer dance."

Sasha thought about mentioning Donald, but she just could not let herself go there. She needed to stay on topic: apology.

"So you see: the pan seemed just one more precious thing that was lost to me. And like I said, I was depressed, not myself. Sadly, I took all my pain out on you, for which I am truly sorry, Evelyn. I am sorry for yelling, and for every other time I've treated you poorly. Please forgive me. In all honesty, the pan as a birdbath has brought me more entertainment and enjoyment than it ever would have hiding in the oven. And I sincerely mean that."

Although Evelyn said of course she forgave her, Sasha was haunted by the look of indefinable sorrow that had settled around Evelyn's eyes. Since Sasha was done with her confession and Evelyn's kind acceptance of same, she waited for Evelyn to take a turn and share what was on her mind.

Instead, Evelyn said that if Sasha didn't need her, she thought she'd go for a long bicycle ride. She would be back in time for therapy home-work, then she would make them dinner. Was there anything Sasha needed from the store? Sasha said no, and out the door Evelyn went, her Life is good–backpack riding on her shoulders, remind-ing Sasha of the terrible day she'd sent Evelyn packing in a driving rainstorm.

Sasha told herself that she should have known her confession about her mom and that pan might make the incident seem all the more terri-ble in Evelyn's eyes. Couldn't she have just apologized without sharing the whole story? Was she that selfish?

Had she always been so self-absorbed, think-ing only about herself?

She sat in the rocker, still warm from Evelyn's presence, and laid the beautiful cane across her knees. She ran her finger softly across the sparkling colors, which reminded her of a costume she'd worn in *Paquita.*

Picking up the snowglobe, Sasha looked directly into the dancer's eyes. "You know, when I was young, I used to look at you and feel the magic. I'd think, *I want to be like you.* And then I was, right down to the inexplicable broken body parts. Now I wonder if the rest of my life is destined to be *exactly* like yours: alone. As if trapped behind glass. Unable to reach out and touch anyone without wounding them."

Soon, when therapy ends—maybe even before—Evelyn will figure out I don't really need her anymore, and that will be the end of her employment. The thought of that loss was nearly unbearable. Sasha would be isolated and alone in her big house, all because of her own bad choices, which began with not telling Donald or anyone about her dizzy spells.

She slowly turned the snowglobe upside down, recalling the first time she'd watched her mother do the same. Determined to once again feel the snowglobe's magic, she fought against viewing the treasure as a trapped image of herself. *I need to erase* that *image!*

Slowly, the dancer's arms floated up over her head and her legs split out, stopping hip-high as she leaped through the air. Sasha righted the globe and watched as the dancer began to settle back into her starting position.

But this time, the dancer didn't stop in her usual static pose. To Sasha's amazement, her knees, which were not jointed, began to bend. The dancer's pointed toes slid back behind her as she continued her descent. Gently, she settled on her knees, head slightly bowed, as if she were in prayer.

"Dear God!" Sasha blurted, holding the snowglobe away from her.

Yes, Sasha? I am here. What do you need?

The voice in her head was clear, calm, powerful, yet gentle, readied, and listening.

Sasha's breathing was so rapid, her voice quavered when she spoke. "I have no earthly idea," she whispered, closing her eyes and cradling the snowglobe in her palms, tears spilling down her cheeks. "I used to think it was to be a dancer. But for the first time in my life, I believe dance might be at the bottom of my list. I just want to belong in this world again, to pay cnough attention to *all* the details to make them matter!

"I want to be able to reach out and touch people, especially those I love. I want," she said, some-thing deep within her cracking open, "to make right the things I've done wrong."

After a long cry, she finally opened her eyes to set the globe back on the table. As if she'd never moved, the dancer stood in her age-old position while the snow settled around her feet, making her appear as if she were standing on a cloud.

Fourteen

Evelyn raced her bicycle to the outskirts of town until she came to the trails at the base of the bluff near the winding roadway. She pedaled as fast as she could on the steepest ascent until her legs nearly gave out. One thing became clear: she could not outrun her mind. She finally gave in and pulled over.

Salty stinging sweat poured into her eyes and off her nose and rimmed her lips. She retrieved her water bottle from her backpack and downed the contents in continuous gulps. Unable to get the kickstand to settle on the rough terrain, she laid her bike under a nearby tree, then flopped down beside it on her back, staring up through the branches.

She needed to settle down. She wasn't going to move, and certainly would not return to Fourth Street, until she got a grip on herself and came to terms with a few of her hot-plate issues. Flecks of sunlight winked through the thick green leaves, causing her to squint. She rested her arm over her eyes and engaged in some deep breathing, aware of an occasional nearby car groaning its way up the hill or the grind of a lowered gear during another's descent. *Just like life.*

Her intimate moment with Ms. Davis—receiving another woman's eloquent and heartfelt apology—should have brought relief and joy, maybe even have helped *her* open up. Instead, from the moment Ms. Davis mentioned that she couldn't be more proud of Evelyn if she were her own daughter, to the final straw about how a parent's job was to both protect and applaud, Ms. Davis had unwittingly hammered on Evelyn's current vulnerabilities, heartaches, and short-comings.

She wondered if her dad had shared with her mom what she'd said about their early pregnancy. If so, Evelyn felt both embarrassed and ashamed. Although she knew she was right about Jorden, low-blowing her parents gnawed at her conscience.

She sighed, finally able to take a deep breath after the exertion of her ride. *There. The problem is officially highlighted: it's you.*

Ms. Davis wouldn't be so proud of her if she knew (a) she had insulted and wounded her parents, and that her early engagement and no-college choice had severely disappointed them; (b) she was fighting the surprisingly potent lure of lust; and (c) she was selfishly worrying that when Ms. Davis got well, she'd no longer have a safe place to live. Her home on Fourth Street might be the only thing keeping her from making an ill-conceived, pressured, and premature decision to marry the man who held her heart.

And speaking of Ms. Davis, Evelyn had felt certain that the confession about the frying pan was leading to the admission of Donald Major being her husband. How was it she could embark on a confession of that proportion but never once mention she had a *husband* out there? *Maybe Ms. Davis didn't mention him because she owes* him *a big fat apology too!*

Good grief, Evelyn! You are despicable and pathetic, trying to blame something—anything— on her. Sorry, Ms. Davis. Sorry, Lord.

Whether or not Ms. Davis had a husband was none of Evelyn's business. She was hired to do a job, nothing more and nothing less. Though she had to admit to growing extremely fond of Ms. Davis, and had in fact been both touched and flattered by her mention of friendship and the compliment—right up until guilt overshadowed everything.

Had Ms. Davis been cranky back then? Of course. But given her circumstances, who wouldn't have been? Now she'd done the good and right and professional thing and owned up to it. Plus, even by Ms. Davis's own admission, her attitude had come around. These last few weeks, Evelyn felt she was finally getting to know the real Ms. Davis, the one who existed apart from her troubles. She was kind, fun, even mischievous, in a good way.

So why does knowing all that make me feel worse?

Evelyn raised her head and put the water bottle to her lips. Empty. She wished she'd saved a few swigs. She settled the bottle beneath the crook of her neck. The ground wasn't very comfortable. But then, this one-on-self session wasn't about comfort. It was about truth.

As much as she tried to find excuses or blame her foul mood on Ms. Davis, there was no getting around the truth of the matter: her wretched emotional state had nothing to do with Ms. Davis and all to do with her disappointment in herself.

Everything Ms. Davis had said upped the ante on Evelyn's self-doubt. When she'd talked about a parent's job being to protect and encourage, Evelyn knew the heart of the conflict with her folks, especially her dad, was built on the fact that they loved her and were trying to look out for her. They wanted the best for her—an education, a good job, a fine husband, a chance to see the world—and they, especially her dad, believed Jorden was keeping her from those things. Or, as her dad implied, she allowed Jorden to keep her from those things.

When Ms. Davis mentioned how her mother delighted in watching her young daughter dance in the kitchen, Evelyn thought about the lifetime of ongoing affirmations she'd received from her folks, especially when she brought home an aced report card, finished another book, swished a nothing-but-net H-O-R-S-E point, or managed to land the biggest sunfish or walleye of the day. They loved her for who and exactly how she was.

They loved her when she'd been accepted into three of her four top-pick college choices, something that pleased and excited all three of them. But she received the acceptance letters just when she'd started dating Jorden and her goals began to shift. And this she also knew: even though she'd insulted them, they still loved her.

A song she once heard on an oldies radio station popped into her mind. The singer wanted to know something like, "If loving you feels so right, how can it be so wrong?" *Exactly my question!*

She drew her left hand in front her eyes and waggled her fingers. She loved her diamond; she loved Jorden's kisses; she loved Jorden, who had never treated her with anything but kindness and respect. Nobody in her life had ever made her feel more of an independent, fully grown, attractive, and feminine woman. Yes, *woman.* Why couldn't her dad see how much Jorden mattered to her?

No, that is not the problem, Evelyn Burt!

She tucked her hands under her armpits, an outward gesture signifying dissatisfaction with her own thinking. *If you are being totally honest with yourself, here, Evelyn, the problem is that Dad* does *see how much Jorden matters to you.*

The last time she'd had a private moment with

her grandpa, which had been far too long ago *(And why are you now even avoiding Gramps, Evelyn?)*, he'd told her the same thing. He'd said that what fretted her father—and grandpa quoted her dad precisely—was her "determination to waste her great mind and wonderful potential on a bad decision to skip college."

"I'm sorry, Sweet Cakes," Gramps had said. "That's not me talking, but it seems the only way your dad is capable of seeing things right now." Gramps told her, because she pried until he did, that her dad thought she was blind to the fact that Jorden mattered more than college or a career. Her dad had also told her directly, "This shouldn't have to be a Jorden or college choice." If Jorden loved her enough, her dad had said, he'd wait for her to get done with college, or he'd apply to the same college and be near her there.

That he was questioning her integrity and judging someone he barely knew made her so mad, out the door she'd flown.

Then again, why *hadn't* she asked Jorden about any of that? She suspected she already knew the answer: he couldn't afford college. But other people figured out how to go after grants and borrow money. Maybe Jorden didn't have the grades though, with all that moving. Or maybe he just wasn't interested. What was wrong with honest factory work anyway? Even Grandma Burt worked at the factory, and nobody thought that was a bad thing. Or maybe Jorden's parents didn't want him to follow a girl anywhere. He'd mentioned his folks were the polar opposite of hers. What had he meant by that, and why had his face turned so dark when he'd said it?

Furthermore, why didn't he share any of that information with her?

For better or for worse, her dad had her thinking.

She sighed, lowered her arms to her sides and relaxed them on the ground. She then turned her palms face up and let her legs fall out to the side. She'd read about the sponge posture in a book she'd checked out on yoga.

Time to relax. Be a sponge. Soak up what you need to know by listening to God for a change. Come on, Lord. Talk to me! But her mind was too locked on Jorden to think about relaxing her calves or to receive a word from the Almighty.

Although she left her arms and legs where they were, her thoughts raced back to a burning question: Was keeping secrets the first indication that Jorden might one day also keep his distance? Which brought her back to Ms. Davis. Now that she'd spoken to Evelyn as a friend, perhaps Evelyn should just outright ask her about Donald Major. Tell her about his call, his pleading—his crying.

Why didn't people just *talk* to each other? Tell each other the truth about things? *Why?!*

"Evelyn! *Evelyn!*"

Evelyn screamed, startled by a hand shaking her shoulder and a voice yelling her name.

"Thank God! I thought you were dead!" Jorden was nearly panting. "Evelyn, what happened?" He leaned over her, a look of fear and concern on his face. "Are you all right?"

She sat up. "Of course. I'm just resting." She looked at her wristwatch. She thought he was still at work, but more time had passed than she imagined. "What are you doing here? How did you find me?"

"First things first. What are *you* doing here, lying on the ground, off the side of the road like this? You nearly scared me to death! I saw you and your bike out of the corner of my eye when I passed by, but since the road is so full of blind curves, I didn't dare stop. I drove to the top like a madman, then parked and ran back down here."

"The bike path is right over there," she said, pointing to the small dirt trail. "I just pulled over to rest a bit and get some shade."

He knit his eyebrows together. "You have tear stains running down your face," he said, gently tracing a finger along her cheek.

"Just sweat, I guess," she said, recalling all the earlier tears she'd shed today. No doubt her eyes were puffy.

"Would you like a ride home? It's too stinking hot to ride uphill. Your face is so flushed . . . Here," he said, holding out a hand to help her up.

"I'll walk your bike up the hill, then toss it in my trunk."

Evelyn started to say no thanks, that she could handle things herself. But the truth was beginning to gnaw within: perhaps she could not.

"Sounds good," she said. Sometimes her stubborn pride didn't serve her well.

Walking up the hill, she made up her mind: she would visit with Jorden for a while, maybe even ask him a few important and pointed questions. Then she would knock on her parents' door. What good was wondering why people just didn't stick it out and talk to each other, when she herself was guilty of the same?

Fifteen

In her bird book, by the picture of the tiny house wren, Sasha put a check mark and noted the date. She felt pleased she'd remembered enough details to definitely recognize the little guy's picture. There was no mistaking the somewhat checkerboard-looking wingtips and tail.

Evelyn had been gone for a while now. Sasha wondered if she'd ever studied Evelyn as closely as she'd studied the house wren. Was it possible she'd been so absorbed with her own journey—

viewed Evelyn as nothing more than someone to help her, never once considering the opposite possibilities—that until today, she'd failed to ever really give of herself to that girl?

One thing she knew to be true: getting stuck in a new rut of self-pity would not be a healthy response to the day's events, for in their midst, there'd been a personal victory. She had owned up to a mistake. She would not be sad the cane wasn't from Donald; she would choose to be glad it was from Evelyn. She would not beat herself up for making Evelyn cry; she would choose to believe there was more to the story and that Evelyn had truly forgiven her. It was, in fact, entirely possible that Evelyn's tears had nothing to do with her.

Remember, not everything is about you, Sasha Davis!

Something special she could do for Evelyn was to finally take a turn making dinner for the two of them that night. She felt fairly confident that, with a little patience, she could handle the rigors of the kitchen during a full-fledged meal endeavor.

She made her way to the fridge, opened the door, and prowled the shelves. She was so grateful to finally be able to bend enough to explore. Such a small gift. "Grace," she mindlessly whispered.

Fresh fruit, yogurt, veggies and herbs from the farmer's market (Evelyn went every Wednesday),

217

lunch meat, leftover pasta salad from last night . . . Evelyn really was the most thoughtful and wise shopper and a far better cook than herself. What could she make that wouldn't be an embarrassment? It was still early enough to thaw something in the microwave, get some kind of dish simmering or baking, so that the house would smell inviting when Evelyn returned. Sasha explored the freezer and found two pounds of ground chuck from the butcher's.

That's it! She'd make a meat loaf.

By the time she gathered the ingredients, as best she could remember them, she was laughing at how nervous she'd made herself about cooking Evelyn a meal. Squishing meat and eggs together wasn't her favorite thing to do—and sadly, she'd already overthawed and partially cooked the ground chuck in the microwave—but she shored herself up, added chopped onions and green pepper, salsa (Donald's favorite trick with meat loaf), crunched soda crackers, salt and pepper, and a dash of milk. She patted it all into a loaf pan, gratefully washed her hands of the grease, and stuck the pan into the 350 degree oven.

She rummaged until she found a few potatoes and selected two similar in size. There was a button on the microwave for baked potatoes; how wrong could she go there? She washed and pared some broccoli, then put it in a saucepan on the stove, making a mental note to turn it on when she put the potatoes in the microwave.

The preparations took much longer than she imagined. Constantly moving and then leaning again, rearranging food items, nearly losing her balance . . . She was, to be honest, exhausted and a little sore from some of the awkward positions. But she decided the weariness likely had as much to do with her earlier retelling of the frying pan story and its attached memories than any physical labors. Moreover, the wild and potent roller coaster of emotions she expended believing Donald had sent her a gift, and that he was actually about to knock on the door, had taken the bigger toll. Still, after meal preparations, she felt productive and proud of herself, excited to surprise Evelyn, and happy to sit in her rocker for a while.

Sasha pictured her mom pouring ketchup on top of the meat, then smearing it around with the back of a spoon. She'd once asked why she didn't use a brush, the way her girlfriend's mom did. Her mom explained that she enjoyed the feel of the spoon gliding around in the ketchup, like a tiny sled. She'd sometimes let Sasha do the smearing. Sasha decided she'd add that special touch in forty-five minutes, then let it bake another fifteen so the ketchup would brown. That seemed about right, she thought, as she leaned back in the rocker and closed her eyes to soothe and rest them for a moment. All the crying had made them burn.

When she woke, startled to discover she'd

nodded off, she smelled something burning. She scurried as quickly as possible into the kitchen and pulled the meat loaf from the oven. It was a little black on top, likely a little black on the bottom too. *Don't worry,* she told herself. It wasn't beyond salvation. She cut the black portions off the top and poured ketchup over it, then worked a little smearing magic, smiling while feeling clever about her camouflage. It looked and smelled okay. She set it back in the oven, which she turned to low.

She checked the kitchen clock, surprised Evelyn wasn't back already. She put the potatoes in the microwave and pushed the Baked Potato button, then turned the burner on under the broccoli. She rummaged through the hutch until she found her mother's crystal candlesticks, which she centered just so on the dining room table.

She laughed at herself. *Goodness, Sasha! You'd think you were preparing for the Queen of England—or Donald!* Still, it felt good to fuss over someone else for a change. She made a mental note about that, so she wouldn't forget.

At 7:30, dinnertime long gone, oven off for an hour, Sasha finally ate. Alone. Lukewarm, dry, slightly burned meat loaf; soggy, overcooked broccoli; and a cold baked potato, the unmelting butter pad sitting on top of it like a party hat.

She might have enjoyed the wretched meal at least a little if she knew why Evelyn had neither shown up nor called. A few times throughout the evening, Sasha had thought about calling Evelyn's cell phone, just to make sure she was safe. But Evelyn had obviously been emotionally upset when she left. A call seemed invasive. Sasha didn't really need her for anything this evening, so . . . what would her excuse be? *Why aren't you here helping me with my therapy homework and eating the one dinner I cooked for us—that you didn't know I was making?* Semivalid issues for a boss, but not so for a budding friendship, a friendship which she herself had earlier claimed. This new level to the relationship might have complicated their work arrangement. Then again, wouldn't a friend on either side of this coin call and check in?

Then *again,* look how long she had ignored her best friend and husband.

Always so much to sort out.

How did parents deal with the dramas and traumas of everyday child rearing, curfews, finding the line between protection and interference? She doubted she'd have been very good at parenting in her younger years. There was a time when she thought that after she and Donald retired, it might not be too late to try. They'd discussed it a few times, but decided to wait and see how they felt when that day arrived. Now, of course, it was out of the question. It was impossible to have a child with someone you never saw, might never see again. It wouldn't surprise her if she were soon served with divorce papers. But when you truly loved someone and believed he would be happier without you, you let him go. Isn't that what people always said, what they believed—what was true?

After Sasha cleaned up the kitchen, she got out her notebook of exercises and set to work. The drill wasn't as much fun without Evelyn, who always managed to make her laugh as well as toe the line, but she didn't want to have to tell Evelyn she'd skipped her homework the one time the girl hadn't been there to supervise. Evelyn could be as devilish about discipline as she was. Sasha pushed herself until she'd worked the maximum reps for each of the exercises.

When she was done, she put on some music. *Time for a library book.* Deflated, she realized Evelyn hadn't had a chance to empty her backpack from her library run that morning before she left.

Good grief! Do you have *a life apart from that girl?*

Evelyn rode in the passenger seat of Jorden's car. She mentally weighed the advisability of when, exactly, to ask her questions. Now that Jorden had calmed down from his scare over her safety—a strong sign of his love—she thought she should give him a little more time to decompress from work before she started in. After all, he had been on his way home when he came to her rescue.

She chuckled. Obviously, she'd read too many articles recently about womanhood in the fifties. *Who do you think you are? June Cleaver? You don't even own an apron!*

"What's so funny?" Jorden asked, shooting her that killer grin.

"Me," she said. "Sometimes I crack myself up."

He nodded. "You crack me up too, Evelyn." He reached for her hand. "It's one of my favorite things about you. That is, when you're not scaring me to death lying by the side of the road."

His hand felt warm, secure, and most of all, manly. Aside from her dad and grandpa, the only other guy's hand she'd held, and then only once, was Phillip's. Although he'd been a year her junior, she'd been most embarrassed by the fact that her hand was larger than his. The first chance she'd had, she'd withdrawn it and made sure it wasn't available again. But Jorden's hand? It wrapped nearly completely around hers.

She looked at the top of his knuckles, which were dark with grease stains. He'd told her on the phone a couple of days ago that he'd been spending every spare minute working on his car. "Your fiancé is a grease monkey," he'd said, as though it might embarrass or disturb her. Instead, his many faceted skills made her proud. From computers to engine repair, he was a jack of all trades. If they ever went into business together, they could do just about everything! *What would we call our company?* She pictured putting their two names together. *Jorvelyn's. Jorvelyn's Rent-A-Couple.* What would the artwork be? Maybe a watercolor of them from the back, holding hands.

"You know," she said, drawing his hand to her lips and giving the top of his knuckles a kiss, "I don't need to get back to Ms. Davis's right away. How about I treat you to an ice cream for your heroic rescue?" She giggled, caught herself nearly batting her eyes. *Good grief. Let someone make you feel womanly, and you go all gaga.*

"Sounds great. You mind if we swing by my place first? I really need a shower."

She bit her lip. "Are your parents home?"

He let loose a riotous laugh. "Good grief, Evelyn! Do I scare you that much?" By this time, they were only a few blocks from his driveway.

"To be honest, it's me I'm afraid of," she said, feeling her cheeks flush.

He did a double take her direction before cutting his eyes back to the road. "Well, to be honest, nothing personal, but you look like you could use a shower too." He looked her way again, let go of her hand, and ran his fingers down what he'd described as tear stains.

She pulled her hands into her lap and leaned toward the car door.

He pried her arm out of her lap and grabbed

hold of her hand again. "You worry too much. The honest answer about my folks is I have no idea if they're home. Or what kind of shape the house might be in when we get there, or what kind of mood they'll be in. They had a bit of a party last night and . . ." He let his voice trail off. "My guess is they slept in, or started partying a little earlier than usual," he said, unreserved disgust in his voice, "to get over last night's party hangovers." He lifted his foot from the accelerator pedal and slowed down. "In fact, it'll be best if you stay in the car until I scope out the situation. Believe it or not, there might be worse things for you to see than my bare behind."

Evelyn's stomach did a flip-flop. "Maybe you should just take me home," she said.

"Relax, Evelyn!" he replied, withdrawing his hand again and putting it back on the steering wheel. "I wasn't planning on showing you my behind, even if my folks weren't home. Why can't you trust me? I just need a shower, okay? It was hot in the factory today."

"Okay. I'll wait in the car till you're back. From your shower. The breeze has picked up a little, and the fresh air feels good."

He pulled into the driveway, turned off the engine, shook his head, and shot her a lopsided grin. "Suit yourself. I'll hurry. Here," he said, tossing his keys on the dashboard. "If you decide to listen to the radio, just turn the car on. All the way on, engine running, please. I don't want to have to charge that old battery again. Stay out of trouble while I'm gone." He laughed like a hyena at the absurdity of his own statement, as if she'd *ever* get in trouble. Then he disappeared into the house.

Evelyn leaned her head back and closed her eyes. Sounds from the neighborhood wafted into her awareness: music from the ice cream truck, which she guessed to be about three blocks away; the maniacal barking of two dogs; the rising voices of kids next door getting ready to play ball, arguing over who would be on whose team, but more importantly, who wouldn't. *That brings back memories.*

Large for her age even when she was young, Evelyn was always chosen quickly for softball or Red Rover. But soon kids learned that her coordination back then (her mom said it was because her muscles just hadn't grown into her body yet) wasn't the best, and she became the one they argued not to have to take. She was glad those days were far behind her.

Glad that Jorden had, over everyone else, chosen her.

The sound of a woman's voice sailed through the open front window of Jorden's house. It took Evelyn a moment to recognize it as his mom's. She'd barely heard Mrs. McFinn speak a dozen words since they'd met. In fact, Evelyn had only seen his folks a handful of times; his dad usually did the talking when she was around. Jorden didn't try to hide his mom and dad, but come to think of it, he didn't go out of his way to bring them all together, either. She thought it odd neither of them had asked her about wedding plans or her family or . . . But then, since she and Jorden hadn't set a date, and they certainly had no plans yet, why would his parents ask? Their original "two years" timeline put a wedding a long way off.

Or maybe they were as unhappy about the engagement as her parents were. She didn't bring Jorden to her house much, either.

The woman's voice escalated, became louder, almost frantic. Evelyn sat bolt upright and leaned her head toward the open car window. She couldn't make out what was being said, but it almost sounded like Mrs. McFinn was begging someone not to do something. Then came a man's voice, not Jorden's.

"Why didn't you bring your latest little piece of honey in, Jorden?" he boomed. "You ashamed of us or something?"

Suddenly the curtain in the front window drew back and Jorden's dad looked straight at her. He wore nothing more than a pair of boxer shorts and a white sleeveless T-shirt. He waggled his fingers, inviting her to come in.

"Shut up, Dad!" It was Jorden. "And for God's sake, get out of the window!"

Jorden's father rocked back, as though pulled. An unseen hand drew the shade. Unspeakable words and angry yelling erupted from Jorden's father, loud enough that the whole neighborhood could probably hear. Evelyn heard the muffled cries of his mother, then a terrible cracking sound, like a slap on bare skin. Then a door slammed; there was a crash and then silence.

What on earth!

Evelyn didn't know whether to run into the house or away from it. Something was wrong. Very wrong.

She bit her fingernail and prayed for Jorden to appear, smiling, fresh from a shower—unharmed. He would say something about the crazy television show blaring in the living room, and she would decide the vision of his dad in the window was a hallucination.

After what seemed like hours, but was probably no more than a minute or two, Jorden stomped out the door. He got in the car, turned over the engine, and backed out of the driveway so fast it scared her.

"Jorden! Be careful! There are kids right there!" she said, pointing toward the tiny ball players who'd appeared from between the houses.

Jorden craned his neck and slowed down. Still, he exited the street going too fast. He drove in silence, his jaw working so hard it looked like he was trying to grind off his molars. When they crossed the rough railroad crossing, her bike banged up and down in the trunk and her head nearly hit the ceiling.

When they reached the park, Jorden careened into the parking lot and turned off the motor. Then he got out of the car and stormed toward the swing set. He sat on a swing, wrapped his arms around the chains, clasped his hands together and dropped his head into them.

Evelyn reluctantly trailed behind, her heart pummeling her chest wall. Did he want to be alone? She hadn't been able to clearly see the front of his face. Had he been hit? She slipped into the swing next to him. With everything that was in her, she wanted to reach out and grab his arm or stand in front of him and wrap her arms around him, but she sensed that she needed to remain still, wait for him to speak.

After several minutes, though, she couldn't take it anymore.

"Jorden, please talk to me. Are you okay?"

"I'm fine," he growled. "As fine as any guy could be after his family makes a complete and total . . ." He moaned, ran his fingers through his hair. Evelyn noticed his knuckles were still black and that he was wearing the same clothes. He hadn't showered.

"Jorden," she said, daring to rest her hand on his upper arm, afraid he might rip it away. "Did your dad hit you?"

"Don't worry about it!" His voice flared.

"Did he hit your mom? *Does* he hit your mom?"

Jorden lifted his head and for the first time looked directly at her with near venomous anger. "What makes you think I didn't hit him?" He spat the question, causing her to reel away from him. "The apple doesn't fall far from the tree. Isn't that what they always say? Isn't that what everyone always expects?"

Did she, had she, ever known enough—anything at all—about Jorden or his family?

Was violence an ongoing part of it?

Had her fiancé hit his father? Or was Jorden just protecting his dad?

He got out of the swing and strode to the car. Evelyn followed, purposefully lagging. He rustled her bike out of the trunk and motioned for her to take it.

"I think you should go home," he said. "But mostly, I think you should get as far away from me as you can. I'm sure that after that little scene, not only is ice cream off the docket, but the engagement is over too. You can keep the ring. You deserve it." He headed for his car.

"Jorden! WAIT!" Evelyn took off after him, running alongside her bike. She didn't reach the car until after he'd already jumped in and slammed the door. When he started the engine and put the car in gear, she threw down her bike and put her hands on the open window. "Jorden! Talk to me!"

"Evelyn, there's really nothing to say. I'm sorry. I'm *truly* sorry. I thought with you, with your faith in me, that maybe this time my life could take a different turn, a better turn, but . . . Believe me, it's best when I tell you the engagement is over."

And then he pulled away, leaving her hands hanging midair.

Sixteen

You can keep the ring . . . the engagement is over.

Evelyn's head felt like it was going to explode. Had he broken up with her? Or after what she'd witnessed, did he just assume he'd beat her to the punch?

She had to get out of the middle of the parking lot. She mounted the bike and began to pedal. As much as she wanted to disappear, her legs were no help. They felt like jelly. The bike wobbled as if she'd never ridden one before. She dismounted and walked, feeling emotionally whiplashed, stunned, betrayed, lost, and utterly alone. Her eyes welled with tears, but she blinked them away. She was stronger than that. Smarter. *Think, Evelyn. Think!*

Could it be true? Had she simply been acting the part of a misguided Cinderella, hoodwinked by a player? The smooth-talking, diamond-giving, bad boy of Wanonishaw, Minnesota, the one her parents tried to warn her about?

What had just happened?

The moment Evelyn's father opened the front door, Evelyn fell into his arms, weeping the first tears she'd let herself release since Jorden abandoned her in the parking lot.

"I'm sorry, Daddy," she whimpered into his chest.

"What is it, honey?" she heard her mom ask from somewhere off to the side. Then Evelyn felt her mom's arm on her back and knew she'd wrapped the other around her dad, nestling her between them. A constricting sorrow moved from the pit of her stomach up her windpipe and lodged in the back of her throat, nearly choking her.

"I can't even talk about it right now, Mom," she said through her sobs.

They stood in a circle until her parents' love soaked thoroughly enough into Evelyn that she could finally dare to look at them. Her mother gasped when she saw Evelyn's face. Evelyn had already cried once that day. The memory of Jorden commenting on the tear stains on her dirty face, the feel of his finger tenderly tracing them down her cheek—the look in his worried eyes when he thought she was injured—made her tear up again.

"Come on," her mom said, taking her by the hand and eyeing the engagement ring still on her finger. She led Evelyn as if she were a two-year-old instructed to keep hold of Mommy's hand. But unlike her stubborn little-girl self who railed against such impingements, now she was glad to simply follow. "Let's sit down in the kitchen. I'll get you an iced tea and a cold washcloth for your face."

Evelyn noticed her dad hanging back, giving the women privacy. "No, come on, Dad. I want you with me too."

She held out her empty hand behind her, which he took. Their family train made its way to the kitchen. Evelyn and her dad sat down at the table. He scooted his chair close to hers while his wife ran a dishcloth under the faucet and filled three glasses with iced tea. Evelyn used to make fun of their ancient yellow Tupperware pitcher. Now it looked like the brightest ray of sunshine she'd seen all day.

Evelyn's mom set a glass in front of each of them and handed Evelyn the cloth, which she held over her swollen eyes for a few moments. After she wiped down her face and nearly drained her iced tea glass, she felt somewhat human again.

The prodigal daughter returns.

"Is it something with Ms. Davis?" her mom asked.

"Or Jorden," her dad said, the words tumbling

over his wife's, his voice dark and concerned.

"Mom, Dad—especially you, Dad—I need you to just listen to me. And to be honest, I'm not sure how much I want to say, or even can say." It flicked through her mind that earlier that day, Ms. Davis had said the same thing to her, that she needed to just listen. *Why is that so difficult for all of us?*

"I'm sorry," her dad said, then immediately covered his mouth with his hand. He removed it just long enough to say, "Awhile back, your grandfather told me I needed to just listen to you. He was absolutely right, sport. And again, I'm sorry. Your mother and I are here to listen, to whatever you have to tell us. And no matter what, we will love you through it." He took his wife's hand —a gesture that swelled Evelyn's heart—both of them clearly and deeply concerned about what ailed their only child, frightened at what might have taken place, given the way she appeared.

Evelyn turned from her mother to her father. Where to begin? How much to share? There was so much she didn't know about what had happened, what she should, or shouldn't, do next.

She decided to start from the beginning, when her day had first run amuck. She shared the entire story about Ms. Davis and the cane and Ms. Davis's comment about being as proud of her as if she were her own daughter. She shared the guilt she'd felt for firing cheap, inconsequential barbs, for staying away from them, and the gratefulness that welled in her heart when she thought about everything they'd done for her throughout her life—including choosing to bring her into this world. She had to hold her hand up a few times to keep her dad from jumping in.

She did not share her concerns about where she would go when she was done at Ms. Davis's. She once opened her mouth to talk about her and Jorden's desire to get married sooner rather than later, then remembered she possibly wasn't going to marry him, or anyone, ever. She swallowed down the thought and went silent for a few moments, trying to decide what and how much, if anything, to tell them about the rest of her day's events, what she'd witnessed at Jorden's, and how crazy worried she was about him.

How oddly afraid his dark anger had made her.

How she couldn't stop wondering who had hit whom, or if she'd misheard or misinterpreted that part of the terrible incident to begin with. It had all happened so fast . . .

No, she could not talk about any of that yet. She could not, would not, talk about Jorden at all right now. She would keep the conversation focused on her regret at the brokenness in her relationship with her folks. She would apologize, again, for being headstrong, and she would tell them how much she wanted things between them to be the way they used to be.

And so she did.

"Of course we forgive you, honey," her mother said, after Evelyn asked for their pardon and grace. "And we hope you forgive us. You know, we haven't done a great job of understanding that you are a grown woman now, with a mind—and a heart—of your own."

Her dad reached out and rested his hand on her arm. "By we, your mother of course means me," he said, a guilty smile on his lips. "And for that, I *am* truly sorry, Evelyn. You are no longer my little tomboy girl. Even though to me, you'll always be daddy's little girl, you are also your own woman. A bright, smart, funny woman. As a dad, I haven't done a very good job of just letting you be that woman. You know how headstrong I can be, and—"

Evelyn cut him off. "Yes, Dad. I do. As headstrong as me, a chip off your old block." She smiled, reached out and touched his cheek. He put his hand over hers and held it to his face. His eyes welled with tears, as did hers. "I love you, Dad. Mom."

"I have a feeling there's something you're not telling us," her mom said, also crying. "Something more. But I respect your privacy."

"There might be, but right now, I'm not sure enough about it myself to delve into it." *I need to talk to Jorden first. We need to set the record straight.* Are *we through?*

The one thing she knew for certain was that she could not marry a man with that many family secrets—or possibly with a violent streak in him. Yes, she would see him again and talk everything out. Getting to the bottom of *all* the truths was now more important than ever.

Her mom said she'd been about to make dinner when Evelyn arrived and asked if Evelyn would like to stay and join them. "It's just gonna be BLTs, chips, and pickles tonight, but I made a peach pie yesterday with a little fresh ginger in it, your favorite."

Evelyn heartily accepted the invitation. She cleaned the lettuce while her mom fried the bacon and her dad sliced tomatoes. They spent the next two hours eating and just visiting, some-hing that used to be so familiar—something Evelyn had forgotten could feel so good. Her dad talked about his teaching job and his fall bowling league start-ing up; her mom shared what books she'd been reading, as did Evelyn. She and her dad bantered about sports. Evelyn realized how far out of touch she'd become with players and rankings. *How far away from what used to be my "usual" I've grown.* Then they talked about fishing, which made her heart pine for days lost.

Thankfully, nobody asked her about college.

Or mentioned Jorden again, which, given her circumstances and their fragile reunion, seemed safer for everyone, especially Evelyn.

• • •

Sasha felt a huge sense of relief when she heard Evelyn come through the back door. There was no mistaking the sound of her backpack thunking onto the table, especially when filled with library books. She got up out of the big chair in the living room and headed toward the kitchen, then arrived to the sight of Evelyn's backside sticking out of the fridge.

"I'm so glad you're home!" Sasha said.

Evelyn lurched and banged her head on the bottom of the topside freezer. Rubbing her noggin, she turned, diet cola in hand, letting the door close behind her. "You startled me! I thought you were in bed."

Sasha had to stifle a gasp. Evelyn's face was swollen, her eyes puffy and half-closed.

"I'm sorry," Sasha said, taking a step closer. "I was just so happy to hear you come in. Truthfully, I was a little worried when you didn't return in time for my therapy. And before you ask," she said, nodding her head, "yes, I did my homework, every last exercise, and to the max."

"That's great." Evelyn said. "I'm proud of you." She popped the can tab and downed a few loud gulps.

I'm proud of you. The simple words lit Sasha up inside.

Sasha wondered where Evelyn had been (likely with Jorden), how she was (why did she look so terrible?), and if she was truly okay. But it didn't seem right to pry. "Did you have dinner?"

"Yes. BLTs and über-good pie at my folks' house. I brought you a piece. I'm sorry; I should have called. It was a last-minute invite, and I hadn't talked to them for quite a while. We had a nice visit though."

She reopened the fridge door and pointed toward the meat-loaf pan. "Looks like you were busy."

"I decided I'd try my hand at dinner tonight. It's been a long time since I cooked, and I finally felt able."

Evelyn eyed a baked potato wrapped in cellophane. "I hope you weren't waiting for me," she said, her brows knitting together.

"No." Sasha decided to fib so as not to make Evelyn feel bad. "By the time dinner was ready, I figured you'd made other arrangements. My cooking was a pretty lame excuse for a meal anyway, but at least I know I can handle cooking if and when I have to now."

Eating alone had not been fun. The thought of not sharing meals with Evelyn made her sad. The emerging image of spending the rest of her days alone made her sadder.

"Not much can go wrong with meat loaf," Evelyn said. "That's what my Grandma Burt used to say. My first Grandma Burt, that is. The one before Grandma Betty Burt." She took a couple more swigs. "My first Grandma Burt died."

"Well, I hate to disagree with someone who is deceased, but I won't let that stop me." Sasha laughed at herself, which felt good. "True confession: I partially cooked the meat trying to thaw it, then overcooked the broccoli. The one-button microwave baked potatoes turned out okay, though. Thank you, whoever invented that little convenience!"

They sat in silence for a moment.

"How were your folks?" Sasha asked, for lack of anything else to say that sounded benign, then wondered why she'd never thought to inquire about Evelyn's parents before, never considered having them over. They must have been a nervous wreck, letting their daughter move in with someone they'd never met.

Then again, Evelyn was self-sufficient Evelyn, so perhaps they didn't worry at all.

"They were great," Evelyn said, leaning back in her chair. "Busy. Same as usual, cranking back into the school routine, getting ready for fall already. They're both teachers here in Wanoni-shaw. Dad had a pretty good fishing season, which was nice to hear. Landed an eight-pound walleye."

Teachers? And Evelyn's not going to college? That must be something for them to swallow.
"Really? I've never been fishing myself. You?"

"All the time," Evelyn said, sounding a bit wistful. "It's been awhile, though. Dad and I want

240

to get out soon. We'll check your calendar, see when it's okay for me to take off."

"Does Jorden fish too?"

Evelyn closed her eyes for the briefest of moments, then avoided eye contact when she opened them and said, "To be honest, I don't know."

Sasha was surprised by the answer, but she made sure it didn't show on her face. What was going on with those two? "Do you eat the fish you catch?" she asked, to help them move on.

"Sometimes." Evelyn ran her finger around the edge of the can.

"Maybe if you catch enough, we could have your folks over for dinner—assuming you do all the cleaning and cooking of the fish, of course." Sasha laughed at herself again. "Maybe we could have them over for after-fishing lemonade or something. Earlier, I was thinking that it would be nice to meet your folks, get to know them a little. I feel remiss in not inviting them sooner."

"Really? They'd like that!" Evelyn brightened. "In fact, they asked about you tonight. I told them how well you were doing. Nothing personal, of course! Dad wondered if you were ready to start getting out and about town. I told him I thought that was a great idea."

Her folks must be anxious for her job to end, so they can get her back home.

Sasha tried to picture herself caning her way

241

into one of the local shops, alone. She wondered if people would even know who she was. She wasn't sure she was up for the scrutiny. She still recalled the way she'd recoiled at the stares of the older couple taking a walk as she waited in the front window for the arrival of her first home therapy visit. She'd also witnessed the nosy neighbor's curtain fluttering every time she got in or out of the car. Evelyn had even commented on it, made fun of it. *"Oh, look! Out of nowhere, a breeze once again ruffles her curtains!"*

"Something to think about," she said in response to Evelyn's reference to getting out. "Maybe we could go for a walk around the block together for a starter." *Your humor can help me grind through the embarrassment of any gawkers.*

Evelyn yawned. "Maybe. In fact, sounds like a good idea to me." She yawned again. "I hate to cut this visit short, but I'm pooped. I took a pretty rigorous bike ride when I left here, then . . . visiting and all. Feels like it's been a long day."

"I know what you mean," Sasha said. "But I must admit, it's also been a sparkling one." She lifted her cane, gave it a twirl. "I want to thank you again, Evelyn, for such a thoughtful encouragement. And I want to say this, too: I can't imagine my last many months without you. I even miss you when you're gone." She took a deep cleansing breath. "It's clear to me I would not be as well as I am now without your devoted care, your tolerance, your kindness . . ." She stopped and swallowed. "Not to get sappy here at the end of the night, but I just wanted you to know those things."

"Thank you, Ms. Davis. Never be embarrassed about sharing your true feelings. I'm coming to the conclusion that brutal honesty is highly underrated." She looked like she was about to say something else, wanted to say something more, but then was overtaken by a yawn. "Do you need anything before I head upstairs?"

"Nothing I can't handle."

After cooking a full meal that night, no matter how lousy it was, Sasha realized that the only thing in the physical realm she really needed Evelyn for now was driving her to therapy, something the doctors still wouldn't allow her to do herself. Sure, she needed groceries, but she could hire someone for that errand. Maybe even Evelyn and her one-woman service company, if she started that back up when she was done here. But at the rate Sasha was recuperating, driving herself wasn't that far off in the future anyway. What would be her excuse to keep Evelyn then?

Evelyn picked up her backpack.

"Wait!" Sasha said. "I do need something! How about one of those library books? What, pray tell, is our topic this week?"

Evelyn unzipped the largest compartment and unloaded three books, which she let bang onto the table, a look on her face that tilted toward disgust. "Take your pick," she said, with a note of sarcasm in her voice. "I'm going to bed."

Out of the room she walked, yawning as she went, uncustomarily leaving the entire stack of books on the table.

Sasha turned the pile to face her. The top book was titled *The Five Love Languages: How to Express Heartfelt Commitment to Your Mate.* The next book, *The Four Seasons of Marriage,* and the final, *Now You're Speaking My Language: Honest Communication and Deeper Intimacy for a Stronger Marriage.*

Sasha didn't know whether to laugh or cry. What timing! Seeing these books on her table the very day her defenses dropped enough for her to think her husband, whom she hadn't seen for six months, could break her stubborn pride and show up at her door. What language had she spoken, she wondered, when she moved away from him without a word, other than, *Don't ever contact me again?* The language of stupid farewells and hateful selfishness?

Was it too late for *any* kind of language to turn things around? Did he already hate her during this likely final stage of marriage?

She stuffed the books back into Evelyn's backpack, wondering what Evelyn was doing with such titles. Were she and Jorden thinking about getting married soon? Or was the topic just one more that happened to catch Evelyn's eye that week?

She made herself a cup of Sleepytime herbal tea and parked in her rocker. The cold, hard reality of Evelyn's impending departure began to seep in. It might happen sooner than anticipated if Evelyn was ready to tie the proverbial knot. *Hopefully not a slipknot like mine,* she thought, grimacing.

She looked around the room. Yes, she would miss Evelyn's quirky self. But there was more. When Evelyn was gone, she'd no longer be able to instruct someone else to look things up online. Evelyn had the only computer in the house, which would go with her. Not that Sasha couldn't buy herself a laptop and have the Geek Squad, or Jorden and his friend, come hook her up. She certainly knew her own way around the Internet. But that would mean she'd have to find the courage to get her own e-mail, answer her own online fan mail—avoid the temptation to Google Donald's whereabouts, check dance review blogs, see how well everyone else was doing with their careers while she wielded her sparkling cane.

She'd have to get her own library books, find new ways to entertain herself, trust her own judgment about bird identification. Keep the frying pan birdbath filled with water.

Get comfortable with being alone in the house, all day and all night.

Decide if Wanonishaw was where she should remain.

Before long, she, too, was yawning. It was time to go to bed and let the day's emotional roller-coaster ride fall away.

When she turned off the final light, it felt as though she'd extinguished every last shard of brightness around her.

Seventeen

For the fourth time, Donald read the most recent rendition of his note. The wording had triggered two late-night bouts of torment. He still wasn't completely satisfied, but it was time to let it go.

Dear Ms. Burt,

I appeal to you in the name of love and in the best interest of your employer to think about the following questions. Is Sasha's new letterhead design based on a shawl she owns? If so, does she ever wear it?

I realize those might seem like odd questions, if, in fact, you have no idea what I'm talking about. But if you do, and the answer to both questions is yes—if it nudges your conscience to learn that I, her husband, the giver of the shawl, have noticed the similarities—please know that it makes my heart exceedingly happy to think (to dare to believe) she still cherishes the shawl for its memories and the private significance it holds between us, enough to wrap her letterhead in it as well as her dear shoulders.

I would approach her directly with these questions, but I fear she would not open or answer my correspondence. As you know, she will neither take my phone calls nor answer my e-mails. So instead, I give you these questions—this message—and hope you will pray over what to do with them.

Sincerely and with appreciation for your grace and efforts,

Donald Major, Sasha's husband,

who loves her always, and forever

In printing very unlike his own, he addressed the envelope to Ms. Evelyn Burt, using Sasha's mother's address. Although he didn't know for sure if Ms. Burt lived there too, he did know she worked many hours, for no matter what time he called, she answered the phone. He included no return address, marked it "PERSONAL," under-lining the word twice, then sealed the envelope and applied the stamp.

He hoped Sasha didn't retrieve the mail and notice the postmark, which might make her suspicious. If Ms. Evelyn Burt opened the envelope and *did* know what he was talking about, he hoped she would, with this personal information, feel compelled to do something worthy with it. Perhaps pass it on to Sasha, or at least let him know the answers to his questions.

Since the weather had cooled, he grabbed his jacket. Rather than put the letter in the drop box in their condo's foyer, he would walk to the postal box five blocks away, which would give him one last pocket of time to consider his wording or change his mind about mailing it. But after setting out for Wanonishaw and then bailing, with every step he shored up his resolve not to let that happen again. As he walked, he reminded himself that he had an undeniably compelling argument for following through: this idea had arrived with a sign.

Some time ago, after he'd retrieved Sasha's rumpled newsletter from the garbage, he'd hung it on the refrigerator with one of the dozens of humorous and often gaudy—"The gaudier the better!" Sasha always said—refrigerator magnets they collected from their travels. Every day he studied the new logo with fresh eyes, trying to decide if it was in fact the shawl. The more he looked, the more convinced he became it was. Maybe Sasha *did* hope he'd notice and reach out. The one thing she'd always been short on was correcting one of her own wrongs, unless it was a dance step, and then she was relentless. He knew it was a long shot, but why else would she broadcast the shawl like that if not to get his attention, even if it was nothing more than a subliminal act of her subconscious?

When the idea struck to send a note to Evelyn Burt regarding the design on the letterhead, a vision of Our Lady of Dance instantly popped into his mind. As many times throughout their marriage as he'd tapped the top of that snow-globe, in its absence, he couldn't picture the face of the dancer within. Yet when he thought about sending Ms. Burt a note, there was the dancer, clear as a bell, smiling right at his mind's eye. Call him crazy, but he even thought he saw a nod and wink.

As he pulled down the mail slot, he hesitated. *Nothing like playing a long shot, Donald.* But a long shot was better than no shot at all. He kissed the envelope, said a short prayer, then released his long shot into the hands of the United States Postal Service and Ms. Evelyn Burt.

The next morning, both women were in the kitchen earlier than usual, each looking bedraggled and wearing a bathrobe, an uncommon sight. Sasha's pink satin robe was cinched at the waist with a matching belt. Evelyn wore a raggedy chenille robe, her buttons lined up incorrectly. While brushing her teeth, she'd noticed the errors. She'd decided the wonky button job made her look deranged, which was exactly how she felt. But by the time she was done brushing, she forgot to rebutton her robe.

"How'd you sleep last night?" Evelyn asked Ms. Davis, pouring herself a cup of coffee, surprised to find it already made.

"Not well. To be honest, I thought I would— hoped to—be sound asleep as soon as my head hit the pillow. Problem was, I couldn't turn off my mind. You're a smart cookie, Evelyn. Think you could invent something for that? A brain key, perhaps?"

"If I could," Evelyn said, turning her coffee cup in circles, "I'd have used it on myself last night. Honestly, I don't think I got more than three hours of sleep total. How can that happen when you're wiped out?"

"My question exactly."

They took turns yawning and sipping.

Evelyn ran her fingers through her tangled hair. "I need some protein. I forget how many eggs we had on hand, and I'm guessing you used one or two in the meat loaf last night. Are there any left?"

"Only one. Sorry about that. Eggs do sound good, but I yield our one to you. I'll have cereal. Maybe the crunching will wake me."

They sat in silence, playing with their coffee cups, staring at them, taking more sips, neither yet energetic enough to actually get up and do something to satisfy her hunger.

"I have an idea," Evelyn said, setting her cup down harder than she intended and shooting dollops of coffee over the rim and onto the table. She stood to get a cloth napkin out of the drawer and grabbed two instead. She handed one to Sasha and soaked up the mess with hers. "Let's go out for breakfast. We can walk to town and eat at the Sunrise. It's time you got out and about anyway, remember? Why not start with a good payoff?"

"I'm sure I look a mess today, Evelyn. When I don't sleep well, my face goes all . . . sideways."

Evelyn laughed. "I'm sorry I checked mine in the mirror this morning. I didn't even recognize myself." Along with her swollen face, she recalled her wacky button job. She took a sip of coffee, then relined the top few buttons. "My face is blown up like a puffer fish. I guess that's what crying buckets of tears does for you." She hadn't meant to let that slip, but there was no reeling it back in.

"Crying? Evelyn! What were you crying about?"

Evelyn wrapped her hands around her coffee cup, and her eyes flashed to Ms. Davis's mug. "Hey! What are you doing with coffee, Ms. Sasha Nothing-but-Tea-Drinker Davis?"

Evelyn was surprised by her own casualness with her boss. Her friend. The woman across from her. Whoever and what-all-ever she was. Her whirligig thinking made her realize how sluggish her mind was this morning.

"I put the coffee on for you, then filled the kettle with water," Ms. Davis said. "By the time the kettle was hot, the coffee was ready. The smell of that rich dark brew made me lonesome for . . . I just thought I'd have a cup of coffee for a change. In another life, I used to drink it every morning. That's all."

Evelyn chewed her bottom lip. Had Ms. Davis almost said it made her lonesome for her husband? Was this the time to jump in and outright ask her or tell her she already knew? Then she thought, *Would I want her asking me anything— anything—about Jorden right now? Likely not. Maybe not.*

But maybe I would. Who else am I going to talk to about him? Definitely not my folks, at least, not first.

I need to talk to Jorden and Jorden alone about us.

But I also need to give myself time to think, to prepare myself for whatever he might have to say. Plus, I need to catch him when he is rested, not right after swing shift, which he's working right now.

Maybe he'll call me and tell me what a terrible mistake he's made. Yes, I need to give him time to do that.

And maybe Donald Major is who Ms. Davis needs to talk to, too. She kept that thought to herself as well.

"So, how about going to the Sunrise Cafe?" Evelyn asked. "They don't serve a full English breakfast like I do." She paused, smiled, and in a sign of bravado, blew on her nails and brushed them on her chest. "But they have a good, cheap special every day, usually a version of eggs, meat, and choice of toast or pancakes. It's only about a six-block walk. You go farther than that in your therapy sessions, I'm sure."

"Oh, I don't know."

"No time like the present. You don't have to know, you just have to go." Evelyn smiled at herself. "Poet and know it. We used to say that all the time in grade school when we accidentally rhymed something."

"I'm not sure I'm ready or that the Sunrise is ready for me."

"Sometimes we'll never feel ready to make the right or brave choice, but sometimes we just need to do it anyway." The rush of emotions Evelyn felt as her knuckles rapped on her parents' front door last night came to mind. "You can wear your sideways face, and I'll wear my puffer-fish eyes. We'll give all the geezers and gossips something *worthy* to talk about," she said, then chuckled. "We can stop at Grandpa's shop on the way home and pick up some eggs. He always keeps a couple dozen or so in the cooler, just for poor eggless folks such as ourselves."

" 'Poor eggless folks such as ourselves.' Well,

now. I have thought of myself in many ways, especially recently, but I have to admit, that's never been one of them."

"If the shoe fits," Evelyn said.

"Wait. I have a pedicure here at the house in two hours. Do we have enough time, you think? I move pretty slowly still. Maybe we should take on Sasha's Great Adventure another day."

Evelyn felt sure Ms. Davis was just reaching for an excuse to postpone her first venture out. She downed the rest of her coffee and set the mug on the table with a thud. "Here's what we'll do. You use your cane, and I'll walk my bike. We'll time how long it takes us to get there. If, when we're done eating, it looks like we might not make your appointment, we'll skip the butcher shop, and I'll ride my bike home and run the car up there to get you. How does that sound?"

"Oh, I don't know, Evelyn. Maybe I should . . ."

Evelyn cut her off. Feeling emboldened, and challenging herself to the same head-on action with Jorden, she said, "Maybe you should what, for *what?* Hide in this house for the rest of your life? I don't think so. Sometimes we just need to activate. Come on, let's get dressed and hit the sidewalk." Evelyn pushed herself away from the table and cleared both their coffee cups, even though Ms. Davis still had half a cup. "I'm gonna race through a shower, and I'll meet you at the front door in fifteen minutes. I'm guessing it'll take us twenty minutes to walk the distance, so that's thirty-five minutes off our two-hour window. Then let's say we take a leisurely hour to eat, but it will probably really only take us thirty minutes, maybe even just twenty. We check the clock, make our call about me bringing the car, and *voila!* Home in time for your pedicure. And as your friend, I insist on buying."

"I can't believe I'm going to say this," Sasha said, pushing herself up from the table and grabbing her cane, "but you have a deal! I have to get ready now, before I lose my nerve."

"Front door in fifteen minutes. GO!"

Eighteen

Sasha buttered her toast, then removed every jelly packet from the metal container and fanned them in front of her. Funny, she thought, that aside from last night's meat loaf, this felt like the first time in way too long since she'd enjoyed—thoroughly enjoyed—a liberating choice over one of life's ordinary pleasures. Not that she wasn't grateful for every last morsel of food Evelyn had presented to her over the last four months, right down to the labeled tea bags.

But that was just it: Evelyn had presented her

with *Evelyn's* choices. Moreover, Sasha had allowed her—gladly enabled her—to do so. *Depression must have stripped away my ability to even know what I'd surrendered and how easily I'd done so.* While fingering the jelly packets, Sasha realized that she had yielded countless choices and details of her life to others. She'd done so with Evelyn, then before that with home health-care workers. Before *that,* months of having doctor and hospital folks make choices for her: how long she could sit up, if she could sit up, what type of diet she'd be on, what they'd put in her IVs . . . Right after her fall, of course, all she was able to do was lie there and benefit from the medical community's decisions about her healing and well-being. But somewhere along the line, she'd never taken back the reins.

The one definitive choice she'd made was to cut herself off from those she loved most.

It's time to start reclaiming *your life!* she thought while pushing first the grape jelly packet aside, then the strawberry, then the blueberry.

"Do we need to ask for another tray of jellies?" Evelyn asked, intruding into her thoughts. "Do they not have what you're looking for?"

"No. I found what I want right here," Sasha said, her heart racing with giddy exhilaration when she spied the orange marmalade. She carefully stacked the rest of the packets back where they came from, then lavishly slathered her toast with the entire packet of marmalade. With each bite, she felt as if she were nourishing her resolve, feeding her power, flexing her growing muscles of enthusiasm. With the last morsel of toast, she swiped up the egg remnants from her over-easy order. "You were right about this place," she said. "Good food at a good price."

Sasha looked around and smiled at those who acted like they hadn't been watching her every move, those too late to divert their eyes before she caught them. At first uncomfortable in the restaurant—feeling, like the dancer in her snow-globe, stuck on display—she was relieved to discover she ultimately enjoyed the cat-and-mouse game of catching them staring. It put her in mind of the times she'd been out for coffee or in a store and one of her fans would recognize her, try not to stare, yet thrash through a handbag or grab a napkin for an autograph.

Everyone here had of course figured out right away who she was. How could they not? Her sparkling cane—likely not another like it in the entire county—stood propped at the end of the booth. She was also with Evelyn, who seemed to be very well-known around town. The behavior she was used to in her past life from autograph-seeking, adoring fans was a little too bold for these "Minnesota nice" folks. Still, several had marched up to Evelyn to say hello, eyeing Sasha while they spoke, obvious in their hopes that

Evelyn would make introductions—which she did, after a good amount of time passed. It was clear that Evelyn enjoyed the catbird seat too.

Nobody mentioned Sasha's dance career. Nobody. She'd heard that was exactly how it went after a parent lost a child. No one brought up the child for fear they'd make the parent sadder. "As though," she'd once heard a bereaved parent say on a public radio show, "they could possibly make us sadder. We *want* to talk about him!"

Maybe so with a child. But honestly, I'm glad nobody's asking me about the death of my career. The day will come, though, and I need to know what to say, how to respond when someone asks if I miss it.

But she wasn't going to think about that now, not when she was having so much fun. She eyed Evelyn's plate. "Aren't you going to eat your last pancake?"

"No. Want it?" Evelyn looked at her watch. "You have plenty of time."

"Yes," Sasha said, momentarily surprised she'd forgotten about her pedicure. It had been the one pampering delight she most looked forward to. Now she realized how good it felt to get back out in the world again, apart from a medical office. Maybe it was time to change her pedicure appointments to the salon.

"Would you mind driving me to my pedicures, if I switch to the shop?" she asked Evelyn. She mounded the pancake with butter. Since the pancake had cooled, the butter didn't melt, but it didn't matter. The syrup was great. *Made by a local,* the label said, the same as the label on the display case at the front of the restaurant where the yummy-looking sweet rolls resided.

"Not at all," Evelyn said. "I think it's great you're ready to make that move!"

Sasha poured the syrup on thick, then swirled a wedge of pancake in the overflow. "You've had a lot of good ideas, Evelyn, but going out to breakfast might be your best." She put the bite in her mouth and savored its goodness. Something about finally changing her surroundings, just for the joy of it, made everything seem better. "You didn't finish your eggs either," she said.

"Not as hungry as I thought." Evelyn waved at someone across the room. "They tasted good, though."

Sasha studied Evelyn, noted the dark circles under her eyes, a drape of sorrow around her mouth. "Are you okay, Evelyn?"

"To tell you the truth, I'm not sure. But it's nothing I can talk about right now. If and when I'm ready, I think you might be just the person to share it with. It has to do with relationships." She gave Sasha a hard stare. "While I'm on the topic, you didn't like my library selections? I see they're in my backpack again."

Sasha nearly choked on her pancake. "Love is

always an interesting topic," she said, getting the sudden feeling Evelyn was referring to more than her library books. "Why do you ask?"

Evelyn looked at her watch again. "Just curious. You better eat up, and I better pay. We need to hit the sidewalk. You feel up to the walk back? We'll just have time. Or should I ride home and get the car? You make the call."

"First, thank you for breakfast. And I think after everything I ate, I *better* walk! Since I've been getting more exercise, my appetite has improved. But I need to watch myself. Extra weight wouldn't be good for my injuries, and a few pounds on a tiny frame is a lot."

Evelyn pursed her lips. "I wouldn't know. Ten pounds on a large, thick frame is not even that noticeable. I guess that's one of the perks of being a big girl, huh?" She grinned, grabbed the bill, and headed toward the cash register. In a few moments, the two of them were on their way home.

Sasha looked at Evelyn's sturdy body and erect posture as she walked her bicycle. She pictured the way Evelyn rode like the wind with such strength, balance, and command. She admired Evelyn's comfort with her own body type. All her life, Sasha had stepped on the scale nearly every day, as did many dancers. But with good reason: gain too much weight, and you might lose your job. In professional dance, a few extra pounds could make a quick dent in your stamina, not to mention give the costume folks valid cause for a hissy fit. If you showed up for a performance and couldn't fit in your costume, life was not happy. One needed to keep a healthy obsession with weight. Although Sasha knew dancers who got caught up in harmful practices to maintain the correct amount of pounds, she was grateful a big appetite had never been her lure.

Grace, she thought, for both herself and Evelyn.

About midway home, Sasha began to fear she might run out of steam before they reached their destination. She noticed Evelyn sneak a look at her watch a few times and silently chastised herself for making a bad decision. They'd be cutting it close, too close. She could feel herself slowing down, her limp becoming more apparent as she tired. But even though she could barely talk, her breath short from sustaining such a heroic effort on a full stomach, she determined not to give in. *If I have to send Evelyn ahead to meet Dawn and tell her I might be a few minutes late, I'll do it.*

Then an idea struck: she should just let Evelyn take her appointment. That way she could sit down on the bench she spied just ahead, and Evelyn could get on home. She doubted Evelyn had ever had a pedicure—although the moment she drew that conclusion, it seemed the height of snobbery. *What are you? Back in high school with the snooty girls, assuming the less prissy girls don't enjoy feminine indulgence?* Whether or not Evelyn had previously received a pedicure, why wouldn't she enjoy a spontaneous opportunity to be treated to one today?

"Evelyn!" Sasha stopped midstride, breathless from walking and the excitement of her own idea.

"Are you okay?" Evelyn asked, already putting down her kickstand to lend a hand.

"I am fine. Well, actually, I'm . . . pooped," Sasha said, gasping for breath. "But that's not the issue. I have a great idea, and speaking as your boss, I simply won't take no for an answer."

Evelyn kicked the stand back up and started to straddle her bike. "I'm on my way," she said, assuming they were diverting to Plan B.

"No! That's not my idea. This one is even better. See that bench up there?"

"Yes."

"I'm going to perch on it like a queen and stare at other people for a change." She chuckled. "Then when I'm ready, I'll take my sweet and sassy time getting back. I want you to go home and take my appointment today."

"Ms. Davis, I couldn't do that! That's not right."

"Yes, it is right, and it would make me happy. Since you bought breakfast, it'll be my treat. And Evelyn, it'll be good for both of us."

"My feet are . . . big. And I have these funky toenails," Evelyn said, shaking her head. "They're not pedicure material, never have been."

"Welcome to normalcy," Sasha said. "Do you

think everyone who gets a pedicure has pretty feet? We get pedicures for the pure luxury of them and to *make* our feet pretty. Trust me on this: you'll love it. I'm guessing from your statement you've never had one. After this, there will be no turning back, I guarantee you."

"I wouldn't feel right, taking your place."

"As a wise woman once told me, you don't have to feel right, you just have to do it. Go on now. I'll pay when you're done."

Evelyn shook her head.

"Evelyn Burt, as your boss, I command you to take my place!"

Sasha watched as Evelyn looked down at her Birkenstock sandals, noted the ragged edges of her toenails and her callused heels. Then she stared at the sidewalk. "I'll tell you what," Evelyn said. "I will take your appointment. But only if you let me pay. Otherwise, no deal."

"Okay. But since Dawn comes to the house, it's more expensive than a typical pedicure. You might be sorry you insisted on that."

"I won't know the difference if it's more expensive or not. Like my dad is fond of saying in circumstances like this, 'I have money I haven't even spent yet.' " She laughed. "Now I know what he means by that, which could probably be summed up as, oh, what the heck!"

"Go ahead then. I'll see your pretty-footed self when I get there."

Evelyn took off on her bike.

"Don't worry about me!" Sasha yelled after her.

"Okay!" she heard, as Evelyn turned the corner and disappeared.

Evelyn was aflutter with mixed emotions, both about leaving Ms. Davis behind and getting a pedicure. But Ms. Davis had insisted. Maybe, Evelyn thought as she pedaled home, the longer bout of sunshine would do Ms. Davis good. She had been smart enough to know she needed to sit down, and she was, after all, a grown woman.

Evelyn arrived at the house just ahead of Dawn, who was a few minutes early. It flustered Evelyn not to have time to wrap her mind around this idea and settle in—or bail out.

Dawn took the switch in plans in stride. She instructed Evelyn to sit in the rocker and remove her shoes, then went to the kitchen to fill the soaker with warm water.

Evelyn did as she was told, her heart racing. She felt like an ugly-footed fool. This was humiliating. She kept twisting her torso in the chair, looking out the window, hoping to catch a glimpse of Ms. Davis through the trees, each time having to remind herself that from this angle, it would be impossible to see her anyway.

She was ready to pull the plug on this whole crazy scheme when Dawn, taking baby steps with the full soaker, returned. Evelyn settled one bare foot on top of the other and drew them both back as far under the rocker as she could. Her fingers tapped on the chair arms, and she chewed her lip, chastising herself for being nervous about some-thing so common. But though she'd long ago come to grips with her size, she was suddenly chagrined as she recalled Ms. Davis's slender legs and tiny, feminine feet when she sat in this same chair for her pedicure.

"Here we go!" Dawn said. "You're going to like this. Trust me. Your first pedicure could be con-sidered a baptism into womanhood."

Evelyn raised her eyebrows. Dawn didn't look much older than herself. And what was up with that black nail polish she wore on both her fingernails and toenails? *Good grief! What have I gotten myself into?*

"Oh, not that you're not fully a woman," Dawn said, noting the look on Evelyn's face and her engagement ring. "That was a bad choice of words. I apologize. Maybe a first pedicure could be considered a baptism, of sorts, into the blissful mysteries of luxury. Yeah, that's more like it. Trust me, your shoes and your fiancé will thank you."

She smiled while Evelyn tucked her left hand under her armpit and tried not to think about its implications, given that she no longer knew *what* the ring signified, if anything. Every time she thought about her dramatic predicament, her heart both raced and sank anew.

Dawn reached under the chair and wrapped her hand around Evelyn's top ankle, causing Evelyn to lurch. Dawn started to pull Evelyn's leg toward her, but Evelyn's reflexes resisted.

Dawn laughed. "Hey, I'm not trying to steal anything here," she said. "I'm going to begin by simply placing your feet in the soak. Just relax. Let me do the tootsie driving, okay?"

Evelyn exhaled and tried to surrender her legs, which suddenly felt the size of tree trunks. At least she'd shaved them two days ago.

Dawn settled Evelyn's feet in the soak. The water was warm, slightly sudsy, and fragrant.

"I'm going to run out to the car and get another pedicure packet. I had Ms. Davis's kit here in my bag," Dawn said, pointing, "but I keep a separate kit for each of my off-site clients, and I always have extras. You just relax, and I'll be right back."

Evelyn was grateful her feet were hidden beneath the frothy bubbles on top of the water. She forced herself to press her shoulders back in the chair. Although she was glad Dawn was serious about hygiene, she didn't imagine herself ever making another appointment, so having her own pedicure packet, whatever that entailed, felt like a waste of . . . whatever. She was distracted by voices out in front of the house, but couldn't make them out due to a nearby lawnmower. She felt imprisoned.

Soon Dawn returned with a sealed plastic bag

that held skinny flip-flops, toe separators, and a few other items. She'd seen her mom use the separators during one of her rare home pedicures, something she was never able to talk Evelyn into. "Fish don't care about toenails," Evelyn recalled once quipping to her mom.

Dawn opened the bag and laid the items out on a short-legged portable tray she brought with her. She used a black magic marker to write Evelyn's name on the outside of the kit, then she opened another large plastic case filled with polish.

"While you're soaking, you can take a look at the polish colors I have with me today. I brought mostly bottles in Ms. Davis's palette, which tend toward the pinks and might not be your cup of tea. I'm guessing you'll either lean toward neutral or bright reds. I do have a few of those in there, but that's about it."

"Bright red?" Evelyn asked, sitting straight up, her voice sounding like a pipsqueak's.

"No?" Dawn asked. "You seem like the bold type."

"Bold, yes," Evelyn said, thinking about the business she'd started, the way she spoke what was on her mind. "But from no polish to red? It seems kind of . . . vampish. And vampish I am not." Evelyn sounded almost insulted, aware her tone verged on that of an old lady. *Old-before-her-time Evelyn. If the shoe fits . . .*

Dawn broke into great guffaws. "Oh, man!

Vampish. Mrs. Oliver—she's eighty-three—will just love that one! She's worn red polish since I've been in business, and according to her, since she was eighteen years old and her mom finally allowed her to wear polish."

"I didn't mean to be disrespectful," Evelyn said.

"No. Seriously, she'll *love* it. I can guarantee she will claim her vampishness with great gusto. She's in the assisted-living residence out at the edge of town now, been there about six months. She lost her husband, let's see, nine months ago, after sixty-two years together. She said the secret to their longevity, both together and in life, was that they danced every chance they got. Square dance, ballroom, slow dance, jitterbug . . . didn't matter. They liked them all. Her walls are lined with pictures of the two of them, and their kids, and grandkids, and great-grands and one great-great-grand. She has a little trouble with balance now, but she can still wiggle her fanny, which she does, just to prove she can.

"She once confessed to me, in front of her husband, that her fanny and her fire-engine-red polish sealed the deal. She said they were also the two main factors that first attracted him to her." As she unrolled a few towels across her lap, Dawn smiled, a true fondness for the couple brightening her face. "When Mrs. Oliver told me that, her husband just nodded and winked at both of us, then told me his wife could still do a pretty mean hootchy-kootchy." She laughed, causing Evelyn to do the same. "They were so cute together. She talks about Samuel all the time. Sometimes she tears up, and then I do too. But that's okay. After all those years together, who wouldn't?"

Evelyn felt herself sink back in the chair. She wasn't sure whether she was finally relaxing or succumbing to a morose bout of sorrow. *Sixty-two years of marriage.* She and Jorden hadn't even started, and they were already over. Maybe.

She wiggled her toes in the soothing warm water. *Then again,* she told herself, *after we finally get to talk, after I feel strong enough to face him, maybe everything will be cleared up and proceed as if nothing happened.* She took a deep breath and fanned the flickering flames of her optimism. Jorden might even call her this very day, come knocking on the door to apologize for the solitary moment in his life when fast driving and crazy talk got the best of him. If he did, she was convinced that marrying sooner than later was the right thing to do. The idea that they were separated for even a short while over a possible misunderstanding—surely he hadn't really broken up with her—was too difficult to bear. Thoughts of the cozy trailer, a wedding certificate, his warm lips, vampish polish . . .

Simmer down, Evelyn.

But if she didn't hear from him and she had to go knock on his door in order to talk, that might be a different ball game. After seeing his dad in the window and that muffled sound of a slap . . . In hindsight, she was pretty sure his dad had hit someone, either Jorden or his mom, not vice versa. If Jorden did have a violent temper, wouldn't she know about it by now? But then, why had Jorden even hinted at such a terrible thing? Just to shock her? To turn her away from him? To deflect his embarrassment over his parents?

Was his diversion the move of a player?

But something else Jorden mentioned tempered her worst thoughts. Her faith in him. Had no one ever believed in him before, the way her folks believed in her? Why should she retract that faith now?

She wiggled her toes again, then moved her feet forward a little, for the first time feeling the bumps in the bottom of the soaker. They felt funny, like a pair of sandals she'd once tried on with rubbery knobs in the soles, which were supposed to massage your feet while you walked. Instead, they just felt annoying and kinda itchy. As she scooted her feet again in the soak, Evelyn noticed these larger bumps felt relaxing.

She closed her eyes and was just about to settle in when Dawn tapped her on the knee to let her know it was time to remove her right foot from the soak.

"Just this one, right now. Relax your leg muscle,

okay? I'm just going to set your foot here on this towel in my lap, exfoliate your dead skin, push back the cuticles, and even up your toenails. By the way," Dawn said, tilting Evelyn's foot this way and that, "you have nice feet. No bunions or corns, and really nice arches. I can tell you've always worn good shoes."

"Yes," Evelyn said. "Thank you. But I wouldn't exactly describe my feet as nice. Large would be more like it, size nine-and-a-half, and pretty unkempt, I guess. But they've always served me well. After watching Ms. Davis go through such a rough time, it's made me grateful to be able to use my feet and legs without having to think about each step."

"You know," Dawn said with a warm smile, "that's a good reminder to be grateful for every-day things I take for granted. Thank you. It's so easy to whine. And to be honest, I've done way too much whining this week. I could hardly stand myself yesterday."

Relatable. Evelyn leaned back in the chair again and gave her leg a yoga sponge posture directive, then instructed herself to give thanks for the moment.

Grace.

Dawn began trimming Evelyn's toenails and cleaning under them, which set Evelyn slightly on edge again. The instruments looked sharp. But Dawn wielded them with the skill of a surgeon.

Before she knew it, Evelyn had again relaxed, and Dawn was on to her left foot. Then Dawn removed a pumice stone from Evelyn's personal kit and went to work on her heels and the sides of her big toes. After the soak, Evelyn was surprised how easily the layers of dead skin rubbed away. Dawn poured a large dollop of a grainy substance, something she called sloughing lotion, onto each foot and began to rub it all over, including on top of Evelyn's feet. When she was done, she set them back in the soak for a moment to rinse, then went to the kitchen to refill the soak with clean water for a further rinse.

After she patted Evelyn's feet dry, Dawn poured some wonderful mint scented cream on them and began to slowly massage, which was when Evelyn got ticklish and could barely hold still. Dawn tried a heavier touch, then a lighter touch, the heavier touch producing less ticklish results. By the time Dawn was nearly done, Evelyn had become more used to it.

"Now then," Dawn said, wiping her hands on the towel. "Did you pick out a polish yet?"

"Oh! I forgot all about it! Let's see." Evelyn eyed the bottles. The longevity of Mrs. Oliver's marriage and her spunk and sassy attitude struck Evelyn's sensibilities. Perhaps those were some good footsteps to follow in, at least this once. Maybe Jorden would find the red irresistible too, if he ever had a chance to see it. "I'll go with that red there," she said, pointing. "Not the fire-engine red next to it, but the deeper one that has more blue in it."

"Oh, you understand colors, huh?"

"Yes. I work with watercolors."

"Wish I was artistic. You're lucky." Dawn picked up the bottle and held it to Evelyn's leg. "Good choice for your skin tone. I applaud you."

It wasn't until after Dawn started applying the base coat that a sudden fit of guilt struck Evelyn: Ms. Davis hadn't come home yet. She'd forgotten all about her!

"Oh!" she said, lurching, causing Dawn to paint the end of her big toe. "Ms. Davis never made it home! Oh, my gosh! I hope she's okay. I have to go look for her!"

"No worries," Dawn said, wiping the polish off Evelyn's toe with the end of her finger. "When I went to the car to get your kit, she was just passing by. My apologies. I forgot to give you her message. She said to tell you not to worry, that she was enjoying herself, and that she wished to give you privacy for your first pedicure. She said she'd return after my car was gone."

"Where on earth was she going? I'm sure she was completely tired out."

"To be honest with you, I've never seen her look so relaxed. She almost had a glow about her. She said to tell you she was going back to her viewing stand, that you'd know what she was talking about. She only stopped by because she knew you'd fret. I guess living together, you two know each other pretty well, huh?"

Evelyn thought for a moment. *Not exactly.* But then she laughed. "Viewing stand. That is too funny."

"I have no idea what she meant."

Evelyn did not explain. She leaned back and pictured Ms. Davis sitting on the bench, staring—gawking—at people going by, which made her laugh again.

"I'm glad you're finally relaxed," Dawn said. "Let's finish this base coat, then see how you like the color you picked. I'll put it on a nail or two, and if you don't like it, we'll remove it and try something else."

If only all of life was that easy.

Nineteen

"The tables have truly turned," Ms. Davis said with a smile. She sat at the little desk and studied Evelyn, who was waking from a waiting-for-her-toenails-to-dry nap, complete with a cat in her lap. "It was finally my turn to watch the drool run down your chin as you slept in the rocker while wearing a TuTu!" Ms. Davis chuckled.

Evelyn blushed and wiped her chin with the back of her hand.

"Just kidding," Ms. Davis said. "No drool. Payback time!" She loosed a riotous laugh. "Do you remember once fooling me with that line about drool, then telling me I took myself a little too seriously? You were, of course, exactly right."

Evelyn stared at Ms. Davis, then at the cat in her lap, then at her own foreign feet at the end of her legs. It was shocking, really, to see her very own toenails evenly shaped, dark red, and on feet without a hint of dry skin. Her feet looked . . . *good!* When she leaned forward to remove the toe separators, TuTu leapt off her lap and wound herself around Ms. Davis's legs before heading out of the room. Evelyn decided she better leave the separators in place. She had no idea how long it took that many layers of nail polish to dry.

She reviewed her circumstance. After she'd paid Dawn, Dawn had packed up her stuff and instructed her to just relax until her polish dried. The sun was streaming in the window, the house was quiet, the neighbors were done mowing, the kitty jumped up in her lap and began purring. She must have dozed right off. She hadn't even heard Ms. Davis arrive. No surprise, though. She'd barely had any sleep last night, and in the end, even after all her fretting and the ticklish part, the pedicure was indeed a baptism into a luxurious and relaxing experience.

"How long have you been sitting there?" Evelyn asked Ms. Davis.

"Not long. Maybe five minutes."

"How long does it take four layers of polish to dry?"

"To be safe? A good while. Just relax. We've got nothing on our agenda. After all that walking and fresh air, I'm ready for an iced tea. I'll get you one too—and no arguing!" Ms. Davis said, pointing her cane at Evelyn.

Evelyn let her head fall back against the rocker. There were a million things wrong with this picture and with her life, yet she felt incapable of doing anything other than accepting every single one of them, at least for the moment. She looked out the window at the birds frolicking in the pan. There was the house finch. Such a bright coral head. *Oh! And the goldfinch!* A robin landed nearby and off the tiniest birds flew. The robin surveyed the situation, looked around for predators, then hopped in the nearly empty birdbath. Evelyn hadn't had time to fill it that morning. She made a mental note to do so after her polish dried.

She turned her eyes toward the snowglobe. Such a delicate piece, so unlike the rocks Evelyn collected from everywhere, including the bottom of creeks and other people's driveways. When she was young, her mom had tried to get her interested in dolls and delicate things, but they were just so boring. She had much more fun foraging, building forts, playing baseball and basketball, fishing, and bantering with the neighbor boys as they drove their trucks and big diggers through the sandboxes and dirt piles, crawling here and there, leaving trenches and piles of chaos behind. Action! That was what she liked. Not tea parties and dress-up and Barbies and all the frilly stuff most other girls her age found fascinating.

Which, she thought as she glanced back down at her feet, was why it shocked her how much she liked her polished toenails. She couldn't wait to show her mom, who would probably keel over.

And hopefully, Jorden. But her heart kerplunked as she looked at her ring.

Evelyn turned her eyes again toward the dancer in the snowglobe. She appeared so serene and feminine. So happy in her life as a dancer. Evelyn wanted to pick up the globe, but felt it might be an intrusion into Ms. Davis's personal life, as she obviously treasured it.

Evelyn tried to picture Ms. Davis wearing the dancer's costume. Although she'd never been to a ballet, she knew Ms. Davis would be up on her toes, hands placed just so, leaping and twirling, garnering applause, traveling the world. It was the first time it truly soaked in for Evelyn how different Ms. Davis's life was now. Of course Evelyn knew this in her head, but sitting in this chair looking at the snowglobe, the weight of the loss—the loss of Ms. Davis's entire way of life, not to mention her husband—settled deep down into Evelyn and made her incredibly sad. Why was this just striking her now? Because she was, for the first time in her life, in such a confusing and utterly vulnerable place herself?

Such a dark time.

She rested her fingertips lightly on the top of the snowglobe and her eyes welled with tears.

Through the blur, she noticed Ms. Davis's delicate hand carefully setting an iced tea next to the snowglobe.

"She has that effect on me too," Ms. Davis said, in a reverent whisper.

Evelyn looked at Ms. Davis and was surprised to feel tears streaming down her cheeks. "You've lost so much," she said. "I'm so sorry for your trials."

Sasha finagled the small chair closer to the rocker, then held up a finger. She made her way back into the kitchen and returned with her tea. After several swallows, she sat in front of Evelyn, exactly where Dawn had positioned herself.

"Dear Evelyn," she said, resting her hand on Evelyn's knee. "Yes, I have lost much. My life has definitely and irrevocably changed. When I hit the floor, the self I knew died. But sitting outside in the sunshine today," she said, her voice gathering energy, her eyes brightening, "watching the sparkles on my cane cast their brilliance all around me—watching a mom push her severely handicapped teenage son in a wheelchair—it finally settled in for good that it's time I stop living in the past and dedicate myself to what comes next.

"I don't know exactly how to express it, but an inexplicable peace enveloped me, followed by an excitement to get on with life! There was that mom, her son tilted to one side in the chair, and yet she was humming, smiling, nodding. She noticed my cane and stopped to ask if *I* needed a hand. The boy smiled too. I was reminded that there are people who carry much heavier burdens than mine. So many circumstances will never change for people, so many will never get to realize their hopes and dreams. Yes, life is, and will be, different for me. But life is not over for me, not by a long shot. Such an obvious realization, but it came to me as a wonderful epiphany. I even had a vision, for lack of a better word, of what that next something might be for me! I'm not ready to talk about it yet. It's just a seedling of a thought. But it even involves dance."

Evelyn rested her hand on top of Ms. Davis's. At their touch, it felt as though their deepest longings and vulnerabilities, their richest hopes and innermost secrets knocked on each other's hearts.

And the curtain fell.

Evelyn's eyes welled again. Ms. Davis spoke not a word, she just sat there, a comforting grip on Evelyn's knee.

"Ms. Davis," Evelyn said, "I am so grateful for you. You gave me a golden opportunity to spread my wings. I'm so glad your life is coming together. But right now, I have to be honest. My life is falling apart." She took a deep breath, exhaled, and before she had a chance to chicken out she said, "I think Jorden broke off our engagement."

The sound that emerged, something between a moan and a whimper, was foreign, yet fully expressed the torrid anguish she'd fought to hold at bay. Saying it out loud brought on a whole new level of *real.*

After Evelyn's crying settled and she blew her nose, Ms. Davis said, "Evelyn, I am so sorry. It sounds like you're confused about the situation, though. Why is that? What happened? Do your folks know about this?"

"No. My parents do not know. Not yet anyway. They, especially my dad, aren't crazy about Jorden to begin with. I'm afraid they'd jump right to conclusions and maybe make a bigger mess of things than they already are. I can almost picture my dad banging on Jorden's door."

Evelyn thought about censoring her story for Ms. Davis, about skipping the rough parts regarding Jorden's family and what she thought she'd heard take place. This was a conversation she'd promised herself was reserved for Jorden. But in this moment, with Ms. Davis's hand on her knee, her own vulnerabilities exposed, and her need to hear herself, for the first time, repeat out loud the whole incident—as if to finally test its truth—she delivered all the details, starting with Jorden's tender and valiant attempt to rescue her from what he feared had been a roadside accident and ending with him driving away, leaving her in the parking lot.

Evelyn looked straight into Ms. Davis's eyes the whole time she spoke, waiting for them to reveal something, anything. Although Ms. Davis's eyes remained focused and sympathetic, they were devoid of judgment, for which Evelyn was grateful.

After a brief silence, Ms. Davis set her left hand on top of Evelyn's, which rested on top of her own right hand. The weight of the chain of union, all resting on Evelyn's knee, felt purposeful, as if it could anchor her in the chair and help her pass through this moment, to weather the raging storm within.

"I am so sorry," Ms. Davis said. "Love is . . . sometimes so complicated. Has there been any other evidence of abuse?"

"Not that I've witnessed. I was blindsided, stunned, shocked, and then numb. I've turned it over and *over* in my mind until, to be honest, I'm not sure *what* happened that evening. It feels so dreamlike, overshadowed by Jorden ending our engagement."

"And you haven't heard from him since?"

"No," Evelyn said, her eyes glazing over, her voice cracking. "I haven't heard a word. As for the abuse thing, he once alluded that everything wasn't . . . normal in his family, but that's it. Abuse never entered my mind."

"You know, Evelyn, if there is a pattern of abuse in Jorden's family, it sometimes trickles down through the generations. People don't know any other way. It can be a terrible cycle, and if that's true for Jorden, it's good you found out now. Perhaps as difficult as this is, Jorden is sparing you a world of worse hurt. On the other hand, maybe he was just mortified you caught his family during such a low moment, and in an attempt to spare both of you further embarrassment and concern, he overreacted and prematurely broke things off. Maybe, hopefully, he just needs some time to come to his senses, then come clean with whatever's going on, so you can get to the truth of the matter and patch things up."

"Maybe," Evelyn said. "I wondered some of those same things."

The idea of Jorden housing a violent streak made her shudder. Then she locked on what Ms. Davis had said last, about overreacting and prematurely breaking things off—and especially about giving someone time to come to their senses. She wondered if Ms. Davis was describing her response after her accident.

"Ms. Davis, is that what happened with you and your husband, Donald Major?" Ms. Davis gasped, withdrew her hands and recoiled as though she'd been slapped in the face. *Well, now you did it, Evelyn!*

"How do you know about Donald?" Ms. Davis asked, putting her hand over her heart, her voice a mixture of shock and anger.

"He told me," Evelyn said, folding her hands together and squeezing so hard her knuckles turned white, the warmth of Ms. Davis's hands still evident on her own. "The day you were in your first outpatient therapy session and you left your cell phone in your handbag. You instructed me to answer it. It rang. And he told me."

"He told you what, exactly?" Ms. Davis sounded almost frightened.

"That he was your husband. He wanted me to tell you that he missed you and that he *loved* you. And then he wanted me to tell you something else too, but you came through the door and I . . . I hung up on him before he could say."

Tears started streaming down Ms. Davis's face, making Evelyn feel like she'd just betrayed the woman to whom she'd confessed her own miseries.

"Ms. Davis, you've been so clear in your instructions never to put him through. I . . . I didn't want to get in trouble. I didn't know what else to do. At first, I wasn't even sure he was telling the truth about being your husband, but then he told me about the picture in the upstairs bedroom, which I swear I didn't go look for. But he knew the layout of the house, about the stained glass in the front door, your mother. And Ms. Davis, he was *crying*. I was afraid if I told you, I'd . . . You were doing so good with your progress, finally getting happier, and . . ." Her voice trailed off. What else could she say that didn't move the purpose of this revelation about Donald's contact toward her own self-justification?

Ms. Davis closed her eyes and bit her trembling lip. She mumbled something.

"I'm sorry, I didn't understand you." Evelyn's throat was tight.

"It's not your fault, Evelyn. Nothing is your fault. It's all mine," Ms. Davis said, burying her face in her hands.

Evelyn leaned forward, removed the toe separators and flung them aside. Then she put her hand on Ms. Davis's knee. "*I* am so sorry. You've been through so much. But you have to know . . . I have to tell you that his voice was filled with such sincerity and love. Ms. Davis, if you still love him, maybe you should just talk to him."

"Evelyn!" Ms. Davis snapped, the look in her eyes a combination of sorrow and sparks. "You don't know what you're talking about." Her volume escalated. "It's just not that simple. You don't know a thing about what I've done!

How awful I've been to those I love the most."

Then, as if punched in the stomach by a mammoth fist, she folded in on herself and wailed.

After a long silence, Evelyn picked up her iced tea and went upstairs, leaving Ms. Davis to herself. What else was there for her to do?

The next couple of days in the abode on Fourth Street were quiet. The two women were congenial, yet often separate, for the most part avoiding each other. Ms. Davis, who left for a long walk every day, often parking herself on the bench for long periods of time, requested nothing of Evelyn but a ride to therapy. Aside from a few mundane pleasantries about the weather, they ate their meals together in silence. Ms. Davis did her exercises, Evelyn cleaned the pantry and the refrigerator, they both read a lot, including the books on love. The music never played. The phone did not ring. Evelyn spent the majority of her time in her room.

It was as if they were a sequestered jury of two, each deliberating her own case.

Evelyn simply could not find the courage to call Jorden, fearing what he might say. As long as she remained ignorant about the dark possibilities, it was easier to hang on to the hope that her fears were unfounded. But the longer she waited without word, the more difficult it became to believe that they weren't.

On day three, the postman delivered a letter to Evelyn marked "PERSONAL."

Jorden!

She ripped it open and read it through, three times, then, shoulders slumped, walked straight into the living room where Ms. Davis sat in the big chair. She carefully set the letter, envelope and all, on Ms. Davis's lap.

"It's addressed to me, but it's really for you," she said, and then she walked straight out the front door.

She circled the house, went to the garage, hopped on her bicycle, and with Donald Major's words "in the name of love" ringing in her head, rode like the wind straight toward Jorden's house.

While her feet pedaled, she thought about the day Ms. Davis had said she'd like to have a new letterhead designed. She'd asked Evelyn if she thought she could put her graphics skills to work and come up with something clever, a challenge that energized Evelyn. She hadn't had a chance to loose her artistic talents in far too long.

"What about a watercolor rendering of your beautiful shawl?" Evelyn had asked.

She'd often pictured how brilliant a painting could be using the shawl as a model, had in fact one hot night in her bedroom even sketched the shawl in her sketch pad, playing with different techniques to duplicate the shawl's intricate stitches. In real life, the pearlescent beads captured the light in brilliant ways, and the satin trim really set it off. It would be a challenge to infuse the shawl with its own sense of life and color apart from Ms. Davis, but it would be a fun challenge.

"This shawl?" Ms. Davis asked, as if there were several of them sitting around. She grabbed the end of the shawl wrapped around her shoulders and rubbed the satin against her neck.

"Yes, that one. The colors are so nice. I believe the pastels will render really well in watercolors. If you like the painting, I could scan and JPEG it, then plunk it into the graphics program. If you don't, we'll go back to the drawing board."

And so the new letterhead came about. Ms. Davis's voice went hoarse when she saw Evelyn's finished piece. She'd whispered how beautiful the painting was, how . . . *special.* Evelyn had no idea her suggestion—and the use of her God-given talents—would eventually set something far bigger into motion.

Yes, she knew exactly what shawl Mr. Major was talking about when she read his letter.

"In the name of love." The simplest words. Such short words. Unspoken signs in a shawl. *Please, God, let Ms. Davis receive her husband's letter with the grace he expected of me.*

"In the name of love." "I would approach her directly . . . but . . ."

Directly. Here I come, Jorden, right at you! No more waiting and wondering.

As she rode around the corner onto his street, her breath caught in her throat. There was a big pile of furniture stacked on the curb in front of his house. When she pulled into his driveway, she noticed a House for Rent sign hanging in the front window.

She dropped her bicycle in the grass and ran to the door, pounding on it like a wild woman. "Jorden! Open up!"

She stopped knocking after a long, silent minute, jumped off the porch, and moved to the front window. The house was empty.

Surely Jorden hadn't left without a good-bye! Yes, he'd mentioned his folks wanted to move again, and he'd all but begged her to marry him, to combine resources so they could get a place for him to stay until they could move in together.

But he would not leave without giving her a chance to . . . without explaining . . .

No. He wouldn't just leave.

Twenty

Sasha sat with the letter in her hand. The paper shook, she trembled so. She'd read it at least twenty times. Each time, the words quaked her core enough to dislodge everything she thought to be true about her ability to release Donald into a life without her. What appeared to be true, instead, was his dogged determination to never let *her* go.

Beginning with "I appeal to you in the name of love," which she read over and over before moving forward, and ending with "Sasha's husband, who loves her always and forever," each time she moved through the passion of his words, she wondered anew, *Oh, Donald! What have I* done *to you, to me, to* us?

"What must I do?" she said aloud, clutching his extraordinary plea to her chest.

She folded the letter and placed it back in the envelope, for the first time noticing the way it was addressed. Personal, to Evelyn. It was remarkable, the way he'd humbled himself, honored her wishes to stay away, given her the space she so selfishly demanded, and yet never, ever, given up on her.

He'd even declared his love for her to a perfect stranger!

"Grace," she whispered. *"Grace."* Salt from her tears curled into her mouth.

He must feel like a caged tiger, waiting to see if anything comes of this attempt to reach out to me in this way. What courage, such restraint, first to hold back and give me space, yet to never give up on me!

She wiped the tears off her face, got up out of the chair and headed for her cell phone, which she'd left in her handbag in her bedroom. The first thing she saw when she entered her room was the shawl, which, when it wasn't wrapped around her, she kept displayed across the end of her bed. She picked it up and set the cane where the shawl had been. Light streamed through the window, casting the cane's reflections all around her. She sat on the bed and caressed her cheek with the shawl.

"Her dear shoulders . . ." Oh, Donald!

She fumbled through her handbag for the phone, wondering at the remarkable chain of events that had led to this moment. If it weren't for Evelyn—applying for the job in the first place, cheering Sasha on toward recovery, recommending she use the shawl for the new letterhead, using her extraordinary talents and patience, passing along the letter—this opportunity to make a course correction in her life would not be Sasha's.

But now, things are about to change, she

thought. A glorious and toe-tingling thrill, unlike anything she'd felt outside the tap of Our Lady of Dance's snowglobe, raced through her as she dialed Donald's number, praying he would, *Please, God,* answer on the very first ring.

Evelyn went back to Jorden's front door and pounded three times with both fists. "Jorden! Are you in there?"

What if something terribly violent had erupted? Maybe his folks had left, but he was still inside, waiting in his bedroom for her to rescue him.

"Hello," a young voice said, startling her. Evelyn turned to find one of the little ball players from her previous visit standing just off the porch. His hair went this way and that, and he sported a dirt streak across his left cheek. "If you're looking for the McFinns, you missed 'em. They moved out night before last. My mom said it was in the *middle* of the night when things were *pitch dark!* She heard noises and saw 'em through her bedroom window, packing up their car and truck with suitcases and stuff. She said she wasn't surprised. She called the landlord yesterday and told him she thought they'd left." The boy nearly worked himself into a breathless lather passing along this juicy insider information.

"They *all* moved?" Evelyn asked.

"All of 'em. Mr. Harry—that's the landlord, and our landlord too—told my mom this morning, when he finally came to check the house, that they'd left nearly all their furniture behind. That's what's in that big pile there." He pointed toward the curb. "Said the Salvation Army would be by to pick it up later today. Don't tell anyone," he said, lowering the tone of his voice and leaning toward her, "but we took one of the recliners."

In his hand he held a ball, which he tossed straight up and caught twice. "Mom said we'll *finally* get some new neighbors now. I hope they have young boys this time." He threw the ball up and caught it again. "My team could use a good second baseman."

Evelyn felt queasy. She thanked the boy, picked up her bike, and started walking it down the street, too shaky to ride. As if to rub salt in her sting, the sun refracted off her diamond ring, catching her attention. She stopped, leaned the bike against her hip, yanked the ring off her finger, and stuffed it into the pocket of her jeans. When her eyes cast downward, they lit on her red toenails, which she'd been so anxious for Jorden to see.

Which was when the tears began to well.

It was official. She was no longer engaged. Her fiancé, her *ex*-fiancé, who'd abandoned her in a parking lot, hadn't even cared enough to tell her good-bye before he left town. She was a woman newly baptized into luxurious womanly ways. Yet somehow, she suddenly felt far short of being a woman at all.

Who had she been kidding?

She got on her bike and started to pedal. *I am a nineteen-year-old fool whose world has just hit rock bottom. What did I think I knew about love anyway? What ever made me believe Jorden, who attracted every girl in town, could be serious about* me?

She pedaled faster and faster. *What a chump I've been! Likely everyone in town knows it, or will know it by the end of the day. That boy's mom probably told everyone she knows that Jorden's family moved out in the middle of the night, and her son is repeating it too—and Lord knows how many other people. Likely everyone. I might be the* last *person to find out he's gone!*

Faster still, she flew. *Wait until my folks find out.*

Fury rising, one important mission suddenly lodged in her mind, its priority rocketing with immediacy. She circled around the block, back toward Jorden's house. She was going to find that little boy and tell him, in no uncertain terms, one thing he needed to learn, and right now: he shouldn't wish for just little boys to move in next door when girls could play baseball—and do just about everything else—just as well!

She pedaled so fast, the heat of her anger nearly propelled her off the ground. As she turned the corner, her bike tires hit a patch of gravel.

The next thing Evelyn knew, she lay near the

side of the road, the back of her head surrounded by a pool of blood.

The little baseball player stood over her, screaming, "MOOOOM!"

Donald was home just long enough to grab a bite, swap out his gym bag for his ballet bag, and get to the theater for rehearsal. He'd just put his workout clothes into the washer when he heard the phone ring. As he sat on a kitchen chair to peel off his left sock, he picked up the phone and said hello.

"Hello?" he said a second time, switching the phone from the crook of his right shoulder to his left so he could remove his other sock.

He barely heard a voice say, "Donald?" But when he did, his foot slammed to the floor, his sock only half off.

He sat erect, still as a chimney yet electrified. "Yes." He heard a sniffle. "Sasha, is that you?" he dared to ask.

"Yes. I am so sorry, Donald!" she said, her words barely decipherable.

He looked at his wristwatch, then removed it and laid it face down on the table. Class, rehearsal, performance, career be darned. His wife was on the phone! "Sasha, no apologies. Tell me how you are. Just tell me you're . . . all right."

He listened while she sniffled. "I don't deserve you," she finally said. "When I read your letter to

294

Evelyn, I . . ." She broke into sobs. "Please forgive me."

"Shhh, sweetheart. Hush," he said in his most tender, soothing voice. "It's okay. It is enough you called." He closed his eyes and pictured her cheek, very close to his own. "Tell me, Sasha, how *are* you? Tell me everything."

He heard her swallow. "I'm recovering. I'm even walking with a cane now."

He gasped. How many months had it been since the fall, and she still had a cane? "I am so sorry."

"No, Donald. It's okay. *Really.* Recovery, both mental and physical, has been difficult and slow. But just a couple of days ago—and I can hardly believe the timing of your letter—I turned an important corner. I've spent a lot of time meditating lately. I've come to grips with the reality that I won't perform again, and I am at peace with that. Finally." She let out a deep breath. "I've dedicated myself to moving on, although I'm not sure exactly what is in store for me. *Please* don't feel sorry for me, Donald. I couldn't bear that. It's one of the reasons I chose to . . . why I haven't . . .

"But never mind that for now," she said. "No more time wasted on regret. Oh, Donald, I have missed you so very much.

"How are you?" she asked. "How's the troupe? What are you performing now?"

His stunning, beautiful dancer, using a cane. It

was an image he simply could not allow himself to conjure. And yet she truly did sound at peace, which flooded every pore of his body with relief. He imagined her sensitive, yearning, pleading eyes. He felt like he once again held her tender heart in his hand, same as he had every time they'd danced together. Only this time, the knowledge of such a blessing was even more powerful, since it was a gift he'd nearly given up on.

Yet, how odd her question. Surely she'd followed the company's schedule on the Internet. But perhaps doing so brought too much heartache? Best not to ask such a question, lest he sound assumptive or arrogant, or his intent be misread.

"We've just opened *Coppélia*," he said, recalling the last time the two of them had danced it together, he as Franz and she as Swanhilda.

Since the accident, *Coppélia* was the first time he'd had to perform in a ballet he and Sasha had danced together. His current Swanhilda, the Mid-Central Festival Ballet's new principal female, was a wonderful dancer. Still, it had taken him some time to emotionally detach from the heart-ache that it wasn't his dear Sasha's waist, arm, or leg he held.

The line was quiet for a moment, which worried him.

"I loved dancing Swanhilda, especially with you," Sasha finally said, her voice strong and energized—maybe too much so. "Such a fun story line, and those hilarious characters. And," she added, her voice quieting, sounding more thought-ful, "such crazy misunderstandings in that story." She paused a long moment, perhaps thinking about the similarities to their lives right at this moment, as was he. "How's it going? How's attendance?"

"It's going fine." He dared not say how much he missed partnering her for fear of bringing sorrow in the midst of this wonderful brightness. *Just focus on the good and stay in the moment. She is right: we have now.* "We're holding our own in this tough economy, which is a surprise."

"Wonderful!"

An awkward quiet set in. What came next? he wondered. He realized their conversation had started with a rush of emotions, then quickly moved to work. *His* work now, he reminded himself. He was suddenly and acutely aware how much of their life together, how much of their dialogue, had centered around their careers, their love of dance, their shared experiences in the studio and on the stage.

He didn't dare ask if she was moving back. It was too soon. And since the new season had just opened, he wasn't available to visit her. Plus, she hadn't invited him. So now what?

"Look, Donald," she said, as if reading his mind, wanting to chase away this shadow, "since you're in production, I'm sure you need to be heading out pretty quickly. I am just so grateful I caught you. Thank you for *taking* my call. Thank you for loving me, even after all . . . this. Thank you. That's all I really wanted and needed to say right now."

Even though everything within him did not want to lose this, their first reconnection, he knew it was time to hang up. He felt sure there would be more conversations, many more.

On the hope of his belief, they began their good-byes. Donald promised he'd call Sasha as soon as he found a pocket of time that would feel more relaxed.

While he scurried to finish packing his bag, he replayed their entire conversation. Sasha had responded to his plea and called. *Thank you, Our Lady of Dance.* She'd apologized and thanked him, neither of which was necessary. She'd called, which was everything. She'd said apologizing and thanking him was all she wanted and needed to say today.

But she had not apparently wanted or needed to say that she still loved him, a thought that put an instant damper on his joy.

Twenty-One

Sasha hung up, kicked off her shoes, wrapped herself in the shawl, and for the first time since arriving in Wanonishaw, lay on her side of the bed, the side she slept on when she and Donald were together.

When she'd first arrived, due to her injuries, the home health-care folks had set her up with a twin-size air bed. Although that rental appliance had thankfully been gone for some time now, its protective function no longer necessary, she'd only allowed herself to sleep in the dead center of her mom's full-sized bed. It was too painful to take "her side" when Donald was not there to occupy his.

But today, at long last, she scooted across to her familiar left side of the mattress. She silenced her breathing enough to pretend she heard Donald's. As she fingered one of the beads in her shawl, she imagined the feel of his body turning her way, his warm arms wrapping around her as they spooned.

An enormous wave of relief expanded inside her, filling her entire soul with an incredible joy. She'd finally unburdened herself from the terrible aching silence—her self-imposed abandonment of the man she loved—and taken an atypical step to right her own wrong. If she'd received the letter before her park bench epiphany about moving on—if she hadn't had the last couple of days to let the truth of the possibility of new beginnings sink in, to allow herself to turn that corner—would she have been strong enough to respond to his out-reach? She didn't think so.

Such perfect timing could only be God's. She'd heard her mother say it hundreds, if not thousands, of times.

Thank you, Mom. Thank you, Donald. Thank you, Evelyn. Thank you, God. Thank you all for your perfect timing and abundant grace.

She was just about to drift off when her phone rang. Certain it was Donald, she scrambled to answer it, accidentally sending her cane to the floor with a thunk.

"Donald!" she said, before she even got the phone to her ear. "I'm so glad you called again already. I was just . . ."

A deep, unrecognizable voice cut her off. "Ms. Sasha Davis?"

"Yes?"

"This is Officer Shumski with the Wanonishaw Police."

Sasha felt a sudden rush of dread. She worked her way off the bed and retrieved her cane from the floor. "What can I do for you?"

"I'm here with Evelyn Burt. She's been in a bicycle accident."

"Oh, no! Is she okay?"

"She refused to let me call an ambulance, and rather than let me take her to the clinic in the squad car, she said I should call you. That was our compromise, of sorts," he said through what sounded like a smile. "She's of age and in her full faculties, so I cannot force her to do anything against her will. She says she's fine, that she can just ride her bicycle home, but it looks like her head hit the pavement pretty hard. She's going to need at least a couple stitches, and I think she should be checked for a concussion before she starts riding her bicycle."

"Thank you, Officer . . . Shumski, did you say?"

"Yes, ma'am."

Sasha's mind reeled. Why did Evelyn have the officer call her? What was *she* supposed to do? She couldn't pick Evelyn up; she wasn't yet allowed to drive. But if Evelyn didn't want to go to the hospital or the clinic, if she rode her bicycle straight to their house, how would she get stitches? Or get checked for a concussion, which was nothing to fool around with?

"Where are you and Evelyn, officer?" Sasha asked.

"We're near the intersection of McQueen and Calvin. Just so you know, one of the neighbor kids saw her take the spill. No other vehicles were

301

involved. He stayed with Ms. Burt while he called his mom outside. Mrs. Casper took one look and called the police department. Blood from a head laceration can make an injury appear far worse than it is. When I arrived, Ms. Burt was conscious. It's unclear if she ever *lost* consciousness. Mrs. Casper was kind enough to get a towel, which we used as a compress, and she brought out an ice pack too. She's been very helpful. The bleeding has pretty much stopped and the ice pack will aid with swelling, but still, like I said, she'll likely need a couple stitches—and maybe a bike helmet for the future." A note of reprimand laced his voice. "Ms. Burt says she left her backpack at home, so she doesn't have her cell phone. I told her I'd make the call if she stayed put. I'll stay with her until you arrive."

Sasha wondered why Evelyn hadn't had him call her folks. Then it dawned on her: Calvin ran north and south on the far end of town where Jorden lived. Something else must have gone wrong concerning him, a thought that caused Sasha to shiver.

"I'll be right there, officer."

With as much haste as she could muster, Sasha made her way through the kitchen, grateful Evelyn always kept the car keys on the hook by the back door. She grabbed Evelyn's backpack, thought about calling her parents. If Evelyn were her daughter, Sasha would want to know right away if she'd been injured. But her loyalties lay with Evelyn, and that's where they'd stay. Like the officer said, she was of age.

Sasha got into the car and sat behind the wheel, but the seat was adjusted for Evelyn. Sasha felt miniscule and was half-reclined. She hadn't driven her mom's big old car for years; it felt the size of a battleship. She and Donald had always owned small cars, and for that matter, didn't even drive them that often. City living had its advantages.

It took her a while to figure out how to adjust the seat. *So many buttons.* When she was too far back, she had to point her toe to reach the accelerator and brake pedal, which caused a bit of discomfort. Like Goldilocks, she adjusted and readjusted all the electronic settings until she got things just right. It was bad enough she was driving against doctor's orders, and toward a policeman! She didn't need further trouble by setting her healing back. Finally, she adjusted the mirrors, took a deep breath, and with a racing heart, put the car in reverse.

She took her time getting across town, carefully winding her way to Carlton, missing the turn onto Calvin her first go-around. The streets weren't exactly as she remembered them. That end of town was barely recognizable. When she was a child, the area had been all fields. Now condos, duplexes, and prefab homes extended for blocks.

Wow! Isn't this where the boys used to play ball and I came to chase butterflies? The sight of a squad car with Evelyn's legs sticking out of it— with her trademark Birkenstock sandals—came as a welcome relief.

When Evelyn saw Sasha pull up, she leapt to her feet and strode toward the old LeSabre, holding the ice pack to her head. "I'll have Officer Shumski put my bike in the trunk. He's dying to do *something* official," she said with a weak smile. "Stay put, okay?"

Sasha nodded. When Evelyn turned and walked toward Officer Shumski, Sasha noticed the back of her blond head was covered with blood. Sasha decided that whether Evelyn wanted to or not, she was going to the doctor, which she said after Evelyn was safely belted into the front passenger seat.

"Fine," Evelyn said. "I'm sure I just need a stitch or two. This all looks way worse than it is. If that little boy hadn't freaked out, I'd have ridden my bike home and that would be that. By the way, thanks for coming to get me. Brave move! Do you want me to drive, now that we're out of Officer Shumski's line if vision?"

"Not if you have a concussion. I'd rather be safe than sorry."

"Oh, and driving without permission is the best way to do that, right?"

Sasha chuckled. "We're quite the stubborn,

disobedient, and clandestine pair, you know that?"

"Yes, I do," Evelyn said, her voice solemn. She paused a moment and repositioned the ice pack. "And I have to say I kind of like us this way. Definitely more exciting than bird-watching, huh?" She smiled.

"Not funny. First you get me hooked on the sport, then you dis it? Where should I take you for stitches?"

"Not the hospital. Just take me to the walk-in clinic on South Main Street. I realize how irresponsible this is going to sound, and it is, but I'm not sure if I have any health insurance coverage. I know I would if I'd gone to college. But since I'm not living with my folks, I'm not sure. I've always been as healthy as a big old horse. It never occurred to me to . . ."

"Is that why you didn't want them to call the ambulance?"

"Heck, no. I just didn't need all *that*. I bumped my head. Not the first time; probably not the last."

"When I lived in Wanonishaw, there was no walk-in clinic," Sasha said. "You'll have to instruct me where to go."

"It's just down the street from the café where we had breakfast. Once you start moving," she said, raising her eyebrows, "we'll be heading the right direction."

Sasha put the car in gear. "Evelyn, I don't mean to pry, but I'm guessing that since you phoned me and not your parents, your accident had something to do with Jorden. Is everything okay there?" Her hands clenched the steering wheel as she puttered down the street.

"Let's talk about it after we're home, okay? I need to hold together," Evelyn said, swallowing hard.

"Fine."

"For the record," Evelyn said, "I know you're just trying to be careful, but you're driving like a geezer who *belongs* in a LeSabre."

Sasha smiled. "Perfect."

"What about you and your husband?" Evelyn asked. "Anything I need to know there? By the way, you need to turn left at the next block."

"After your stitches. If I tell you now, I'll start crying and then I won't be able to see to drive. Just so you don't worry, though, it's very good news."

"You talked to him?"

"Yes," Sasha said. "Yes, I did." Her voice cracked. "I'll never be able to thank you enough, Evelyn."

They drove in silence for a couple of blocks. Evelyn pointed out the parking lot of the clinic and told Sasha to wait in the car.

"Not on your life," Sasha said. Into the clinic they went, Sasha using her cane, Evelyn holding the ice pack to the back of her head. Sasha smiled. "They'll probably wonder which one of us they're supposed to see!"

Sixty-five minutes and four stitches later, they

returned to their abode on Fourth Street, this time with Evelyn behind the wheel. She'd been cleared of a concussion, although the nurse suggested Sasha still watch her for the next twenty-four to forty-eight hours.

The two women sat at the kitchen table for an hour, sharing their good news and bad news, their joys, their hopes, their crushing heartaches, and their tears.

"You know, Ms. Davis, when I was waiting for you to arrive at the scene of the accident, as Officer Shumski so dramatically kept referring to it, I thought about the day I applied for this job. I couldn't wait to tell you about my fiancé. I was on top of the world. I remember saying something to the effect that love is as love does, and our love *does*. It turns out, it's your love, which at first I didn't even know existed, that truly does, while Jorden's and mine obviously didn't. Whatever that means." Evelyn shook her head, glanced at her left hand, then tried to reach into her pocket. She stood, checked deep into her right pocket, then into her left, then turned her pockets inside out.

"Oh, no!" she said, her cheeks flushing. "The ring must have come out of my pocket when I crashed. I have to go look for it!"

"You had the ring in your pocket?" Sasha asked. Evelyn nodded. "It's getting dark already."

"I won't sleep if I don't find it." Evelyn grabbed the flashlight and her backpack.

"Evelyn Burt, do not ride your bike again tonight! If you're determined to go, take the car."

"That's probably a good idea. The headlights will be helpful. Thank you."

"Do you want me to come with?"

"No. Nothing personal, but I could use a little time alone."

"How does your head feel? Come over here and let me look at your pupils first, to make sure they're not dilated."

Evelyn moved in front of Sasha and made bug-eyes at her. "I have a slight headache, but I think that's just an overflow of pain radiating from my heart."

"Okay. Take the car then. But if you feel the slightest bit funny, *you call me!*"

"And you'll come get me in what?"

Sasha tilted her head. "I saw a wheelbarrow in the garage."

"Like you could push me in a wheelbarrow."

"You, my dear, have no idea what I'm capable of when I set my mind to something."

Evelyn grabbed the keys.

"Be careful!" Sasha hollered as she went out the door.

An hour later, Evelyn returned exhausted and with a banging headache, but no ring.

After breakfast the next morning, her headache down to a dull ache, Evelyn rode her bike through yesterday's exact route—including her double-back to give the little boy a what-for, which in hindsight seemed like a ridiculous notion —and looked everywhere again for her ring. She combed the streets, which were unusually quiet that Sunday morning, and surrounding yards. No ring.

The one thing she did discover in the daylight was that the stack of furniture outside Jorden's house was gone. Although it probably shouldn't have, its absence made her even sadder. At least the pile had served as evidence he'd existed. From their first meeting to the breakup, the whole of their relationship now seemed almost surreal. Not even the ring remained to serve testimony.

The story the little boy had told her about the Salvation Army popped into her head. She remembered how he'd confessed his family had taken one of the chairs. Last night when she came back to look for her ring, she'd noticed him peeking out the window of his house. When she spied him, he drew the drapes tight and didn't appear again. Now it made her wonder if, when he and his mom had helped her, they might have also found the ring and pocketed it. She thought about knocking on their door, then decided to just let it go. If they hadn't, it would feel pretty rotten to accuse the people who had helped her of stealing. And if they had, they likely wouldn't admit it.

If she was still engaged, everything would be different. She'd seen dozens of lost items reported in the local newspaper, with offers for rewards. But now that she was likely the laughingstock of town, the last thing she needed was an ad in the paper for an engagement ring that only reminded her she'd been jilted. Yes, jilted.

What would she do with the ring now anyway? Stare at it every day as a sad reminder? Besides, she told herself, anyone could have picked it up. Maybe it even rolled down the sewer drain.

She got on her bike and headed toward her grandpa's shop. She could use a dose of him about now.

But what if the shop was already buzzing with questions about his granddaughter's fiancé, who they'd heard left town in the middle of the night? She remembered the lukewarm reactions when people learned she was engaged to Jorden, the way her own Grandma Betty offered nothing more than how she saw him at work, but had shared no enthusiasm or kindness about his work ethics. The way the little boy's mom had said she wasn't surprised his family had left after dark.

The way her dad almost instantly formed a negative opinion about him.

Judgments were so unfair. Then again, had she just been blind? Duped? Had she been taken in by a bad boy?

Her head itched from the stitches, her heart

ached from her loss, her self-confidence was down the tubes. What was she going to do? She couldn't lock herself up and hide in Ms. Davis's house forever. Wasn't that what Ms. Davis had done to herself, what Evelyn had worked so hard to help her overcome?

Sooner or later, she'd have to face the world.

Just not yet. Not with stitches in her head. *Good grief! Everyone likely already knows about my spill too.* They'd probably put the pieces together, figured out she'd gone looking for him, maybe tried to off herself in the aftermath. That was how rumors spread.

Yes, she was better off without the ring, for now and forever. Even a lost item ad would be embarrassing.

She pulled into the Fourth Street driveway and parked her bike in the garage.

"Any luck?" Ms. Davis asked when she walked into the kitchen.

"Maybe," Evelyn said. "I didn't find it, which I'm beginning to think is the good news. What would I do with it anyway?"

"Oh, sweetheart," Ms. Davis said, moving toward Evelyn and giving her a quick hug. "I am so sorry."

Evelyn bit her lip, which trembled.

"Your mother called while you were gone. She heard about your accident and was worried when you didn't answer your cell phone. She said she tried to call you twice this morning."

"Yeah," Evelyn said, slumping. She pulled out a chair and sat down at the table. "I saw her number on my caller ID. I'm just not up to getting into it with my folks yet."

Ms. Davis seated herself across from Evelyn and leaned her cane against her knee. "She also asked if I knew anything about you and Jorden. She said she'd heard . . . things."

Evelyn put her head down on the table. Word *had* already spread. "I just can't face *anyone* right now," she said, "especially my folks."

"Evelyn, I don't want to interfere in your life any more than you've interfered in mine." The words were barely out of Ms. Davis's mouth before she broke out in a fit of laughter, which made Evelyn raise her head and offer a limp smile. "Well, let me rephrase that. I don't want to get in the middle of something I've not been invited to get in the middle of. But just as you felt compelled to pass Donald's letter along to me, I have to tell you that the tone in your mother's voice was heartbreaking. She's worried sick about you. I didn't share anything with her, other than to assure her you were okay, but I did promise her I'd let you know she called."

"Thank you," Evelyn said. She yawned and rubbed her eyes. "If it's okay with you, I'm going to try to catch a quick nap before we head to your therapy."

"Sure thing," Ms. Davis said. "If you're not down by eleven, I'll holler up the stairs."

"If you don't hear me rustle, call the undertaker."

"Evelyn! Don't even say such a terrible thing! Is your head throbbing?" Ms. Davis asked, looking hard into Evelyn's eyes, inspecting her pupils again for signs of enlargement.

"No. My headache's pretty much gone. But right now I feel like I could outright die of humiliation. I've been so stupid and gullible!"

Evelyn broke out in sobs as she ran through the house and up the stairs.

Twenty-Two

Sasha made herself a cup of hot peppermint tea —leaves from the plants Evelyn grew behind the garage, then dried—and settled into her rocker. Evelyn had barely made an appearancc the rest of the day yesterday. Sasha closed her eyes and focused deliberate wishes toward the girl's peace and healing. She wasn't praying, just thinking. Then again, maybe she was praying. How could one really tell the difference? What else could she do for Evelyn, aside from be there for her, same as Evelyn had been there for her? Some wounds needed to run their course. Of this, she was well aware.

She opened her eyes and focused on the bird-bath, which she'd filled in Evelyn's absence. Two stunning bluebirds had stopped by for a drink that morning. Somehow, the old adage, "the blue-bird of happiness" felt spot on when they landed so very close to her life.

It would be less than two months before the full blast of Minnesota's harsh winter arrived and the birdbaths would be put away. Evelyn had suggested that when the time came, they get some ground fat from her grandpa's shop and make a variety of suet balls to hang in the trees and off the porch rails so they could continue to attract as many birds as possible. She'd mentioned all kinds of special seeds and seed blends for this species and that. Sasha blew into her teacup and watched as three raucous sparrows splashed and shook, splashed and shook. She could no longer imagine sitting in her rocking chair without enjoying this simple bird-watching pleasure. She smiled at the way she and Evelyn had joked about it.

She expected Donald to call today. She knew the daily schedule by heart; he hadn't called yester-day because Sundays were jam packed. Mornings were busy too. Even so, more than once already, she'd caught herself staring at the phone. He might call during his lunch break, though, which was exactly when she'd be in rehab. She sighed into her cup of tea again and felt the warm steam flow back under her nose.

As anxious as she was to hear his voice again, and as grateful as she was they'd taken a step in the right direction, the obvious lull in their previous conversation was not easily forgotten. It had quickly become clear to both of them that apart from the topic of dance, and especially after such a lengthy time of *no* conversation—and so many personal questions hanging in the air—the waters of ongoing communication might be tricky to navigate. This was a stunning surprise after thirteen years of marriage, during which they'd spent most of their waking and sleeping time together.

This semi-fretting led her straight to the impossible question she kept trying to ignore: given the states of their lives, was reconciliation *really* possible? But nearly every time that dark question reared its fear-mongering head and blasted a fiery breath on Sasha's hope, she found herself responding to it with a powerful one-word whisper: *"Grace."*

Evelyn had made her a believer.

She set the tea on the side table, got up, and retrieved a pad of notebook paper and a pencil from the desk. After reseating herself, she patted Our Lady of Dance on the head. Across the top of the page, she wrote, "THINGS TO TALK TO DONALD ABOUT." While pondering, she picked up the tea and took a small careful taste, then began.

1. How much Wanonishaw has grown
2. Evelyn (nothing personal)
3. How I've come to enjoy the rigors of therapy (make joke about the familiarity of sweat)
4. Arabesque and TuTu
5. How much I've been reminded that as opposed to city living, where nobody knows you, here, everyone knows you and your business (Good or bad?)
6. BRIEF overview of my progress (do not dwell on difficulties! STAY POSITIVE!)

Enough about me, she thought. She drew a double line under her six topic points, then wrote, "THINGS TO ASK DONALD ABOUT."

1. Has he spoken with Janine? If so, how is she?
2. How has his health been holding up? Any long-term effects from the fall? (Good to finally talk about the incident so we can move beyond it—hopefully)
3. Who replaced me in the company? Anyone I know? (Let him know he can talk about this) NOTE TO SELF: Make sure you are okay with this first and keep tone of voice light and normal! (He will ask why you haven't looked on the computer. Are you ready to tell the truth?)
4. Ask about *Coppélia*?

Ask him what, exactly, about Coppélia? she

thought as she quickly withdrew her hand from the page. She felt like she'd suddenly appeared at the top of a massive cliff, where either a magnificent view or a fatal fall awaited her.

As if to back away, she rested the pencil on the tablet and picked up the snowglobe.

During idle moments since Donald had mentioned *Coppélia*, she'd rehashed the story line and relived their magnificent time together during that run. *Coppélia* was often considered dance's greatest comedy. But it was also referred to as a love story in three acts, or a sentimental love story. Early that morning, after Evelyn left to look for her ring and Sasha was done filling the frying pan with water, just thinking about *Coppélia*'s music inspired her to pull out her mother's album containing music by Clément Philibert Léo Delibes, his name itself lyrical. Several pieces from *Coppélia* were in the mix.

On rare mornings when she and Donald could loll in bed together, how they'd loved listening to their double CD set of *Coppélia*'s entire score. Sometimes at the start of the wedding *pas de deux* in act 3, they'd spontaneously rise from beneath the covers to casually dance its festive romance. That morning, while listening to Delibes's music on her mother's old phonograph, picturing every step the way they'd performed it and using her cane for balance, Sasha had danced a slow, care-ful waltz around the living room, through the sitting room, to the kitchen and back. When she envisioned the lifts, she'd paused and imagined she felt Donald's strong hands guiding her, holding her, settling her to the floor . . . loving her. She heard the thunderous applause when the final curtain drew.

It wasn't until she sat in the rocking chair to catch her breath that she realized she'd never once relived the terrible fall.

I am truly healing!

In *Coppélia*, Franz, the character Donald played —was *now* playing, she reminded herself—was smitten by a handcrafted, life-size doll named Coppélia. Coppélia had been crafted by the eccentric and somewhat questionable, perhaps even unsavory, Dr. Coppélius. Of course Franz (nor in the beginning, Swanhilda, whom Sasha loved portraying) didn't know the doll wasn't real. After Dr. Coppélius placed Coppélia on a balcony, seated, as if she were reading, she looked every bit the lady. She was to Franz simply a beautiful woman who captured his full attention, and he blew her a kiss. Swanhilda, Franz's lover, caught him in this act and became jealous.

As the story progressed, Swanhilda and a band of friends broke into Dr. Coppélius's studio to find out about this Coppélia woman, which was where she discovered Coppélia was but a doll. Swanhilda donned the doll's clothing, causing Coppélius to believe his creation had come to life. How Sasha enjoyed dancing those fun, uncommon steps, pretending she was a life-size doll, falling over at the waist, splitting to the floor, moving in very clunky and unladylike—unballet-like—movements as Coppélius, her creator, reveled in the notion she actually lived.

There was, of course, more to the story, but after all the misunderstandings and falderal, Swanhilda and Franz were married.

And they lived happily ever after despite all that chaos in the middle—all caused by a handcrafted doll, she thought.

Sasha studied the dancer in the snowglobe. Something inside her quickened and her heart raced with nervous energy. For the first time ever, a curiosity sprang up inside her as to the maker of the dancer in the globe.

Curiously crafted dolls, sometimes seemingly capable of surprising events. Unexpected events. Life-changing events. She'd never before thought about the tangential similarities between the handcrafted Our Lady of Dance in the snowglobe and the twists and turns in *Coppélia*.

Sasha studied Our Lady of Dance's face as though expecting an explanation, something to tie all her swirling thoughts together, something to help her make sense of so many senseless things.

Something to help her believe that the maker of the figure in the snowglobe had only kind and good intentions (after all, the gentleman who sold it to her mom did seem a bit of a fortune-teller), rather than the objectives of the shadowy Coppélius, which seemed more aligned with deceit.

She needed to hear words that helped her never again return to the questions: *Can* we get back together? *Is* grace enough?

Then something astonishing occurred: as she heard the strains of the music from *Coppélia*'s act 3 dance commemorating *Prayer* swell to life all around her, the dancer nodded.

And just like that, the seed planted inside her on the park bench began to grow. She knew what her next endeavor would be, to whom and what she would dedicate herself. At the assured awareness, a bolt of energy, alive with hope and possibilities, ran through her.

Thank You. This time she had no doubt to whom her quick thought was aimed, and yes, it *was* a prayer to *her* Maker.

She crumpled the sheet of paper and tossed it in the garbage can. If a woman needed to rely on a cheat sheet to engage in conversation with her own husband, she did not deserve a happy ending.

At five minutes till eleven, Evelyn made her way down the stairs. Her eyes felt nearly swollen shut. While not happy she had to get up and out of the house, at least her ongoing obligations were a built-in remedy to locking herself up forever. That is until Ms. Davis no longer needed her, a moment now destined to soon arrive.

"How are you doing?" Ms. Davis asked when she entered the kitchen. "It looks like you could use some cold tea bags."

"Tea bags?"

"For your eyelids. Old dancer's trick. Well, probably a common trick among many. But we always kept a couple of used tea bags in the fridge. When our eyes were swollen—so many late-night performances and early-morning classes—we'd lie down for a moment and place them on our closed eyes. Helps with swelling. In fact, I don't know if you've ever noticed, but I keep a sealed plastic bag of used tea bags in the butter compartment."

"I wondered about that. It kind of looked like wet cigars, so I just left it alone. Tea bags. Huh. Something to keep in mind for the future. Maybe when I go to bed tonight. Right now," Evelyn said, looking at the kitchen clock on the wall, "we have to get going."

"You hungry? To the best of my knowledge, you haven't had any breakfast yet."

"No. But if my stomach wakes up, I can grab a sandwich while you're in therapy. There's a Subway right down the street."

"Okay," Ms. Davis said. "*Are* you feeling any better?"

"I'd say I'm somewhere between pathetic and resigned."

"I know it's cliché, but time is a healer, Evelyn. I guess you could consider me Exhibit A."

"Have you spoken with your husband again then?"

"No. I didn't expect him to call yesterday, and mornings are busy. He might call on his lunch break today, while I'm in therapy."

"Want me to answer?"

"No, thank you. Just let it go to voice mail. Hopefully he'll leave a good callback time."

"You sure he won't think you're avoiding him again?"

Ms. Davis grabbed her handbag and started for the back door. "You know, you might be right about that. Maybe if he does call, you should answer and pass along that I'm sorry I missed his call. You can tell him why too."

"Deal," Evelyn said.

"You know," Ms. Davis said, passing through the doorway, "maybe Jorden will still contact you. Maybe he's in a nearby hotel, or . . ."

"Ms. Davis, I know you're trying to help. But I don't get that feeling at all. I'm beginning to wonder if he didn't buy diamond rings by the dozen and give them to every naive girl in every town he ever lived in, just to try to get them to . . . just because." *I'm so glad I didn't cave in to his sexual insistence. Think how I'd feel now that he's gone!*

Ms. Davis didn't respond. The two of them got in the car and didn't speak again until they were almost to the clinic. Then Ms. Davis said, "I've been thinking about what you said. About Jorden maybe buying rings by the dozen. I suppose that's possible. There are plenty of guys like that out there. But maybe that's not the truth at all.

"Evelyn, I don't think you'll do yourself any favors by projecting the worst-case scenario onto the situation. Besides, I believe you're too smart to have been taken in by nothing more than a smooth-talking con artist."

Evelyn sighed. "I don't know about that," she said, shaking her head.

"From everything you've told me, it's possible you *were* the best thing that ever happened to Jorden. Maybe you were the first person who looked beyond his exterior and believed in the best . . . about, in, and *for* him. Maybe that's what made it so humiliating when the worst in his family showed up, with you nearly on his door-step when it happened."

Evelyn's foot eased up on the gas pedal, an outward sign of the internal pause she felt in her thought process.

"Maybe, Evelyn, Jorden was just trying to protect the one good thing in his life, and the only way he knew how to do that was to take all the bad with him and leave you, the good, safely behind."

Evelyn sniffed. "Maybe," she said, turning on the blinker. "Is that what happened with you and Mr. Major?"

Ms. Davis reached over, rested her hand on Evelyn's shoulder and gave it a squeeze. She didn't remove her hand until they turned into the parking lot. In that gesture, she admitted volumes.

"Just in time," Ms. Davis said. She grabbed her purse and cane and got out of the car.

Evelyn didn't follow. "I'm just going to wait in the car today," she said. "You wanna leave your purse with me?"

"Okay," Ms. Davis said.

Evelyn watched Ms. Davis until she disappeared inside. She was almost down to a small limp and growing stronger every day. *No, it won't be long. She will go on to her next thing and leave me behind too.*

Ms. Davis's phone rang, startling Evelyn. She grabbed it out of Ms. Davis's purse and checked the caller ID. Donald Major. "Hello. Evelyn Burt here, Ms. Davis's assistant."

"Ms. Burt," Donald said. "It's not that I'm not happy to hear your voice again. But I hope this doesn't mean . . . I mean, is Sasha there?"

"She was genuinely looking forward to your call, sir." Evelyn made sure she added plenty of perk to her tone of voice. "She thought it might come while she was indisposed. She asked me to answer and let you know that's she's in therapy.

She hopes you leave her a good time to call you back."

"Where is her therapy?"

"La Crosse, Wisconsin."

"How long does therapy last?"

"It depends if they're running on time or not, but they usually keep a pretty tight schedule. Sometimes they work with her first, then give her a regimen to follow on the machines. She's almost never shorter than forty-five minutes or longer than ninety, if that helps."

"How long has she been in there today?"

"I just dropped her off."

"Oh," he said, sounding dejected. "This is my only window of time today."

"Maybe she could call you tonight?"

"It's an hour later where I am. By the time I get home . . ."

"She doesn't have therapy tomorrow," Evelyn volunteered. "Well, she has homework therapy, but she can do that any time. Might you be able to call around this same time then?"

"Yes! Yes, that would be good!"

"I'll tell her to expect your call then. She'll be glad."

After a short pause he said, "Really?"

"Mr. Major, she'll be exceedingly glad." *As happy as I am miserable.*

"Thank you, Ms. Burt. And Ms. Burt, thank you for taking action on my note. Thank you for your patience with me, for being our reuniting cupid, of sorts."

Too bad I can't fire an arrow for myself. "You're welcome, Mr. Major."

"I hope to meet you sometime, Ms. Burt, to thank you in person."

"Are you coming for a visit?" *What an inappropriate and nosy thing to ask.* "I'm sorry, sir. That's not really my business."

"That's quite a fair question. Believe me, it's not for lack of wanting. But at the time, it's impossible for several weeks."

Weeks before they can finally see each other? After all this time? It doesn't seem fair. But then maybe nothing is ever fair about love.

"Ms. Burt, are you still there?"

"Yes."

"Tell Sasha I look forward to talking to her tomorrow about this same time. And Ms. Burt, if I could be so bold as to ask, how is she, *really?* I mean, she told me she's using a cane now, but . . . how well is she?"

"Sir, that is something you'll need to talk to her about."

"I thought that's what you might say," he said. She could hear the smile in his voice. "You're a good woman, Ms. Burt. I'm glad Sasha has you in her corner."

After they hung up, Evelyn looked at her empty ring finger. With her fingernail, she traced the white line across the remnants of her tan. She sighed and rested her hands together, ring hand on the bottom, then put her fingertips to the back of her head near her stitches.

The last week still felt so "otherly." If it weren't for the telltale signs, it could be easy to convince herself that nothing was out of the ordinary, that the whole terrible breakup and aftermath had been one long nightmare.

Ms. Davis's words echoed in Evelyn's head and in her heart. *The tone in your mother's voice was heartbreaking. She's worried sick about you.* She was glad Ms. Davis hadn't pressed her to call her mother back, a thought that made her glad Ms. Davis was in *her* corner.

Still, her folks were probably indeed worried sick. They'd likely heard everything through the grapevine by now, and who knew in what form. She felt bad for Grandpa Burt, who'd probably been put through a buzz saw of questions all day too.

Knowing her parents would both be in school, she got out her cell phone, dialed their number and left a message on the machine.

"Hi, Mom and Dad. It's me." *Your disobedient daughter and the talk of the town.* "Ms. Davis told me you phoned her yesterday. I'm sorry I didn't pick up or call back. It's just that . . . You've probably heard the talk by now. Yes, Jorden's family left town, including Jorden. Just so you know, before he left, in fact just before I came to your house the other day, he broke up with me." She had to stop and steady her voice. "Yes, I took a spill on my bicycle in his neck of town. I have four stitches in the back of my head, nothing to worry about. Ms. Davis took good care of me." She stopped and took a breath. "I couldn't bring myself to face you but . . ."

Beep. The machine cut her off.

She dialed again. "Anyhow, I just wanted you to know I'm okay. I'll be by to see you this week. I love you both," she said, her voice wavering. "Thank you for your patience. Thank you for loving me. Thanks for giving me space. And Dad, it looks like you were right about Jorden all along, but then I guess you already knew that."

Tears rolled down her cheeks. She cracked the window. The day was crisp. The air felt good, the sun warm against her shoulder. She started to rest her head against the seat, but it hit right at her stitches. She winced, then leaned the side of her head against the window as she wiped the tears from her cheeks.

The next thing she knew, Ms. Davis was getting into the car.

"I'm sorry I woke you," Ms. Davis said. "I'm sure you're exhausted. When we get home, you should just go back to bed. In fact," she said, flinging the door open and getting out, holding her thought until she appeared at the driver's side door, "scoot over and go back to sleep. I can legally drive us home!"

"That's wonderful news!" Evelyn said, striving to keep her voice cheerful while moving across the seat. But she felt gut-punched. Surely her job would now come to an end. It wouldn't surprise her if Ms. Davis moved back to Boston.

"I have more good news for you," Evelyn made herself say. "Mr. Major called. I told him you'd be home tomorrow. He said he'd call at the same time, which was right after you went into the building today, so sometime around eleven-forty."

"That's wonderful!" Ms. Davis, suddenly looking youthful and all atwitter, began to fiddle with the car seat adjustments.

Evelyn nodded and tried her best to deliver a genuine smile. It *was* great to see Ms. Davis so happy. To know that a heart *could* mend.

Ms. Davis turned over the engine. "Evelyn, I want to tell you something a very wise woman once taught me. The whole time I was on that terrible bicycle torture machine, I couldn't stop thinking about it."

"Ms. Davis, I don't mean to be rude, but I'm not in the mood for a lesson right now."

"It's not a lesson, Evelyn." Ms. Davis looked right at her. "It's just one word. *Grace.* Grace covers it all. That's not only a direct quote from your mouth to my ears, but I've learned it's absolutely true." She smiled, cocked her head and lowered her voice. "It might be hard to see at the moment, but hang in there. First, though, put your seat belt on, your head down, and go back to sleep. You can take a nice nap on the way home. That'll be good for you."

Evelyn leaned her head against the window and watched Ms. Davis adjust and readjust her seat. After a full minute of the lengthy procedure, which still hadn't ended, a snort-chuckle escaped Evelyn, which felt good.

"What's so funny?" Ms. Davis asked, readjusting the rearview mirror for the third time.

"By the time we get home—never mind finally out of the parking lot—I'll have had a long enough nap that I won't be able to get to sleep tonight, or maybe even tomorrow."

Ms. Davis put the car in reverse. "You know, Evelyn, that might be true. But so is this: driving isn't going to be nearly as much fun, now that I'm doing it within the law. I rather enjoyed our little foray toward *Thelma & Louise*."

Evelyn full-out laughed. She'd seen the movie where the two women created their own freedom by driving full bore off the edge of the Grand Canyon. "Ms. Davis, I hate to be the one to break this to you, but seriously, as slow as you drive, you'll be lucky if you can propel us out of the parking lot."

By the time Ms. Davis cautiously puttered her way to the street, they were both laughing so hard Ms. Davis had to pull over to wipe the tears out of her eyes.

Same as yesterday, when Sasha was in therapy, Donald experienced a niggle of trepidation when he dialed her number. Their first call had been sincere, wonderful, and tender. But in the end, too careful and very awkward. His heart pounded. Thankfully, the phone rang only once before Sasha picked up.

"Donald! It's so good to hear your voice again. I'm so sorry I missed your previous call."

"I understand," he said. "I'm glad you're hitting it hard with the therapy. How'd it go?"

Sasha chuckled. "It was smashing. No barre, no *plié* or fifth position, no music in the background. Just an outpatient drill sergeant who knows how to make me sweat. But I can't begin to tell you how invigorating it is to feel my strength returning. And guess what? I can drive now too!"

"That's wonderful," he said, then added, "I hope. *Have* you driven yet?" Donald recalled the last time she'd been behind the wheel. She didn't drive often, but when she did, *oy*. To say she was a little skittish behind the wheel was an understatement.

"In fact, I have."

"How'd that go?" he asked.

"Same as always." She chuckled. "Not well. You know driving's never been my favorite. But

Evelyn hung in there with me, and it's good to have my independence fully returned."

"Bravo," Donald said. "Bravissimo!"

"Oh, Donald. I've missed you so," she said, her voice low and sincere. "Your humor, your encouragement, the *you* of you. I love you so very much."

And there they were, the words he'd been waiting to hear. Before he could respond, she carried right on, as if the question about her love had never entered her mind.

"You know, after the awkward ending to our last call," she said, "I actually made a list of things to talk to you about."

"Have you checked something off already?" he asked.

"I have no idea. I threw the list away. I decided to just let us find our way. When haven't we?"

"Listen to this," Donald said. He held a piece of paper up to the receiver; it crackled as he wadded it up.

"What was that?" Sasha asked. "It sounded like static."

"Nope, it was *my* list! You are exactly right."

They broke out in a bout of grace-filled, cleansing laughter. They were ready to trust that both common sense and their solid, intimate history would move them forward. It was clear they were back in life together. Perhaps not physically yet, but committed to the rest of their journey, whatever that would be.

Twenty-Three

Donald walked out of the hour-long meeting with the artistic and executive directors of the Mid-Central Festival Ballet. He felt an odd combina-tion of elation, excitement, and fear.

What *would* it be like to retire, to *be* retired, at least from a performing career? It was one thing to experience a sudden, career-ending injury, such as his wife had. But even though he always knew the day would come, it seemed quite a different creature to make a deliberate choice to bow out. Yet it was a decision, an announcement, he'd just made to his employers, one he had not yet shared with his wife.

The meeting had gone well; they'd received his news in stride. They would be sorry to lose him, but, they added, they looked forward to his retirement gala. They even took a moment to bat a few event ideas around, discuss how to handle the press. They also didn't seem the least bit surprised at his decision. They knew Donald and Sasha, whom they knew and loved too, were talking about the when and how of their perma-nent reunion, news he'd happily shared after his and Sasha's second phone conversation. Everyone also knew he was about to age out anyway.

So, I've given my notice, he thought as he walked down the hall. *I can't wait to tell you, darling.*

They were a married couple still very much in love.

During the last month, they'd spoken countless times, each conversation taking them less guardedly into the nuances of their highs and the terrible lows. It was a tender time, aided by Sasha's decision to buy a laptop and get herself back online, which she'd done. After that, when they, and especially Donald, found spare moments, they were able to read and reread each other's thoughts, and cull and edit their own. Luckily, written expressions came easily to both of them. They attached photographs ("Another picture of the floor where TuTu sat a moment before I pushed the shutter button"; "My costume for the second act"), pointed to websites, forwarded jokes, shared reviews, chatted about small-town progress versus big-town choices, and discussed YouTube videos of performances.

After each conversation, Donald discerned a growing trust and strength in Sasha's voice, one that enabled her to discuss the art of dance without feeling remorse or longing, although he knew she still had to have those moments. What dancer wouldn't? They'd even started sharing thoughts about how their future might look after

Donald retired. In a leap of faith, Sasha shared her hopes, her dreams—her vision.

The vision that grew sturdier every day, one that still energized her.

Although Donald had initiated the discussion on the possibility of his retirement, he could tell from the tone in Sasha's voice that the topic worried her. She fretted that because of her condition, he might make a premature decision. She opened up her soul and admitted that had been one of the reasons she'd bowed out of his life: she hadn't wanted her circumstances to remove a gifted and remarkable dancer from the stage before his time—still didn't.

He promised both of them that such a decision would be made on his readiness, and his readiness alone. He also assured her that his body was already presenting its own signs that retirement grew near. He implored her to remember that a life of performing dance was finite, at least in their chosen genre. Even if he'd never met her, the day would still come, and soon, when he'd have to step off the stage.

After the evening's performance, with his permission, word of his forthcoming retirement spread quickly through the troops. It would be difficult to leave this family of dancers and friends who had circled around him, sustained him, seen him through after Sasha left his life. How on earth had she found the courage to just walk away, without even saying good-bye? Then again, now that he'd told them he'd be leaving at the end of this run, he began to understand how it might have been easier for her to simply disappear than to see the looks on everyone's faces if she stayed. He could already read the sorrow and concern in some of their eyes. It silently whispered, "Another one bites the age-out dust. My day will come one day too. Then what?"

But for him and Sasha, the "then what?" answer was already clear. *Please, God.*

Evelyn arrived at the butcher shop over an hour before it opened. It was Thursday, Durve Day, sometimes the busiest day of the week at the shop. On Durve Day, her grandpa handed out the hors d'oeuvre of his choice and making. One per customer. Today, he told her it would be meatballs with a spicy flair, something warm to start people thinking about Thanksgiving. The holiday was still nearly a month away, but he did whatever he could to inspire early orders.

Mostly though, he told her, he had a taste for those meatballs with the rice and cherry pie filling. He'd made a quadruple batch last evening in his two giant Crockpots. One double batch for the shop and the other for his dinner. "Can't stand to smell those things all day and not have a big plate of them when I get home!"

"Sounds good," she said.

"How's it going, Sweet Cakes?" he asked, as she slipped the white butcher's apron over her head. He gave her one solid, happy nod. "You're looking better."

"I'm hanging in there, Gramps. Thanks for asking. In the end, you know what they say: what doesn't kill you makes you stronger. For a while there, though, I kinda wished I was dead." Her grandpa raised his eyebrows. "Well, not really. But you know what I mean. Getting jilted is not much fun. You ever been jilted?"

"Ha! Who hasn't been?"

"I guess people just don't talk about it. When it happens to you, it feels like you're the first person on earth to experience the pain, yet somehow the last person to have seen it coming."

"Evelyn, people have already forgotten about it. Sure, I heard mumbles that first week. Outright nosiness, to be exact. But the gossip soon wore off. Then when news spread that you and your dad caught that outstanding stringer full of walleye the day nearly everyone else on the river got skunked, it gave them something else to yammer on about."

"I just wish I knew what *really* happened, why Jorden broke it off and left without a word."

Ms. Davis was the only person with whom she'd shared the whole story. As far as everyone else knew, he'd just dumped her and he and his family moved on. Since she didn't know the truth of the suspected abuse, what was the point of bringing it up, other than to further cloud an already questionable family reputation? Even Grandma Betty Burt seemed glad Jorden was gone.

"Sweet Cakes, some things are just not ours to know. We just need to trust the good Lord to keep us moving forward."

"Thanks, Gramps," she said, giving him an extra long hug.

He looked at a list he'd scrawled on a piece of butcher paper. "You can get those little white cups out of the cabinet over there and the toothpicks. I think we'll just put a meatball in each, and not even offer special mustard with them today. The sauce is too wonderful to ruin—although I might stir in a tad of hot sauce before I serve it. Did you lift the lid and smell those meatballs?"

"No need to lift the lid. I caught the aroma as soon as I came in the door." She retrieved the items and laid them out on the counter, away from the slicer. "In fact, I already snuck one," she said, smacking her lips. "A dollop of hot sauce sounds perfect. As for those walleye, did Dad show you the pictures?"

"Like a proud papa. I told him to make me a copy so I can hang it up in the meat case window. I've got a couple annoying braggarts I'd like to have a look-see. I'll tell them to go right ahead and bring me their shots, then we'll see how soon they button it up."

"It feels good to be out on the river again," Evelyn said. "There's just something healing about the mighty Mississippi that, no matter what, just keeps rolling along. Dad and I had a great time. We had to bundle up pretty good for those walleye, but the sun was shining. It was a little windy, but the water temperature was really cooling, which helped the bites."

Her grandpa laid a few knives on the counter. "Your dad was just beaming when he told me about it. I think I heard a replay of nearly every single cast. When your dad is beaming, he makes his dad beam," he said, giving his granddaughter a wink. "Sure, he was proud of the fish, but he's just glad to be back in the boat with you—and you can interpret that however you wish."

"Did he tell you Ms. Davis had them both over for dinner?"

"No! When was that? But before you answer, you wanna grab the napkins and put them by the Crockpot, then start packaging up a few two-pound containers of ground beef? I have it on sale today."

"Sure," Evelyn said, getting right on task. "We had them over last Thursday."

"Funny. I don't recall you picking up any meat. You two-timing me and shopping across the river?" he asked with a playful wink.

"Wait till you hear this. Ms. Davis is a terrible cook—information not to be shared—but she didn't want me to have to cook for my own parents. She said we were all three to be guests at the table. She asked if they liked pizza and I said sure, so we kept it simple and ordered in. She did make a side salad. I baked some brownies, those ones with raspberry jelly on top. I can't believe it took this long for all of us to get together. But then, thinking about it, it was probably better this way."

"How'd it go?"

"Great. Mom and Dad were so grateful to her for taking such good care of me. Ms. Davis nearly gushed about how clever and smart I am, how much she loves my artwork. She did a little show-and-tell with the letterhead I designed for her. I told all of them how nice it was to have people who stood by me . . . It was one hug short of a sappy lovefest."

"Love is good," her grandpa said, wiping his hands down the front of his apron, donning a pair of plastic gloves, then slapping a giant pork loin onto the counter. He reached for his heavy-duty knife, checked the blade and got out his whet-stone. As quickly as he began the sharpening process, he stopped. "You know, a person cannot collect too much love. In fact, come over here right now and let me give you that one hug you were short of for that lovefest. The truth is, I could use another hug too."

Evelyn didn't need to be asked twice. It was a

quirky hug, each of them holding their gloved hands away from the back of the other, but nonetheless, it was a strong hug. "Thanks, Gramps. Thanks for always hanging in there with me."

They quickly got back to their tasks. Time was flying by and the shop would soon open.

"So, it sounds like Ms. Davis is pretty self-sufficient now, capable of driving and all. Your dad told me you helped get her new computer set up. I know you like to stay busy, so what's she had you up to?"

Evelyn dug the scoop into the ground beef. "Thanks for not asking directly what I'm going to do next. It seems clearer by the day that I'll have to figure that out, and soon."

She plunked three scoops of meat into the container and weighed it. She was four ounces short, so she added another chunk or two. "That's okay with me, though. Right now, she's got me paint-ing, which is fun. We're tackling one room at a time. First she's going through her mother's stuff, setting aside giveaway piles we disperse between Goodwill and the local thrift store. We bought a bunch of plastic bins for things she wants to keep, or isn't quite sure about yet, and I'm putting them in the third bedroom upstairs. Then we move everything else to the middle of the room and I paint, after much discussion about colors. I'm happy to say, we're really brightening the place."

"She's going to stick around then?" her grandpa asked.

Evelyn stopped weighing. "You know, Gramps, I've probably said enough. And the truth is, I don't know much more. I know she and Mr. Major are definitely planning on getting back together, but that's it. In the meantime, I'm just a happy painter, still happily earning my room and board."

"And," he added, drawing a giant heart in the air with his fingers, "living smack dab in the middle of a lovefest!" He laughed.

Evelyn looked at her grandpa with wide eyes as she sucked in her breath. Happy tears sprang forth from an unknown reservoir. "That is so true, Gramps! Grace! I'm not exactly wonderful yet, but the reminder of grace is washing over me from all directions. Yay, God!"

It didn't take Donald and Sasha long to figure out that if they wanted to see each other sooner rather than later, she needed to be the one to travel. Since her therapy appointments were still only twice a week, she could be away for several days without setting herself back. She could do her homework therapy anywhere.

Even so, at first she balked. Yes, she was getting around well, and her desire to see Donald was nearly all-consuming. Yet the idea that her first solo outing would take her halfway across the country felt a bit daunting. Yes, she could drive now, but even when she did, she invited Evelyn to either come along or take the wheel.

"Don't worry," Donald told her, "I'll make the reservations, line up the limo, and make sure our private time together is just that."

She asked him to give her a day to think about it.

That night at dinner, Sasha laid out her concerns to Evelyn. How insecure it made her feel to have Donald witness her gait, which was still far from the agile grace with which she used to move. How guilty she still felt for shutting him out, even though he told her he never wanted to hear another word about it.

When she finished, Evelyn didn't respond. She just stared at Sasha, not moving a muscle. Finally she said, "And?"

"And what?"

"Exactly," Evelyn said, shaking her head as if Sasha were silly for such concern. She pursed her lips, then took a long, slow drink from her water glass. Standing up, she walked up to Sasha's side, stretched her body to its maximum height, and said, "Do we need a full-out intervention here? Do I need to get right up in your face, so your own lame words echo back at you? The love of your life is waiting for you! This isn't just about you, you know. It's about the two of you."

Sasha bit her suddenly trembling lip. "You're right, Evelyn. Why is it that since the day you moved in here, you are almost always right?"

Within fifteen minutes, Sasha'd called and left a message on Donald's phone, telling him to "Make it happen!" Soon after, she started packing her bag.

Evelyn drove Sasha to the Twin Cities. She didn't have to change planes if she flew out from there, which they all decided would be best.

As promised, a limo driver met her near the luggage carousel, holding a sign with her name on it, and escorted her straight to the door of her and Donald's condo.

Donald wouldn't arrive till late. She had plenty of time—way too much time—to refresh, nap on the couch, eat, and fret some more.

Should she be standing near the door when he arrived? Sitting at the table? In bed?

What could her first physical action be that wouldn't reveal the hitch in her gait? What if her coccyx wasn't yet healed enough for intimacies without excruciating pain?

Thirty minutes before Donald's expected arrival, Sasha was a nervous wreck. In order to occupy her mind, she unpacked Our Lady of Dance. Where should she display her special surprise? On the table? Or maybe she should be holding their beloved talisman? Place it on the center of his dresser?

Yes, she decided. The dresser. That way he

could quietly discover her on his own.

She made her way back to the bedroom. When she flipped on the light, her eyes widened. Donald had removed their wedding blanket from the wall and placed it back on the bed. Sticking out of the top pocket on her side of the bed was a blue piece of paper with a long blue ribbon attached. She sat on the side of the bed and unfolded the small note.

My Dearest Sasha,
Welcome home.
With all my undying love, Donald.

She closed her eyes and held the note to her heart for a long while. When she opened them, Donald stood before her, arms open wide. He was early. How she hadn't heard him enter, she had no idea. But she also needn't have worried—about *anything*.

Late into the night, their tender reunion held them close. Donald's MP3 player delivered the perfect quiet accompaniment. He'd loaded all their favor-ites. There was not much talking, other than to share a few of their deepest longings. In fact, after their initial bout of lovemaking, there was very little movement. The gift was simply in their coupling—hand to shoulder, arm to waist, toes to toes.

Sasha's last thought before dozing off was, *Not even dancing together delivered such sweetness.*

Twenty-Four

Sasha, sparkling cane leaning against her knee, sat in the audience, eyes closed, listening to the overture. She pictured the musicians down in the orchestra pit, horns to lips, bows dancing across strings, the principal percussionist poised with a padded drumstick lifted high in his hand, waiting for the precise moment. After years of acute listening to the music for dance cues, Sasha noted the tinkling of chimes as she counted the beats, felt the musical transitions shift her somewhere deep inside. In her mind's eye, she envisioned the slightly messed hair of the conductor.

Then she pictured Donald in the wings, in full costume, patting the head of Our Lady of Dance. This would be the first time she'd seen him dance since the accident. Her heart, filled with such a multitude of emotions, was with him. She felt her heels spontaneously lift off the floor.

It would be difficult to see the magnificent Donald Major dancing Franz with another Swanhilda in his arms. Yet she was determined to dance in *his* spirit, to feel *his* joy—and yes, *his* range of emotions as he took the stage for his final curtain as a professional dancer.

Evelyn leaned over to whisper in Sasha's ear. "I'm about to faint from nerves, and I'm just sitting here! How on earth did you get through this on stage for so many years?"

"The same way you learned to do all the things you do. Practice."

They sat back in their seats as the music indicated the curtain was about to open. Sasha heard Evelyn, who'd never been to a live ballet performance, gasp at the colorful bounty of the staging. Soon after the second curtain lifted, the dancer playing Swanhilda would perform one of the most strenuous dances in the ballet. She'd also dance nearly all of act 2, then return for act 3. Rigorous, but oh, so much fun.

Sasha found herself on the edge of her seat with nerves. Her own heart raced, as though she were about to face the audience. She mentally coaxed her body into relaxing. *No, dancing is not your job tonight.*

Out came the dancers. Finally, Donald took the stage. Sasha felt slightly dizzy. It was so surreal, having to watch from a distance. She reached over, grabbed Evelyn's hand, and squeezed with all her might. Evelyn, who seemed to be holding her breath, leaned slightly toward her, as if to communicate *I am here for you.*

Donald was a beautiful specimen of a man. Still so strong, appearing to leap without effort. Although they'd been together—she flying in for two brief but delicious visits, the first three weeks ago—this was the first she'd seen him in his white tights since the accident. Tights accentuated every flaw in a dancer's legs, but his were still perfect, beautiful and powerful. She blushed, for this she knew firsthand. From the back, he presented the perfect male dancer's compact muscles.

Yet, there were tiny evidences of his age, perhaps only things she would notice. Dear things, like a slight wrinkle above his brow, a hint of gray hair above his ears. Tears streamed down her face as he launched himself and his partner around the stage. She discreetly dabbed at her eyes. Evelyn squeezed her hand several times, aware of Sasha's every overwhelming moment.

At the first intermission, right after the lights came up, Sasha told Evelyn she just wanted to remain in her seat, but she insisted Evelyn head to the lobby and get herself refreshments. "Lots of great people-watching!"

"Are you sure you want to stay here, alone?" Evelyn asked.

Sasha tucked a twenty into Evelyn's palm. "Absolutely," she said, nodding her head and swallowing. "Go! Enjoy!"

Soon after they'd arrived in the theater, Sasha had taken out the twenty for just this purpose. She was sure she would need this time alone to collect herself, to process her emotions, sans conversation and another's concern. Time to catch her breath. Exhale. Keep her eyes stage forward, hoping no one recognized her.

She'd entered this evening wearing a silk scarf nearly completely covering her head. This was Donald's farewell gala night. Evelyn had two bouquets of flowers under her seat to take to the stage when it was time: one from each of them. Sasha didn't wish a single moment of his deserved adoration and attention diverted to her.

As Evelyn headed for the lobby, Sasha was glad for an unintentional bit of comic relief. It was a riot watching Evelyn walk in a pair of heels. Although they were only two-and-a-half-inches high, Evelyn handled them like she was playing dress-up. But she'd insisted on "dressing worthy for the ballet."

"Worthy for the ballet." Recalling the phrase jettisoned Sasha back onto her mini emotional roller coaster ride. She'd caused so much pain . . . Yet, able to step outside her personal journey, she couldn't imagine *anyone* unworthy of witnessing the magic, power, joy, beauty, and yes, the blessing of dance. By the time the lights went down for the second act, she'd pulled herself together, determined not to lose a moment of this, Donald's final dance, to regret.

The dancer who'd replaced her in the company was graceful, musical, slightly smaller than herself, and so much younger. She partnered beautifully with Donald, and probably everyone else she danced with—although Donald was known for his strong guidance. Sasha silently sent her wishes for good health and a long career.

As the performance continued, Donald seemed to become stronger. He'd told Sasha he hoped to perform his best that evening. Apparently Our Lady of Dance had done her job. *So many jobs,* Sasha thought, smiling.

The closer the story line moved toward its happy ending, the more her heart felt linked with Donald's. When they got to the act 3 wedding *pas de deux*, the one she and Donald used to dance in their nightclothes—or nothing—Sasha felt a slight wave of nausea, not her first over the last few days. She added that to her tender breasts and missed period, and she knew. Much to her surprise, her initial vision on the park bench would have to wait. Her new dream, her deepest longing, the next thing she would dedicate herself to, was the child within.

When she and Donald were together for their two brief visits, Donald had brought up the topic of children. "We're getting up there," he said, "but we're not aged out of parenthood yet." Sasha thought her heart would erupt with sheer joy over the possibility and told Donald that having Evelyn under her roof had brought to life how much one could cherish a child. In response, Donald wept, relieved they'd been given the same heart's desire.

Perhaps they were too old. Perhaps the window of time had passed. But nonetheless, Sasha had been off her birth control pills since her accident, so they decided to love freely and see what happened.

What a gift. She watched as the soloist performed *Prayer*, the music and motions moving Sasha to her core. She rested her hand on her abdomen and imagined she felt the dance within. She pictured herself sitting in her mother's rocker—the rocker in which she herself had been nursed and cuddled—with her own tiny little bird in her arms. Or perhaps their child would take after Donald's mother's side: large, stout, stubbornly determined. And that, too, would be wonderful.

Who could ask for more than a bright and kind child like Evelyn?

Of course it was too soon to share the news. She'd wait to see if she carried. Early miscarriages seemed more common in her age group. But she had a good feeling and was glad she'd cleared a pregnancy when she last met with her doctor. She was done with official therapy now, though the faint limp would remain with her always, especially when she was tired. But the pain was gone, her body was strong, and she only used the cane when engaging in strenuous things, like walking several blocks to watch her husband perform.

Goodness! She'd drifted so far into the future, she almost missed the present. There were only a few moments left of the evening, and then, after curtain calls, Donald's special presentation and the after party would begin for his retirement.

That night in her hotel room, Evelyn relived every moment of this amazing adventure. From the day Ms. Davis handed her the surprise airplane ticket to Boston (prearranged with her folks, who insisted on paying for her hotel room), to the look in Ms. Davis's and Mr. Major's eyes when, after the party, they'd parted ways with her to head for their condo, Evelyn's heart swelled with grateful-ness. She'd never seen such an intense light between two people. Their shining adoration for each other was almost blinding. *"Lucky thirteen,"* Mr. Major had told her. *"That's how many years we've been married."*

Evelyn was glad she'd instantly liked Mr. Major yesterday when she first met him. It would have been difficult if she hadn't. After all, she'd settled into a solid friendship with Ms. Davis—Sasha, as Ms. Davis kept reminding Evelyn to call her, especially since she no longer officially worked for her. It would really stink if her husband, who would soon be moving to Wanonishaw, was a pickle. But the way he looked at Sasha in and of itself was enough to cause Evelyn to warm to him. They'd shared a good laugh when Mr. Major told her how he'd pictured Evelyn all this time: a prune-faced old lady. And he'd thanked her profusely for caring for his wife, who he said couldn't say enough good things about her.

Although it was difficult to compare the long-lived love of an older couple to that of a twenty-year-old and his nineteen-year-old fiancée, still, she'd never seen *that* kind of look in Jorden's eyes. It was one she would not soon forget, one she longed to see, hopefully in her future husband's eyes. Sasha and Mr. Major must have really been something when they danced together. *Glowing. Radiant.* Thoughts of Mr. and Mrs. Oliver, the older couple Dawn told her about, ran through Evelyn's mind. How lonesome Mrs. Oliver must be without her husband, for they had danced together too.

In hindsight, and the more she studied marriages that weathered storms, she realized that she and Jorden wouldn't have started life together with very good odds at lasting love. Their foundation was all wrong. They didn't share faith, long-term goals, their deepest thoughts . . . trust. She wished him well, but she'd also dedicated herself to uncurling her emotional fingers from his last remnants of claim to her heart.

Before they'd left for Boston, Sasha had finally invited Evelyn inside the room at the top of the stairs, the one Mr. Major had told her about during the call that freaked her out. The only room she hadn't painted. The walls were filled with pictures. She saw the photo of the two of them together, the one Mr. Major had talked about, but there was so much more. Pictures from Sasha's school days, early recitals, framed memorabilia from all over the world.

Sasha had pulled down the first in a row of scrapbooks, passion lacing her voice as she told Evelyn about her mother's special knack for keeping so many pieces of her daughter's life and career between these pages. She'd fingered the little pieces of fabric, stroked the face of her mother in the pictures, then had Evelyn bring up chairs when they got to the part—what album number was it?—where Sasha and Mr. Major started dancing together.

To think they would soon both end up in Wanonishaw, Minnesota, was actually kind of funny. Sasha had told Mr. Major about the disabled boy she'd first seen from the park bench, and then countless other times around town. She and his mother, Debra, had even started to form a friendship.

Sasha had shared her park-bench vision: a dance studio that welcomed everyone, regardless of age or ability, not just the perfect little dancers. She now knew what it felt like to no longer be the flawless artiste. Yet, *she* still wanted to dance, to be back in a class again where she felt safe and accepted, even with her limitations.

"Imagine, Evelyn, something for every level of dance skill and physical need. A place where even a young man in a wheelchair can come and learn to feel the music, find ways to express it," Sasha had explained, her enthusiasm overflowing. If Sasha were to one day teach, she'd be quite the inspiration, that was for sure.

Mr. Major caught Sasha's vision and added to it. He proposed a combined dance studio and strength center. It would be financially risky, but they were both so excited, talking about their vision every time Evelyn was available to listen. Apparently he'd already been in contact with a Realtor, checking for vacant buildings for sale.

Evelyn relished the enthusiasm in their synergy. Perhaps they'd even talked about dance classes for the likes of Evelyn's clunky self. Who knew? Maybe she'd one day meet *her* Mr. Right while learning to dance the . . . well, the Hokey Pokey felt most likely.

Evelyn laughed and laughed, then slipped off her shoes and studied her pedicure. Dawn was right. There was no turning back once a woman was baptized into this luxury. Now, though, rather than prettying up for Jorden, she did so for herself. For this trip, she'd even had her eyebrows waxed, something she'd quickly determined she'd never do again.

The music tonight had filled her with such happiness. She stretched out her right leg and pointed her toe, trying to imagine what it felt like to fly across the stage, all petite and aglitter. If that was what you knew you were born to do, it would be magnificent. But she'd been born to fix things and fish, to read and to enjoy. But mostly, to paint, create, and design. Yes, those things made her feel like *she* was flying.

She sashayed her painted toenails to the hotel room window and stared down on the bustling throngs of traffic. She was a long way from Wanonishaw, to be sure. But the liveliness of the city was catching. Being here, she found herself getting truly excited about heading off to college in January. She'd be living right here in Boston.

According to the concierge, Waltham, Massachusetts, was only twenty-four minutes from this very hotel. She'd been accepted into the Center for Digital Imaging Arts at Boston University, entering its full-time graphics and web design certificate program.

This, of course, was the reason her parents were doubly excited and supportive of her trip with Ms. Davis to see Mr. Major perform: it gave her an opportunity to spend a full day in Boston, visiting the campus and attending the Boston Symphony Orchestra, for which she'd purchased a ticket online. Tomorrow, she would check out her living arrangements, which felt like a miracle.

Sasha and Mr. Major—"please call me Donald" —offered to let her live in their condo for a price she could definitely afford. They claimed they needed to keep the place secure for a couple of years, in case their dreams in Wanonishaw did not work out. They'd given her a list of fix-it projects (work in exchange for some of the rent) and told others in the building about her capabilities. She already had a waiting list for her services. Between college loans, the financial support of her parents, and her own income, she felt pretty sure she could monetarily make it through the two-year course.

In hindsight, Evelyn could be nothing but grateful she hadn't gone off to college earlier, for this career path would not have been her choice back then. But now she knew it was the only right one.

Although she still thought of Jorden, missed his touch, his strong hand wrapped around hers—prayed for his safety and wellness—in her heart, no matter if he were sincere or not, she now believed that he'd arrived as a divine appointment. Without his holding power to keep her in Wanonishaw—to give her time to find her roots in design, via Ms. Davis's letterhead and other projects for Mr. Major's dream studio—she surely wouldn't have chosen the certificate program through Boston University. The graphics and web design program was the perfect way to combine her traditional fine arts with a practical way to make a living. With her entrepreneurial business experience, she had no doubt she'd be successful. Now that she'd already received so many accolades and fully cultivated her artistic, creative, and designing side, she felt perfectly on track for what came next in her life.

Since Evelyn still lived with Sasha in the brightly painted and organized abode on Fourth Street, she'd taken care of the place and the cats when Sasha visited Donald. When it was first announced he was retiring and that he'd be moving in, Sasha said it would be the perfect trade, Donald for Evelyn. "I couldn't imagine living in this house alone, Evelyn. You've brought both me and this house so much goodness and life. Donald is a whirlwind of those same attributes."

Evelyn thought about his beautiful love letter. *Goodness, indeed.*

"If—no make that *when*—we get our studio under way," Sasha had said, "I told him I know just the handywoman to help him fix it up and make it bright. And the graphics person to design the logo and advertising. I already gave him one of your old cards."

Evelyn blushed, just thinking about the motto on her card. EVELYN BURT'S HELPING HANDS, HELPING *YOU*. NO ODD JOB TOO ODD. Her first order of the day when she returned home: replace the graphic of her hands with one that didn't include an engagement ring.

She already had senior Wanonishaw citizens lining up, wanting her help with outdoor Christmas decorations.

Evelyn hung up her clothes, put on her pajamas, brushed her teeth, and climbed into the luxurious and many-pillowed bed with her laptop. She'd paid extra for the hotel's Wi-Fi, so why not use it? She quickly found a couple of dance blogs raving about *Coppélia*'s wonderful close and the great tribute to "one of dance's finest contributions." She was shocked to find a picture of herself handing Donald bouquets of flowers. It was taken from the back, but it was definitely her.

She opened her e-mail program and started typing.

Dear Sasha,

Imagine this, if humanly possible: me with no words. The trip, the theater, the performance, the party . . . the last many months of my life. THANK YOU! My red toenails wiggle with giddiness. I have a feeling your pink toenails are doing a happy dance too.

Perhaps you and Mr. Major already discovered this, but if not, here's a link to a nice review of the evening. Check out the picture to the far right!

It won't be long before you and Mr. Major will be living together in the Fourth Street abode and I will be off to college. In case I forget to tell you one more time, and in case you or I forget this ourselves, I'm cc-ing myself on this message:

Grace covers it all. Amen.

Your friend forever, Evelyn Burt, soon-to-be college student

A Note from the Author

This I know to be true: curiosity drives my writing; the element of surprise is my favorite payoff. But when an injured ballet dancer showed up in my head (how curious!), the thing that most sur-prised me was that I couldn't make her go away. *Please move along, whoever you are. I don't know* anything *about ballet!*

My only formal training in dance took place in the early fifties. Tap lessons. For the recital, I was a dancing pack of "Phyllis" Morris Cigarettes. For real. The routine was a takeoff on a then popular Philip Morris cigarette commercial. Can you imagine that happening in this day and age?!

After it became clear that Sasha was here to stay, the research began. I read books on ballet, watched countless YouTube videos, went to a ballet, interviewed dancers, read more books. The more I learned, the more paralyzed I became. It was clear I was in way over my head. *Only a real dancer should tackle a story like this!* I spent several weeks avoiding any actual writing. I just couldn't get a picture of Sasha's youth, which is where I thought the story would begin.

While I was walking along the Mississippi River one day, avoiding my keyboard, I began to picture Sasha sitting in a rocking chair, a beautiful shawl wrapped around her shoulders. (Curious.) *Just start there. You can always write a new beginning later.* So to the keyboard I went, and in that rocking chair with Sasha I began. Within a few paragraphs, the scene began to run like a movie in my head. (Surprising energy!) Within a few pages, a pair of young hands showed up, picking up shards of broken glass. (Curious.) By the second chapter, it was clear that the story wasn't just about a dancer; it was about the unlikely pairing of two strong females. (UTTER SURPRISE! I had no idea there was an Evelyn.) Off to nail-wizard Dawn I raced. "I need two colors of polish if I'm going to keep up with them!" (See pictures at www.flickr.com/dontmissyourlife.)

By the time I wrote The End, through them, and Dear Donald, I had learned so much about life, love, friendships, and the pursuit of longing. But most of all, I'd learned a great deal more about grace. Thank you, dear Evelyn, for that lesson in simplicity.

Whether you're young or old, brilliant or stumbling, dancing or wishing you could dance, remember this: grace covers your every step and misstep. Amen.

Please visit www.charleneannbaumbich.com and subscribe to the TwinkleGram (www.twinklegram.com) to stay in tune with what comes next for me. Who knows who might show up in my head!

Charlene@charleneannbaumbich.com

Acknowledgments

My dear Zen Cows, thank you for slowly waltzing up over the ridge, then posing outside my window to quietly cheer me on. You are, indeed, subtle voices of the universe. (See the top of my dedication page for that explanation.) Pictures of said cows are posted at:
www.flickr.com/dontmissyourlife.
To Greg and Linda, this land, and your friendship and ongoing support, spark my creativity. Thank you for sharing so kindly. Who knew one of the rewards of all that would make the cover!

Dawn Merrill, your fancy nail-polish jobs, especially the alternating colors, energized my keyboarding fingers to hang tough with two equally determined female characters.

Jennifer Reed, thank you for gracious time given to the stranger who tracked you down off a health Internet bulletin board in search of *real* information about the horrors of coccyx injuries.

Kerri Olson at Boston University Center for Digital Imaging Arts, a special thank you from Evelyn for helping her find direction.

Dick Heibel, you dear man and snowglobe fixer *extraordinaire,* you inspired my creative soul. Thank you again for your generous time, and for helping restore others' memories.

Although this book is dedicated to you, thank you AGAIN Kenneth von Heidecke, Tresa Mott, Misty Lown, Sondra Forsythe, and Kim Moss for your help and the beauty you bring and give to the world of dance. I hope I did Sasha proud. If I didn't, it's sure not your fault!

I'd like to thank Melanie Doskocil for her time, clarity, and honesty.

Shannon Marchese, without your trust, this book would be nothing but a wallflower. XO. Jessica Barnes, your editorial direction upped the story's rhythm. Pamela Shoup, YAY for finessing production editors! To the entire WaterBrook sales and marketing team, a rousing flash mob dance!

Danielle Egan-Miller, your agenting prowess boogies on and on.

Bret, Brian, Katie, Jackie, Bridget, and Colleen, my dear family, I am overwhelmed with gratefulness for your sparkling, whirling grace, presence, and inspiration in my life.

George John Baumbich, without question, you are the dancing winds beneath my words, even when you are just sitting in your recliner. I love you.

Readers Guide

1. Which character was your favorite? Evelyn, with her thirst for knowledge and unflagging optimism? Sasha, prim and proper but struggling to find hope and purpose in life? Or perhaps Donald, unwilling to give up on love? Do you identify with one character more than the others? Why?

2. At first glance, Evelyn and Sasha are complete opposites. As the book unfolds, do you think they remain opposites, or do they have certain things in common? What are some of these things?

3. What did you think of Evelyn's relationship with Jorden? Have you ever been in a similar situation? Do you think Jorden really loved Evelyn, or was he just using her?

4. How do Evelyn and Sasha impact each other's lives? What effect does Evelyn's presence have on Sasha's depression? How does Sasha help Evelyn in turn?

5. How did you feel about Donald's reaction to Sasha cutting him out of her life? Do you think he should have tried harder to win her back? Do you think he pushed too hard? What would you have done in his place, if your loved one shut you out?

6. The book contains detailed descriptions of the life of a professional ballet dancer. What characteristics do you think a person must possess in order to succeed as a dancer? How do these personality traits affect the rest of Sasha's and Donald's lives and their journey back to each other?

7. What role does the snowglobe play in Sasha's fall and recovery? If she had heeded the snowglobe's warning, how would her life be different? Do you think it would be better or worse? How does the snowglobe help her heal?

8. Evelyn's parents don't approve of her decisions to put off college and marry Jorden. The tension between Evelyn's right to make her own choices and her parents' desire for what is best for her causes a rift in their relationship. Who did you sympathize with more? Have you ever been in Evelyn's shoes? Or her parents'? How did you resolve the conflict?

9. Evelyn's safe place, where she goes when she needs comfort and acceptance, is her grandfather's butcher shop. Does Sasha have a place like this at the beginning of the novel? What about by the end? Where is your safe place?

10. Grace plays a large part in both Evelyn's and Sasha's journeys. How does Evelyn bring grace into Sasha's life? What role does grace then play in Evelyn's own healing? What other ways do you see grace working in the novel?

Center Point Large Print
600 Brooks Road / PO Box 1
Thorndike ME 04986-0001 USA

(207) 568-3717

US & Canada:
1 800 929-9108
www.centerpointlargeprint.com